THE GIRL IN THE WHITE FUR HAT.

D1555803

ry

RICHARD FREEBORN

Dynasty
Press

Dynasty Press Ltd.
36 Ravensden Street
London SE11 4AR

www.dynastypress.co.uk

First published in this version by Dynasty Press Ltd.

ISBN: 978-0-9553507-6-4

Cover artwork design by **Rupert Dixon**

Typeset by **Biddles**, Blackborough End, Norfolk.

Printed and bound in the United Kingdom.

Also by Richard Freeborn:

Academic Studies

Turgenev, A Study
A Short History of Modern Russia
The Rise of the Russian Novel
The Russian Revolutionary Novel
Dostoevsky
Furious Vissarion: Belinskii's Struggle for Literature, Love and
Ideas

Translations

Ivan Turgenev, Sketches from a Hunter's Album
Ivan Turgenev, Home of the Gentry
Ivan Turgenev, Rudin
Ivan Turgenev, A Month in the Country
Ivan Turgenev, Fathers and Sons
F.M Dostoevsky, An Accidental Family.

Fiction

Two Ways of Life
The Emigration of Sergey Ivanovich
Russian Roulette
The Russian Crucifix
American Alice
The Killing of Anna Karenina
Mr Frankenstein
Watching the Accident Happen
The Grand Duke's, er, Great Idea

THE GIRL IN THE WHITE FUR HAT

During the Cold War, if you're a young British diplomat photographed naked next to a naked Russian girl wearing a white fur hat, you're likely to have been caught in a Soviet honey trap. Your career as a diplomat is probably wrecked. Ironically it may have an opposite effect by leading to friendship with a girl from the U.S. embassy and a joint involvement in creating a fictitious network of informants. But why does it have an immediate connection with a maverick Soviet rocket being retrieved from the North Sea and a threat, thirty years later, to assassinate the recently elected U.S. president?

In Soviet Russia the answer was to be found in a so-called 'forbidden zone.' Against all good judgement the British diplomat visits such a zone, meets a family member renowned as a rocket scientist and subsequently helps him to defect to the USA. Thereby the fictitious network is justified and the scientist is granted his lifelong wish. However, thirty years later Washington becomes deeply concerned when it is reported that someone, possibly the scientist, intends to assassinate the president during a one-night visit to London. A certain amount of available Cold War expertise is called into play to thwart the likelihood, but the real secret is revealed by the girl in the white fur hat who was there at the beginning and at the end.

A novel about sexual relations and betrayal, genius and the genie of mockery, the dagger of God and the cross of forgiveness, it exactly reverses the likelihood of assassination and replaces it with everlasting love.

'*Each one of us is undoubtedly answerable for all people and all things on earth, not only because of the universal sinfulness of the world, but each one singly for all people and everyone on earth. To be conscious of this is the crowning achievement not only of the monastic way of life, but of every human being on earth. For monks are just like other people, except that they are as all humanity on earth ought to be. Only when this comes about will our hearts become tender enough to have an insatiable, eternal, universal love. Then each of you will have the power to conquer the whole world with love and wash away the sins of the world with your tears...*'

Starets Zosima's address to his brother monks
on the last day of his life.
From F.M. Dostoevsky's *The Brothers Karamazov*.

PROLOGUE

'See that. Prophetic, eh?'

'Okay, okay. So you got a pot o'gold. We strike lucky.'

'We'll strike lucky,' said Wilbur Oldfield. 'No more prospecting. Just so long as... Yeah, what's that?'

The voice spoke in his ear. It was from a hundred feet below him in the waters of the North Sea. A confirmation. He pressed the scrambler button.

'Sure. Safe? Goddam it, I don't want a live nuclear warhead here in the North Sea... Sure... Sure... Sure... Okay, so it's in the cradle... Okay, insofar as the ROV's done it and you've got it in the cradle... Okay, fine... That I understand. You want me to decide. Right.'

Opaquely, as if fired within the tall, cloud-mottled walls of the kiln of sky surrounding the area of North Sea at that point, the rainbow rose and arced from west to east. It was fragmented. Bits of it, Turneresquely fashioned in liquid oil colour, stuck to greyish-white ranges of far cloud, while a whole section of its arc shone in clear neon brilliance over a patch of sea. Captain Lamb of USN 'Glenarvon' had a clear impression, for one brief instant, that the whole – the rainbow and its reflection, however fragmented by the sea's movement, however shattered by wave-tops and the slow, longitudinal surge of cream-laced water playing in each wave-wake – would make a circle uniting sea and sky. And it did. For one instant.

Then the sign came from Wilbur Oldfield.

'Bring it up,' Captain Lamb ordered.

The motors fired and the winches slowly moved. It would take a while to lift the object to the surface and the one thing he did not want was that the Royal Navy Commander seconded to oversee the operation should make any objections. That, for Wilbur Oldfield, was the trickiest part.

After all, the Brits were allies and they had a perfect right. Whatever the technicalities, these were British waters. Also, there was no denying that, within a mile of them and clearly visible, was a North Sea oil rig. Standing off at a discreet distance was a Royal Navy frigate, HMS 'Arcturus'. You do not send a Royal Navy frigate, or have a special observer placed on board the salvage vessel USN 'Glenarvon', or have a helicopter on constant watch, unless you're pretty sure something unusual is happening. Something more unusual, in short, than the retrieval of a maverick torpedo. That was the reason given by the Navy Department.

'Prepare the covers,' Wilbur Oldfield ordered quietly.

As soon as it broke surface, the object was to be covered. Why he gave that order right now into his intercom he couldn't be sure. It was a sign of panic he regretted at once. What preoccupied him was the attitude of the Brits.

Commander Barraclough of the Royal Navy had binoculars to his eyes already. They were trained on the point where the cables from the huge derricks swung out over the sea were slowly winching the object upwards and the navy and the CIA divers in their black wetsuits waited for it, circling the area slowly in inflatables. One glimpse of it would tell him it was no maverick torpedo. The length of it alone would tell him that. So the divers had been instructed to cover the steel cradle the instant it broke surface.

'They're not going to be fooled,' said Wilbur Oldfield.

'Nobody's going to know they've had the Mickey taken or not taken,' said Captain Lamb softly beside him. 'We're all going to behave like this is an experimental design, as we said it was, and we don't want anyone seeing what might not be good for them. It's just Murphy's Law the maverick should have come to rest so close to the rig.'

The other knew the captain of USN 'Glenarvon' had no real idea what it was all about. The Navy Department often had good ideas and always did their job well, but this Captain Percival Lamb, known familiarly as 'Pepsi' for some reason to his colleagues and subordinates, had to face the fact that this was no normal salvage operation. The Brits were naturally sensitive about it. Whatever the object was - say, for the sake of argument, it was a ballistic missile, which was exactly what Wilbur Oldfield of the CIA knew it was — you wouldn't want it sitting next to a North Sea oil rig. Or likely to destroy the pipe-work on the seabed.

'Because you know as well as I do,' Wilbur whispered in the captain's ear, his eye, like the other's, on the movements of Commander Barraclough as he studied the surging waters where the cables rose dripping, 'they'd have seen it on their advanced warning radar. They'd want to know why we're here so fast, wouldn't they? Boy, if this were the other way round and they were wanting to raise something off Cape Cod, we wouldn't let 'em near it! We've just struck lucky, that's all.'

Commander Barraclough sidled towards them. He used the guard-rail to pull himself along. The deck pitched a little but not enough to unsteady him.

'Mr Oldfield,' said the upper-class English voice. It had a pleasant, slightly ringing authority to it like a fine piece of porcelain struck by a knife blade. 'Mr Oldfield, you're using a cradle, aren't you?'

'Yes, sir.'

'Very sensible precaution.'

'I'm glad you think so, sir.'

'You know what I'm thinking?'

'What, sir?'

'We're going to be observed. You'll need to cover it.'

'Yes, sir. That was exactly what...' Wilbur Oldfield exchanged a quick look with Captain 'Pepsi' Lamb. The captain saluted.

'Comander,' he said, 'excuse me.'

The salute was returned. The captain then made his apologies - he was no real diplomat, Wilbur Oldfield thought – and ran briskly up the stairway to the next deck and the wheelhouse.

'Have I said something?' asked Commander Barraclough.

'No, sir,' said Wilbur Oldfield and gave a faintly sarcastic smile.

'I was only meaning...'

'What, sir?'

'I mean there'll be one of the Russkies over soon, you bet. They'll want a picture of what we're doing.'

'Yes, sir. Well, sir, Captain Lamb was only saying a moment ago we ought to cover it.'

'Very sensible precaution. Ah, I thought so. Look!'

He hardly need have spoken. Two jet interceptors with RAF markings sprang out of the far reaches of the sea at less than a thousand feet and stormed upwards in a huge rising arc towards the patch of clear sky where the neon rainbow had been. All on board USN 'Glenarvon' were deafened. It caused a visible shock on Wilbur Oldfield's face. In the wake of the sound wave he heard Commander Barraclough say:

'On your part, I mean.'

'Sir?'

The American looked into the Englishman's eyes. He saw they were the colour of the North Sea and about as unfathomable – bottle-green, restless, gleaming.

'I suspect all sorts of people may want to nose round this one, know what I mean? All sorts of people.' Commander Barraclough watched the jets disappear. The helicopter now hovered closer. 'You see, we know it came down by parachute in the final stages. That's always their way with test firings. They don't want to lose hardware unnecessarily if they can help it. Very sensible of them, too. The only puzzling question with this one is: Why here? They wouldn't have a cat in hell's chance of retrieving it here, would they?'

That, thought Wilbur Oldfield, was not the only puzzling question. 'No, sir, they wouldn't.'

'And you're not exactly in the business of being Mister Nice Guy in retrieving it for them, are you?'

'No, sir. Right, sir.'

'Then what do you think the answer is?'

Wilbur Oldfield put his strategist's hat on to answer this one. 'Maybe it's strategic... North Sea oilfields... maybe your oilfields and the Norwegian...'

'Oh, yes, we'd thought about that one,' the Commander interrupted light-heartedly. 'An expensive way of going about it, though, don't you think? In any case, why give us - or *you*, I should say - this free gift of one of their rockets?'

Ah, thought Wilbur Oldfield, that was the really puzzling question. But he continued to pursue his own line of thought. 'I'd like to guess they just wanted to show us they could do it. If you couple that with a new targeting strategy, then they might be wanting us to change our whole thinking.'

'Thinking on deployment, you mean?'

'Maybe they simply want to confuse the whole of NATO strategy.'

Commander Barraclough scratched his chin. 'Yes, perhaps it's as grand as that, but to my mind it didn't quite happen like that.'

'Oh, so how do you reckon it happened?'

'I reckon,' the Commander grinned and chuckled, 'it's just possible some Johnny over there simply made a bad mistake.'

'A mistake?'

'Yes. They fired the bloody thing and, God knows, the complexities of the control system may have worked in our favour, if you see what I mean, and so it landed up here. Something like that.'

'Human error?'

'Human error. Call it good luck, if you like. It happens with us. Why shouldn't it happen with them?'

'Sure,' said Wilbur Oldfield of the CIA a little reluctantly, 'we can mess things up.'

'No offence intended, you understand.'

The American smiled. He was beginning to like this Brit. 'No offence taken, sir. But as for what we're dealing with here, I think this is not wholly human error.'

'What exactly do you mean?'

'I mean we might explain it better by saying it was – I say maybe, just maybe – an act of betrayal.'

'So they've got traitors there, you mean. That I can believe.'

Commander Barraclough gave a laugh and turned away. As the vessel pitched a little in the increasing swell, he swung himself back towards the side-rail and once more lifted his binoculars to his eyes.

Wilbur Oldfield wondered at once how much the Commander actually knew. More than he was prepared to admit, that was obvious. Treachery would mean something quite clear-cut to a naval mindset, but to Wilbur Oldfield it only meant a compromised loyalty, a small tract of territory gained by dishonest means. This whole business, he told himself, was just an act of betrayal. Someone somewhere had betrayed something. Now he was landed with the responsibility of bringing the betrayed thing to the surface and finding out whether or not it had been worth betrayal in the first place.

More words sounded in his ear over the intercom. He had ordered that such communication be kept to a minimum, knowing it could be picked up by HMS 'Arcturus', not to mention two or three other sources, but also knowing that excessive use of scrambler would be provocative. It was confirmation of the ETA.

Seven or so minutes. He looked at his watch and moved to the ship's rail to give the agreed hand signal to his own CIA men. It was their responsibility, once the covers were on, to ensure the object was fit for lifting onto the deck. In the water it was the navy's responsibility; out of the water it was the CIA's.

Basically Wilbur Oldfield was concerned with only one thing: the inspection. If it told him what he expected to find, then a bargain had been struck between the Brits and the Navy Department, between London and Washington, between two administrations, between two little spots on the globe. Nevertheless what bothered him most was whether Commander Barraclough would demand to make an inspection as well.

Just below the surface of the waves the object that had been winched from the depths had an odd geometric appearance. The derricks had not been correctly aligned and the winches properly synchronized, so it looked a bit like a huge rectangular skeletal fish, one end only at the surface and the other sunk at an angle below the waves. It took several minutes for the levelling process to be completed. In that time the navy men expertly deployed the covers. They'd done this before, was Wilbur Oldfield's thought, and no doubt they challenged the CIA men to do it as well. The CIA men thankfully didn't mess up but took over at the point when the whole rig was just above water level and stretched the covers over the upper structure of the cradle while simultaneously fastening them round the sides.

A long coffin, Wilbur Oldfield thought. A long black catafalque. The waves broke against the black plastic sides of the object as it was winched higher and higher and then, as it was lifted clear of the sea, the only sound apart from the motors was the sharp smacking of the plastic against the steel cradle as the increasing breeze caught it. Two of his CIA men remained on the upper surface of the structure helping to balance it while it was raised to deck level. Wilbur Oldfield spoke to one of them through his intercom.

'See anything?'

'Nope.'

'Okay.'

It was a disappointment. Orders were issued for the cradle to be hoisted well above deck level before it was swung aboard and the deck was to be cleared of all personnel, including Commander Barraclough. Captain 'Pepsi' Lamb's voice suddenly came over the tannoy. He wanted to high-tail it out of there as soon as possible.

'Okay, okay,' Wilbur said. The vessel was beginning to pitch quite badly. He watched the huge cradle as it swung in slow arcs with the pitching motion. Inwards it came, gouts of water dripping out of it. He stared upwards, clinging to the ship's rail. The thing was like a huge rectangular dirigible above him, its upper surface and both sides covered in flapping black plastic. Within it, as within a womb, was this obscene metal foetus.

He stared at it. It showed damage, a buckling of the metal skin in parts. All right, so a ballistic missile does not come down in the North Sea without doing some damage to itself. He raised binoculars to his eyes as it hung suspended above him. It went slowly backwards and forwards with the pitching. He could read CCCP clearly enough. He was not looking for that. He was looking for something smaller, something more readable. And then he saw it running down the length of the central section.

The letters had been painted on quite roughly. There were six of them. They spelled success so far as Wilbur Oldfield was concerned:

R
A
D
U
G
A

'Okay!' he roared into his intercom. 'Bring it down!'

Down it came, swaying, flapping, a sinister steel cage containing God knows what, but as the twin ends reached normal eye level and men rushed forwards to steady the whole structure there was no concealing the giant metal tube and the fins. They could not be covered in time. It was a Soviet ballistic missile. By several slow stages it was lowered onto the deck of USN 'Glenarvon' and secured.

Of course Commander Barraclough had seen all he wanted to see. He was entirely confirmed in what he already knew. Quizzically, and with a wry smile, he could not help saying to Mr Oldfield of the CIA:

'It's your cargo now, eh?'

Wilbur Oldfield could have been very angry. He had one more essential task to perform and yet here was this Englishman pre-empting him at every turn. The word 'cargo' alerted him.

'I am not,' added Commander Barraclough, 'referring to this cargo, you understand. An excellent job has been done here. I congratulate you. Not this cargo, no. You know what I mean, I think. Do I have to spell it out?'

Wilbur Oldfield permitted himself a sour smile. 'No, you don't have to spell it out, sir.'

He knew the signal would be sent. The whole point of this mission from his point of view depended on that one word. As an operation, the retrieval of this missile had merely been a preliminary stage. They were responsible now for a quite different and much more volatile 'cargo'.

Of the many acts of betrayal in which Wilbur Oldfield found himself involved during his years of service for the CIA this one proved to be the trickiest and the longest-lasting in its impact. Half a lifetime later, when in retirement, he would find it all exploding in his face quite by chance when he least expected it, long, that is to say, after all the surreptitious games of the Cold War had been played out. The safety of the president of the United States would be involved. In retirement he would think that maybe it would have been best if he had never sent the signal, never obliquely contributed to the 'cargo' coming out of Moscow, never have seen that particular rainbow.

But right now, turning away from Commander Barraclough as he did, he took a final look at the seascape. Mottled, high-walled, stone-like, cloud upon cloud, if not threatening immediate rain then certainly offering no promise of bright sunlight, the curtain of sky above the choppy surface of the North Sea was cast in an iron of its own, he thought, and had about it an impregnability, a sinister coldness that made what had just happened seem like a minor miracle. All the pipes on the seabed were apparently still intact.

'Dear God,' he whispered, 'dear God.'

He was not to know that the image of a white cross being carried aloft above a crowd of heads would go round the world as an ultimate symbol of this moment in his life.

PART I

1

One summer in the second decade of the twenty-first century Father Christoph shaded his eyes against the hot sun and the glare off the sea. He was waiting for the arrival of the first ferry of the morning.

It was late, but then it was always late. Timekeeping was no part of the daily rota of ferry services plying the coastline.

Mostly here it was big tourist liners. On of them already dwarfed the adjacent dockside and was disgorging passengers down the walkways. In the peacock bright colours of their summer clothes and with their loud, show-off voices they seemed to Father Christoph truly foreign and incomprehensible. He crossed himself, letting his hand finally come to rest on the chain of the little bronze crucifix hanging down the front of his black cassock.

He was nervous and anxious. If the ferry did not arrive soon, it might be too late to do what he hoped to do. He ran a forefinger along the top of his forehead, gathering the perspiration from the inside rim of his priest's hat. Could there be a sign of comfort for him somewhere in the hot morning? He looked round. The blue funnel of the liner with its white emblem was in brilliant silhouette against the sky's deeper blue. Was that a sign? Just above it a speck rose into the sky. Sunlight struck a star-flash from it. An aircraft was taking off – a sign, perhaps? Would Brother Peter be raised up also?

He was sure this particular morning prayers were needed – oh, not necessarily for the summer visitors, no for those travelling into the sky within the metal sheaf of the aircraft — no, not for them, but needed for the ferry itself and its unusual cargo, for whom he would offer as many prayers as he could to a wise and forgiving God. Because… Ah, because what he had feared had already happened! While his eyes had been diverted to the sky and the rising aircraft, the black Mercedes had driven up and was already parked in the shade of a warehouse.

The sense of urgency, the sheer panic caused by the sight of that sombre vehicle, made him clasp his fingers together. Was there enough true goodness in the world for God's word ever to take root in men's hearts? He would try to dissuade with God's help, but would anything dissuade a passionate heart once it was sure it was acting in God's name?

Oh, Brother Peter, he thought, Brother Peter!

He heard the chugging of the ferry's engines as it approached and pressed forward among the small group of people on the quayside. There would be no trouble in recognising Brother Peter — was he not the Great Peter? Had he not seen him in his Athos cell? Had he not heard his threat? What worried him was that he might miss the small compact figure and the thin dark face with the pointed beard if there were a lot of passengers alighting.

The reversed screws churned the water at the ferry's stern into a creamy mousse of seawater and harbour flotsam. In the instant of berthing, as was its custom, the ferry appeared to open itself to the world. The stern ramp came down with a brisk cranking. It clattered on the stonework of the quay and passengers sprang down it, most carrying goods for the market.

The sun was just at the wrong angle for Father Christoph. He shaded his eyes with his right hand while the fingers of his left hand played nervously with the chain on his chest. He glanced at one face, then another. They were all unfamiliar.

He was quivering with an old man's nervousness. He could see no black monk's habit. Perhaps he had made a mistake?

It astonished him when a voice said softly in his ear, 'Thank you, Father.'

He would have recognised the dark-brown eyes anywhere. For a moment he could hardly catch his breath. He sensed that nothing he said, let alone his presence there on the quayside, let alone his love, would have any effect on the fine-boned, fine-featured man standing in front of him.

Although a wide-brimmed hat shaded the forehead, there was no hiding from the sun the pallor of the usually rather sallow complexion and the way the skin tautened ascetically over the newly clean-shaven cheekbones. A little self-consciously and rather abruptly Brother Peter disguised himself by putting on thick-rimmed dark glasses. He was dressed in a neat, old-fashioned, double-breasted, pin-stripe suit. The dark glasses made him anonymous. Save for the incongruously new black shoes and a hold-all slung over one shoulder, he looked as civilian and slightly down-at-heel as the majority of the alighting passengers.

'Brother!' Father Christoph embraced him impulsively. '*Brat moi!*' is what he actually said, offering the Russian as a reason for holding him tighter than he should have done. Something about Brother Peter, his innocence, his idealism, perhaps his cleverness and his vulnerability, his courage and his conviction, made Father Christoph feel deeply protective towards him as if he were his own son. 'Why?' he breathed.

Brother Peter put his hand up to his open neck when Father Christoph released him. It was a gesture partly designed to tidy, partly to ward off. 'My American clothes?'

'American!' Father Christoph had forgotten he had come originally from America. 'No, no. I mean why are you leaving us? Why are you doing this? You know we love you. We want you to stay.' Brother Peter resettled the strap of the hold-all on his shoulder. Without his beard his face looked twenty years younger, Father Christoph thought. 'Why?' he asked more persistently.

'It is God's will. You know that.'

These were exchanges best left to a monk's cell, the old man admitted to himself. He knew there was a certain justice in what Brother Peter hoped to do, and he could only do it in the world of public affairs. Rather timidly he started saying:

'You cannot expect the world to be silent. Think a moment. Do you want me to be silent?'

The other turned even as Father Christoph was speaking. He appeared to be trying not to hear the words. He strode along the quayside in a determined effort to keep up with the rest of those leaving the ferry.

'Look!' Father Christoph seized him by the arm. Dribbles of sweat were beginning to run down his cheeks. 'You are likely to put yourself in the hands of the living god! Please, please, stop a moment and think!'

'I have thought. I have thought for decades.'

'I know, I know. But just think again!'

'And I have decided. I am doing God's will.'

'You have threatened someone's life!' Father Christoph protested. 'That cannot be God's will!'

'I have been dead for more than thirty years,' Brother Peter said.

'I know that.'

'And I am rising from the dead to do what I have to do.'

Father Christoph could not deny it. He could not deny that Brother Peter had been denied his true identity. Worse, he had been declared dead. What he was doing now was a kind of resurrection.

He saw the two men then. They came forward out of the

shade of the warehouse, more, it seemed, in recognition of him than of his companion and Father Christoph suddenly realized what he had done by coming down to the ferry.

He had inadvertently identified Brother Peter to the very people from whom he had wanted to protect him!

It was already late, perhaps too late, but Father Christoph suddenly, uncharacteristically, in an awkward, elderly tantrum-like explosion of energy, seized Brother Peter and began pulling him backwards, towards the ferry, against the flow of people, trying to force his protégé to come with him and to persuade people to make way. He would protect him from evil!

All he could catch hold of was the strap. He heaved at it and Brother Peter did yield for several paces, letting himself be pulled along a short way. And then one of the two men yanked the strap hard and Father Christoph found himself spun off his feet.

Maybe it took half a second but in his mind's eye, remembering it, he could say it took ages, ages of slow backward tilting, of eyes noticing in child-like curiosity the wooden awning of the warehouse, of the sun bending towards him in its bright occupation of half the sky and the deep, deep blue of the rest of it, the turning, tumbling shape of the blue funnel of the liner and the flat stonework of the quay coming up towards his face, one hand outstretched towards it, a fleeting prayer for divine assistance already on his lips before the stonework struck him a blow to the side of his face and, before all the pain, before the blood started, he was looking at a yellowing sliver of orange peel lying within a few centimetres of his eyes.

Beyond it, carried away as if they belonged to a doll, the two almost unmarked soles of Brother Peter's new black shoes dangled a moment and were rushed away despite his continuing pleas. Hands were reaching down to lift him up. He was lifted. Already the Mercedes was moving away. Its dark, tinted windows were black as coal as it edged out of the shade of the warehouse and people moved aside for it to enter the dazzle of the sunlight and move off briskly down the quay into the other exiting traffic, past the air-conditioned coaches receiving the tourists from the liner, and on into the city.

'You're hurt, Father! Your cheek is bleeding!'

'No, it is my heart, that is what bleeds!'

He stood upright, thanking his helpers. For the first time in his life he knew he had to violate the vow of secrecy that he had always observed in hearing another's confession. Bewildered, he could not understand why there was such a feebleness in his knees. His hat had come off and the sun was burning his head.

'Father!' A man caught him. He knew he was about to faint. Then a woman dabbed at his cheek and he saw the blood.

'I must te-le-phone... te-le-phone... Kind people, I must...'

***

The Mercedes left the harbour area and entered a boulevard. Brother Peter licked his lips and prayed. He had tried to struggle against his captors, but he knew it was God's will that he should bide his time. It might well be that these people had been sent to help him despite appearing to hold him captive. He particularly hated the man on his right. He was plump and sweaty, in a wrinkled suit and dark shades, with a two days growth of beard blackening his jawline and cheeks. And he had puffy, red, permanently half-open lips. Brother Peter prayed to be forgiven for hating him.

He could not tell right from wrong. All he could tell was that the world was feminine. It was full of girls.

They walked to work, waited at bus stops, strolled under the trees, gazed in shop windows. How he tried to shade his eyes from the sensual allure of their bosoms and their swaying hips and their long brown legs! He could tell just from fleeting glimpses through the car window how delightful it would be to run his hands over the naked skin of their shoulders and breasts, hold their hips, feel the curves of their thighs and clutch their soft roundnesses, their shapeliness possessing not a cold marble statuesqueness but a living naked warmth that required to be stroked and caressed by a loving touch.

It was a shining sin! Shame on you, Brother Peter!

Years and years, half a lifetime too long. Except for books and pictures and statues he had not seen a girl, a living girl. Now here was a world full of girls. They were more gorgeous than the luscious oleander flowers he had loved to watch from his cell window, more lissom than the tall cypresses. He had not imagined there would be this much temptation facing him once he had left heaven and been resurrected into the world of men.

He watched the boulevard go by and the streets grow narrower, walls separating the houses from the streets and trees obscuring their facades. It was a world made dark by the dark glasses. The men either side of him were dark presences. He did not look at them but stared ahead of him between the two front seats. The inverted V of the street scene came towards him as the Mercedes climbed almost silently and passed through gates into a small courtyard in front of a house.

The man on his right pulled him sharply by the arm. Brother Peter resented such treatment but would not show it. He eased himself along the leather of the rear seat and out into the sunlight, the hold-all still over his shoulder. He had not sweated yet. He was not going to display any anxiety. The man indicated with his thumb he should follow.

They entered a wide, cool hall and crossed it and a woman approached and took the hold-all from him. He could read people's faces and he trusted her. It was pleasantly cool in the house but he did not take off his hat. He was making no concessions.

At the back there was this large room with a mosaic floor and pieces of expensive furniture. Double doors led onto a wide vine-covered verandah overlooking a small walled patio. At its centre was a fountain. The single jet caught the sunlight and resembled a vertical diamond necklace of water set against the dark green of cypresses. Brother Peter paused to admire the sight.

'Ah, Piotr Nikolaevich! Welcome!'

A white-haired man rose from beside a table where he had been sitting and extended a hand. He had a cultivated appearance and a cultivated voice. The cigarette in an onyx holder in his other hand drew a skein of smoke through the air that formed a large letter O.

Brother Peter saw this, enjoyed the sight, but found himself pushed from behind. Resentment turned to anger in an instant. He rounded on the plump man behind him and said quietly:

'Do not push me.'

He took off his sunglasses as he spoke. The plump man ignored the rebuke. He laughed and repeated the movement.

Few things annoyed Brother Peter more. He knew he should suppress his anger, but he could not. He slowly placed his folded sunglasses in the top pocket of his jacket.

The man's hand was still outstretched. Brother Peter seized it and with a firm, vice-like movement pulled the fingers apart. He had two fingers in each hand. Then he jerked them sharply backwards.

The puffy mouth fell wide open. The man dropped to his knees gasping with the sudden pain. Agony creased his face into a replica of a small boy's on the verge of tears. The mouth went square in a silent yell and the forehead broke out in a cluster of sweat beads.

'*Bozhe moi! Pal'tsi! Pal'tsi! U-mol-ia-iu...*'

Brother Peter held the fingers until they were within a hair's breadth of breaking. He knew how the pain would go right down the length of the arm and would feel like the fires of hell. He released the fingers only after leaning forward and gazing for a second or two through the dark lenses of the man's shades into the depths of his eyes.

The plump man gasped with pain. He was too agonised and ashamed to look at his tormentor. He merely glanced at the white-haired man and, without even climbing to his feet, scampered backwards on his knees through the double doors, clutching his fingers and still gasping. A moment later he could be heard running across the mosaic floor.

'So...'

The white-haired man had remained standing during the finger-bending exercise. He drew the cigarette slowly from its holder and stubbed it out.

'So, Piotr Nikolaevich, where did you learn that?'

He was reassured by the sight. He had the sense that he was not dealing with a monk, as he had anticipated, but with someone more like an assassin.

'Special training, God forgive me.'

Both knew what he meant. They were both products of the former state of things, trained in a former life to do things that they had now outgrown or no longer found relevant.

'Then please sit down.' The white-haired man offered a glass of wine but it was refused in favour of a glass of orange juice. He poured the juice from a jug. 'I do apologise for my Kolia's behaviour. You dealt with it quite appropriately.'

Brother Peter sat down, sipped the orange juice and watched the play of the fountain's jet in the sunlight. He hated himself for having been angered.

'I am, as I think you know, Koursaros,' said the white-haired man. 'It is a suitable name to have here in Greece. Please call me Pavel Ivanovich.' He stretched his neck. It was sun-bronzed but worn like his face and looked particularly thin against the smartness of the open collar of his neat blue shirt. He crossed his bare sunburned arms and showed he was wearing a gold Cartier watch on his left wrist. 'You show no surprise at being brought here?'

'You sent a message.' Brother Peter glanced at his questioner.

'I know. But we did not know – well, how much you might have changed.'

'I deserved more courteous treatment.'

Koursaros smiled. 'Of course. I apologise again. You see we are very similar in a great many ways. Our identities, for instance, have changed many times. We have had to work in secret, haven't we? And you have been so secret you have literally ceased to live – in the real world, I mean.'

'I have been in heaven,' Brother Peter said.

'Really?'

'Among my spiritual brothers.'

'You call that heaven, do you?'

'A life without temptations of the flesh – that is heaven. If you are spiritually strong enough. If you are at one with God.'

'But you are not at one with God?'

There was a teasing tone in the question that Brother Peter ignored. 'God has summoned me to act on the ideals of our intelligentsia, in the name of our old pre-revolutionary intelligentsia. I am doing God's will.'

'Of course. I understand that. You have always been an idealist. I respect you for your ideals.' Koursaros unfolded his arms and took a cigarette from a packet lying on the table. He did not put it in the onyx holder but slowly ran its tube backwards and forwards between forefinger and thumb. 'Perhaps you believe we have been cheated of those ideals, the old ideals, I mean?'

'I do.'

'Yes, I can understand that.' He went on rolling the tube of the cigarette backwards and forwards. 'They are only measured in dollars or euros these days. Permit me to say this, dear Piotr Nikolaevich – if the only way to act is to follow Bakunin in assuming that *Die Lust der Zerstoering ist auch eine shaffende Lust*, then let us assume it is true – that the love of destruction is also a creative love.' The speaker pushed the cigarette into the onyx holder. 'The power to strike at the top is itself power enough.'

'They did strike at the top. On March 1st, when the emperor was mortally wounded. They did it all for the people.'

Koursaros contemplated the small man opposite him and again smiled. 'True.' A lighter was ignited. 'Let us be practical.' He blew smoke towards the verandah ceiling. 'You can speak quite openly here. No one is listening. How do you intend to get close enough? You know what I mean.'

Brother Peter did not even deign to look at the speaker. He gazed at the fountain again and said quietly:

'Someone I know.'

The other gave a sigh. 'Would he perhaps be English?'

'English?'

'Yes, the person you know. English?'

'In my former life the only person I ever trusted completely was an Englishman. He was family and you shot him.'

'Ah.'

This monk who looks like a gangster, Koursaros thought, will be difficult: he *remembers*. He remembers too much. Koursaros scratched his chin and yawned. 'You are talking about an English diplomat, I think?'

'Why did you shoot him?'

Out of the mouths of babes and sucklings... Koursaros winced. 'Shoot? I?'

'You!'

'No, no, Piotr Nikolaevich, I appeal to you. Do not be so naïve. I did not shoot to kill. In any case, it was not serious enough to cause lasting damage. All it did was destroy his career, but then we have all of us lost our careers.'

'I trusted him,' Brother Peter said quietly, 'and he was family.'

'So he will help you now?'

A nod.

'I cannot see how he will get you close.'

There was a silence between them filled with the faint splashing of the fountain and the hum of insects. A vehicle changed gear loudly on the other side of the wall.

'There is someone.'

Koursaros respected the other man's right to secrecy. He knew when not to ask too many questions, especially if it were a matter of family connections. What is more, he did not want to deter this genius from doing what he wanted to do.

'We will shock the world,' he said, raising a glass of wine. 'To our success!'

It was not clear whether his listener heard. The noise of the water splashing in the fountain seemed excessively loud.

***

The Air France charter flight to Paris that evening from Thessaloniki had two extra seats occupied. Separated by an aisle and three rows, the two men did not speak to each other or acknowledge each other throughout the flight. On arrival in Paris they stayed at separate hotels near the Gare du

Nord. Both spoke French of a kind and were able to pass as businessmen with international connections.

Pavel Ivanovich Koursaros attracted more attention than the other. Interpol had been alerted to the possibility that he might break cover and coded information had been passed to London and Washington. He was considered dangerous as a fixer rather than an operative in his own right. He was known to be an ex-member of the Soviet KGB who had built up a network of international business connections linked to people trafficking and the drug trade and what was vaguely known as the Russian Mafia. Various media reports from Russia claimed he was involved in the formation of a new political party.

The next day the two men caught the Eurostar from Paris to London. Seats had been booked diagonally opposite each other so they scarcely ever needed to exchange looks. To all appearances they were travelling separately, but Pavel Ivanovich Koursaros mistrusted his companion.

Throughout the journey the man called Brother Peter looked inconspicuous in his corner seat. His hat pulled down as if he were asleep, he had his face turned to the window and surreptitiously watched the reflections of a French girl and her mother seated opposite. They were talking in busy whispers. When the train entered the channel tunnel their words went on and on just like their reflections going flicker-flicker, flicker-flicker in the darkened window glass.

He was enthralled by the girl. She was beautiful. He watched her because he could tell she knew she was. The self-conscious way she moved her eyes to meet the glances of men passing down the central aisle excited her. He could tell her body, like her eyes, had antennae. She enjoyed the game of being beautiful. He watched her reflection and waited for her to look at him.

She did. It was the first time a beautiful girl had looked at him in more than thirty years. Had she any idea how full his heart was? None. She glanced away even from his reflection.

For the rest of the journey he prayed unceasingly.

It was madness, insanity. He knew it was. But he hoped against hope he might meet the girl of his dreams.

2

Raoul Cyrus Smithson was black and had been in the CIA long before positive discrimination was politically correct. He did not resent racists. He was known to be a stickler – plan speech, minimum jargon, good sense, no crudity. But that morning he resented being summoned to the White House.

He parked in one of the bays reserved for CIA personnel. Colonel Howarth's black assistant Darlene Audubon even asked after his wife because she knew they shared the same name, Darlene, and Smithson said his Darlene was fine. They chatted as she and an armed civilian guard accompanied him along corridors to Ed Kalthorst's office.

Ed had risen in the world. He had long ago cast off the diffidence of a liaison officer with CIA and State Department connections. Now he was a fully-fledged White House official temporarily delegated to the presidential security committee. The smile he directed at his visitor and the firmness of his handshake were an index of his self-confidence.

'R.C., good to see you. Please sit down. This is between us, between you and me, you understand.'

Smithson sat down in a brand-new button-backed green leather armchair. He deemed it an accolade to be seated in something so squeaky new. A button-backed leather armchair was pure Ed, pure Ed Kalthorst – correct, old-fashioned, smart, fastidious, neat. Lifting his right ankle negligently and placing it on his left knee, Smithson looked at tastefully framed eighteenth-century watercolours on the walls. They were all good, some probably good reproductions, some probably genuinely good originals. That was Ed, pure Ed Kalthorst. The same could be said of the rest of the furnishings, including the desk and the ormolu clock on the top of an attractive drinks cabinet – some good repro given a degree of respectability by the occasional genuine article. That just about summed up Ed as it summed up the credentials of the present incumbent of the oval office.

'I apologise for two things,' said Ed. He adopted a chummy tone. Smithson was known to close friends as 'R.C.' so Ed affixed that badge to his remarks. 'R.C., I mean it when I say it's good to see you. And I apologise for asking you to curtail your final vacation before retirement, that's one thing. I know you may feel resentful…'

'I am resentful.'

'Right. And with good reason. It's understandable. But, as you know, the president's security must have priority. I know you'll understand it if I say we, all of us here – and I'm speaking on behalf of everyone here at the sharp end – will be deeply grateful to you for sparing the time to help us. I hope that doesn't sound too unctuous. I apologise if it does.'

Unctuous. Ed, you ball of grease, you could sell 'unctuous' for Christmas! Smithson snapped his fingers.

'And the other thing,' said Ed unctuously, 'I must also apologise for involving you at this late stage,'

'How late?'

'Well, the president's due to fly to England in two days' time.'

'So?'

'I mean there's not much time.'

'You mean I ought to be out there? When?'

'Not later than today.'

He was being hassled. Smithson knew you did not decline assignments involving presidential security. But he also knew he was being hassled.

'I see.'

Ed Kalthorst had a way of simultaneously shaking his head and tightening his lips. He used this kind of reinforcement rather than use his hands. It made him seem inscrutable and authoritative.

'It has to be today. I mean it. Mrs Van Straubenzee's already in London, otherwise she'd be here to tell you all this herself. It's like this, R.C., we've known each other a long time and there's a whole new generation out there who have no idea what it was really like during the Cold War. You and I know what it was like then, back under Brezhnev and a bit later. I'd say we were buddies then, wouldn't you?'

Smithson conceded they were work buddies. He would never have considered Ed a close friend. Ed had a way of redesigning himself to suit every change of decade and political fashion. Evidently he was now in a kind of patrician eighteenth-century phase of benevolent democratic absolutism.

'Yes, well, let me add something. Mrs Van Straubenzee has picked up a little item you and I know about and she's anxious.'

'You're talking about the Interpol report?'

'I'm talking about something else, which we both know about. Pinckney?'

The name could have had a shock effect. For Smithson it was shocking, but he did not respond as the questioner expected. Certain matters in their past were covered by a prohibition of such secrecy it was a sign of bad taste to refer to them. For one thing, they belonged to the Cold War and the Cold War was over. For another, Smithson did not like being reminded. He merely said, almost under his breath:

'Pinckney's dead.'

'I know that. But you know who I mean?'

'Pinckney's dead.'

'You've checked?'

'Of course, I've checked. The files have been erased. Extreme prejudice.'

'Surely there must be something.'

'Just explain to me who the hell it is we're talking about?'

'You know who I mean.'

Ed looked directly at the other man. It astonished him how little Raoul Cyrus Smithson had changed. The fresh, unwrinkled look of the brown face, the firmness of the line round the jaw, the strong, protuberant shape of the lips, the way the returning look of the charcoal eyes could have been that of a self-confident twenty-year-old, as firm and strong and straight as his tall, lithe figure. Ed again shook his head.

'R.C.,' he said in as much lower, more confidential voice, 'it's why I wanted you and me, just the two of us.'

'So?'

'You and I were the first people to interview him. Well, we were, weren't we?'

'I don't remember any *him*.'

There was a short silence.

'Of course he was a man!' Ed said.

'I saw a woman.'

'R.C., it was *not* a woman!'

'I interviewed a woman!'

'You did not interview a woman!'

Ed's voice had risen. He was almost shouting. Smithson made a face. 'You say so.'

'I do say so! I admit I may have thought he was a transvestite but it was a *he*, not a *she*! Let's be clear about that.'

'You may be clear about it. I'm not clear about it.'

'For God's sake!' Ed was angry at being contradicted. He breathed in deeply. He could do without this. 'But you'd recognise him, wouldn't you? If you were to see him again, you'd recognise him, wouldn't you?'

'Consider the facts, Ed,' said Smithson in a pleasant, level tone of voice, pouring an oil of common sense on the suddenly troubled waters. 'I interviewed a person dressed as a woman. The person was a transvestite maybe, or gay, but he, she, it could have been a woman. We interviewed her, him, it, - what? God knows how many decades ago? Eh? Within an hour of the person in question appearing in the embassy. And you expect me to recognise this person - her, him, whatever – from that first interview? And as I recall it, Ed, you and I were both rookie agents of the firm out there in the US embassy in Moscow, under a lot of pressure to acquire sensitive information about the Soviet rocket programme, right? And suddenly this *person* turns up claiming to be a leading rocket scientist.' He paused and held his hands wide. 'Tell me if I'm wrong, Ed?'

'No, no, okay, that's all correct.'

Smithson licked his lips. 'So, from what I recall, we obtained information, right? You know what I mean – *Raduga* and all that. Then what I remember is that specialist – remember him, 'Thorough Thoreau', of blessed memory – he insisted the whole thing should be put under wraps at once and, rightly or wrongly, that's what was done. The story we reported was that a Soviet maidservant had defected. She was on sovereign United States territory and we respected her human rights, etc., etc. *That's* who we had! Not a rocket scientist, just some poor woman who wanted to get away from a drunken husband. She, he, whichever was concealed. In one of those converted suites. Remember? And we were told on pain of death or worse not to say a word about it.' This was where Smithson's resentment showed itself for the first time clearly and unequivocally. 'I didn't have charge of anything to do with her, him, whoever being cargo-ed out. In any case, let me remind you we didn't exactly trust her, him, it. It took two years, didn't it?'

Silence.

There was a tired note in Ed's voice when he spoke eventually. 'All right, all right, I accept your version.'

Smithson said nothing to that. He disliked the atmosphere developing between them and felt it better not to stir things further.

Ed Kalthorst sucked his teeth. He patted a file on the desk. 'All the evidence in here suggests the person we're talking about was given the identity of a certain James Pinckney.'

'What file's that?'

'Mrs Van Straubenzee's.'

So that's it! No computer data, nothing online! Everything on file here in the White House! Smithson shook his head in disbelief and some admiration. 'Okay, so what's it say? If you feel I'm a fit person to know, of course.'

Ed smiled sourly. 'You're fit, R.C. It doesn't say much, as a matter of fact. It says what you've already said about extreme prejudice, that there's a burial plot in his name in Forest Lawns, so he very likely lived somewhere in the Los Angeles area. Doing what, I don't know.'

'No certification?'

'In a manner of speaking, yes, there is. But I have to say it's questionable. There is an address in West L.A. but it's so old it probably means it's now a freeway or a shopping mall.'

The atmosphere between them was changing. Smithson struck his thigh with the flat of his hand. He even permitted himself a brief laugh.

'I'd say he, she, it was awkward, didn't play along! So what's the connection with the Interpol report?'

'I don't know. It's Mrs Van Straubenzee – her hunch.'

'Jees-*us*!' Smithson again snapped his fingers. 'So you've got me here just to tell me it's one of her hunches!'

'R.C., please! Her hunches have been very reliable. Mostly very reliable.'

Loyal ole Ed Kalthorst! Smithson thought. 'Alright, so what's this reliable hunch?'

'I know it may seem tenuous, but there is a connection.' Ed stood up and went over to the window. The Washington Memorial shone distantly through sunlit spring greenery. He said softly:

'Konovalov, Pavel Ivanovich. Ring a bell?'

'Konovalov, Kostomarov, Kalganov, Koursaros – all the Ks, clickety-click!'

'So you know who I mean?'

'Sure.'

'He's broken cover.'

'So what's new?'

'There's been a report from Greece. The report is private intelligence and may not be reliable. It is that this Koursaros, with his numerous different identities, is planning something spectacular, like, quite probably, the assassination of the president of the United States. And we ought to take the threat seriously.'

Smithson had been responsible for keeping an eye on Koursaros for many years. He had first come across him in connection with what was known as 'the *Raduga* incident' in the last years of the Soviet era. He had seemed to wield quite unusual authority within the KGB, to the point of being able to spring one of the key figures of the Soviet rocket programme to the West and to do it so blatantly that it left US intelligence wondering whether or not the key figure (code-named Pinckney) could be trusted. This may have been intentional, of course, although certain valuable information was imparted.

Meanwhile, in the post-Soviet era, Kourasros had undergone several changes of identity for various reasons and was now rumoured to be a major financial supporter of a newly formed political party.

'Private intelligence? What private intelligence?'

'An elderly priest, as a matter of fact.' Ed fiddled with his silk tie. He stood by the window and looked well-tailored and trim in his black suit. 'He has said that a threat has been issued.'

'You mean Koursaros has issued this threat?'

'Yes. And he's been traced to London. And surprise, surprise, the president's due to fly to London in a couple of days.'

'It's not his style,' Smithson said.

'What isn't?'

'Assassination. Koursaros, or whatever his name is. Sure, he's got political ambitions, that's why we've kept a watch on him, and he's got the money. There've been anti-American statements attributed to him, true, but statements like that by Russian politicians don't count for peanuts. His methods have always been covert. Why should he want to assassinate the president? I tell you it's not his style. Not on the available evidence.'

'I don't care what his style is,' said Ed Kalthorst. His voice had acquired a sharp edge of authority. 'He poses a threat and you've been looking after him, R.C. He must be neutralised. Stopped. This new party, the Party of the People's Will, has proclaimed itself anti-American and it advocates terrorism as a legitimate means of achieving its political aims. In my book that constitutes a serious threat.'

Smithson knew he was right. 'So what do you want me to do? Fly to London and do what?'

Ed returned to his desk and sat down.

'The situation is this. Their MI5, their anti-terror people are working on it. They know about the threat. They know he has connections in London. They're keeping an eye on him, but they know he's slippery. They'd like your help. After all, the threat nowadays is mostly jihadist. That's what's being concentrated on. Something like this doesn't have priority. So they'd like help over *this* threat.'

'Surely we've got people over there already?'

'Of course, of course. But they don't know Koursaros. More important, they never interviewed the *person* we interviewed, the one who became Pinckney, the one who's most likely Mrs Van Straubenzee's hunch.'

'Who are we now talking about?' Smithson cried. 'The living dead? You want me to look for the *living dead* as well as Koursaros?

'Okay, cool it, R.C.! No, no. Let Mrs Van Straubenzee look after her hunch. No, there was a British contact, wasn't there? You met him, you knew him.'

Contact?

Smithson looked up at the ceiling. It was so many years ago and, God knows, there had been so many changes. The name was associated with some kind of germ, germ-something. It was a strange name, one he'd never been thoroughly familiar with. All he could think was how hopelessly different everything was now, particularly in the ambience of Ed Kalthorst's sparkling new office with its smell of new leather and wax polish and smartness.

'You must help me on this. Come on, Ed. Germ-something, germ... germ...'

'You can check it out yourself.'

Smithson agreed he could. But if he were due to leave today, when would he have the time?

'There was a senior member of the firm over there,' said

Ed. He flipped open a pad and consulted it. 'Oldfield. Wilbur Oldfield. Remember him?'

Smithson remembered him. Wilbur Oldfield bore a resemblance to Clint Eastwood. It was a silly way of thinking about someone he hadn't seen for maybe twenty years and yet that's what he remembered: the same kind of tight-skinned face if slightly broader.

'Wilbur won't be much help,' Ed said. 'He's retired.'

'I thought he ran things his way and wasn't sort of…'

'If you mean he had a reputation for working on his own, that's right. They like that over there.'

'So I go to London. With what empowerment?' asked Smithson.

'To keep that maniac away from the president.

'To what degree of prejudice?'

'For God's sake, you know the protocol, you don't have to ask that, R.C.! I leave it to your experience and good judgement. I just want to be able to assure the security committee that the threat has been taken seriously and we have an experienced agent already assigned to deal with it.'

Smithson nodded. 'Okay, Ed, I get it. Darlene won't like it. She'll scream at me. She'll remind me I should have taken the offer of retirement and put on my slippers and been done with all this stuff.'

'You'll do it,' Ed said. 'I knew you would. By the way, there'll be a ticket waiting for you out in the travel desk. *Bon voyage!*'

Damn you, Ed Kalhorst! So he'd had me lined up for this from the start! Smithson received the gentle pat on the shoulder with a smirk and strolled loose-limbed out of Ed Kalthorst's office, exchanged a pleasantry with one of the outer office staff and heard the electronic release work the locks on the outer door. A small packet was presented to him just before he left by a middle-aged woman at a very tidy desk. He signed, nodded regarding passport and visa and stood for a quick mugshot. He then stepped out into the corridor to find the civilian guard ready to accompany him back to the other Darlene who was glad to remain with him until he had returned to his car in the parking bay.

Germ, germ, germ, he muttered. It annoyed him not to get the name right. He followed the filter lane into the traffic and breathed in and out hard trying to remember. Vehicular movement was slow as usual but the sunshine bounced off metallic paintwork and chrome fenders and gave him a sense of wellbeing. Springtime in Washington always had that effect. London, though, was something else. Those cabs like top hats on wheels and the poor coffee, not to mention the habit of driving on the wrong side.

He had this white kid assistant, newly graduated from Yale, it was said, Ivy League coming out of his ears, not honest NYU as he was, and it amused him to send him off on a wild goose chase after this and that. Having reached his own office, he unbuttoned his shirt collar and drew off his necktie.

'Okay, Joel, I know I shouldn't be here. I'm meant to be on vacation.'

'Sir,' said Joel Seabrook, the Yale graduate.

'Just one thing. I want the latest update on Koursaros. Send it to my cellphone. So I can bone up on the flight.'

'What flight, sir?'

He said he had to fly to London. Joel raised an eyebrow.

'Since I'm going to London, no more of this *sir* stuff, if you please.' Smithson smiled to himself. 'I'm likely to be associating with royalty. Lord Smithson from now on.'

'Your Lordship.' Joel gave a mock bow.

'Cut it out. Oh, another thing. See what you can find on an English diplomat at the British embassy at the time of

Brezhnev or maybe a bit later. Germ-something, a name like that. Germ… germ… Jermin, that's it! Jermin! J-e-r-m-y-n. Got it!'

Hell, it was all so vague, but at least the name had come to him. Joel Seabrook was keen and reliable. Smithson traded on that. He was responsible for initiating him into the firm.

'Remember, I'm still on vacation,' he said as he left the office. 'Do your best.'

One thing, of course, would not be in dispute: security for the president's visit would be tight. The present incumbent of the White House was of a nervous disposition. The president *liked* security. That was one of the reasons why Ed Kalthorst was where he was and wanted to cover his ass with the security committee by having this extra precaution taken.

The presidential stopover in London was scheduled to take in one night. Hopefully, Smithson thought, he would not have to accompany the presidential entourage to its final destination of a global peace conference in Geneva. So it was perhaps three days in London.

Darlene was not happy. She had an overnight bag packed for him but again pressed the retirement angle. 'Raoul dear, it's what we've talked about.'

But the adrenal had been set going. 'Three days, honey. Can you just let up about it for three days?'

'You're a junkie! You know it! You want a new fix!'

Smithson shrugged. 'Maybe you're right. Maybe I can never get it out of my blood.'

But he held his wife close. That was what he could never get out of his blood: his love for this woman he had spent almost twenty-five years with, the feel of her body against his, the sheer delight of that trusted and secure intimacy.

3

He did not first think the envelope contained more than an item of promotional literature. Maybe it was some glossy brochure or calendar featuring either exquisitely photographed landscapes or exquisitely photographed nude girls.

Such stuff came daily. It lay there on his desk because he had only flown in from Tokyo that morning and had been busy meeting colleagues ever since. He had phoned home but received no reply.

The wall clock showed 8.15 p.m., his watch showed 8.18. His desk computer shone brightly but was annoyingly undemonstrative. It showed him the day's emails and otherwise gave no sign of life. He waited for it to tell him what he wanted, which was why he was very likely the only member of staff left in the entire block of City of London offices. He sat back in his high-backed swivel armchair and muttered impatiently: 'Come on! Come on! You said at the latest by 8.00 p.m. GMT.'

There was one last mouthful of tepid coffee to be swallowed. Then he binned the styrofoam cup. Eighteen or nineteen minutes late. Damn them. He knew their computer system had been down and there'd been apologies and promises, including the 8.00 p.m. promise, but he still felt irritated and tired by the delay. He yawned, wiped his mouth with the back of his hand and felt the silence of the place encroach moment by moment. He knew if he closed his eyes the aircraft noise would be back.

Folding his arms and deliberately fighting his tiredness, he stared at the ceiling. Neon strip lighting set into grey panels emitted the dead whiteness of subdued snow-glare. He moved his head, exercising his neck and shoulder muscles, and thought about the Tokyo agreement. If it worked as he hoped it would, then IIC, his insurance group, would be set for the best results ever.

Very distantly, through double-glazing, he heard vehicles pass in the street below. The electric wall clock gave a sharp tick. Another minute had passed. He thought about the kitchen at home when he was a boy and the sound of the old kitchen clock. His mother had loved having the kitchen as her world.

Her world. She had talked about it with a mixture of fondness and disgust as if it were a distant illness from which she had long recovered. Her Russian world, that is, the world of Russian emigration in which she had lived as a child, a world really belonging to *her* mother, his grandmother. From it he had acquired the language as a legacy and a faint sense of never being a true participant in the English world of his birth.

A door closed somewhere. He was startled and unfolded his arms. A cleaner? Some of the cleaners would be mustering about this time. A ghost? This block of City of London offices was hardly old enough to generate a ghost. Anyhow why now?

He jumped up from his desk. He knew his nerves were frayed but this was ridiculous. He was made jumpy by the slightest sound.

Then he jumped again.

Someone had tapped on the door. He saw the shape of a man in the mottled glass panel.

'Who is it?'

'Just me, sir.'

It was Flying Officer, the night janitor. He poked his familiar thin face round the door. He was of pensionable age but had a waxed moustache and a habit of wearing an old blazer with brass buttons that made him look like an elderly fighter pilot. Hence his nickname. He saw the look of shock on the other's face.

'Sorry, Mr Jermin, sir, I didn't mean to disturb you.'

'No, no, I was waiting for an email.'

'You got it then, did you?'

'Got what?'

'It was delivered by hand. The envelope, sir.'

'Oh, yes, thank you. Delivered by hand, you say?'

'Yes, sir.'

'You didn't see who it was, did you?'

'No, sir.'

At that moment an email was announced on the computer screen and he saw it had an attachment. That was what he had been waiting for.

'You've done me a favour,' he said to Flying Officer. 'You've come just at the right moment.'

'Well, sir, I...'

Bob Jermin asked about Flying Officer's wife who was in hospital.

'Oh, sir, improving, yes.' Flying Officer's hand rose to his moustache and lightly twiddled a waxed end. He couldn't help giving himself an air of authority. 'Her colour's better, that's one thing. I'm worried she's so thin. I keep trying to get 'er to eat but she says she doesn't feel like it. She can be very stubborn.'

'So the operation was all right?'

'Oh, Ella's well over that, sir. She's improving, yes, sir. Thank you for inquiring.' He gave a smart, bent-fingered salute. 'I'll just check on some of the other offices.'

He closed the door behind him and Bob Jermin concentrated

on the email and its attachment. It was as he had hoped. The longstanding arrangements with Tokyo for reinsurance had been renewed and on much more advantageous terms. He glanced through the dense script of the attachment to check that the paragraphs were roughly as had been agreed while simultaneously using a paper knife to slit open the envelope. It took him at least a couple of minutes to scan the succeeding lines of formal script before he reached the signatures at the bottom. It was exactly as had been agreed.

Only then did he extract the material from the envelope. What he drew out was not promotional material. It was an enlarged black-and-white grainy photographic print. Two figures appeared in it, one recognisably himself and the other a girl in a white fur hat. Both were naked. They were depicted facing the camera with light falling from above. Her shorter, thinner figure looked child-like beside his. It seemed more vulnerable through the way in which the white fur hat accentuated the unsophisticated pose of the outward thrust of her small breasts and the immature slope of her shoulders. Her features were largely in shadow because the fall of her hair curtained either side of her face. Somehow her apparent childishness, with her arms hanging loosely at her sides by her slender hips, almost accentuating her sex and her long, thin, attractive legs, emphasised by contrast his masculinity. Particularly conspicuous, as if deliberately drawing attention to his penis, was a scar running at an angle across his stomach, the result of a boyhood cycling accident.

A shiver went down his spine like lightning. He was paralysed by what he saw. His thoughts raced.

Flying officer had said… He took in several deep breaths. By hand. The envelope had been delivered *by hand*. He dropped the print on the desk and dashed out into the corridor. He ran as far as the landing, stopped, knew he was being silly and returned to his office. He rang down to the reception desk. There was the usual answerphone monologue asking callers to leave messages after the tone. Obviously reception was unmanned.

But Flying Officer knew. Staff would have left by 6.30 at the latest. It meant the stuff had probably arrived during the past hour and a half. Flying Officer had not seen who delivered it, so...

And then he found it. Inside the envelope was a single sheet of paper with a handwritten message in felt-tipped capitals: WE SHOW YOUR WIFE?

He slumped back into his chair.

The last time he had seen this blown-up print, for all its blurring of detail, his naked figure had been recognisable enough and the implication that he had been engaged in lewd behaviour with a girl-child dressed in a funny white hat was as obvious as daylight. Certainly obvious enough for its smell of scandal to have cast doubt on his diplomatic career and finally ended it.

It had *neutralised* him. That was the Foreign Office verdict. Of course, that was before he married Marsha. Would Marsha recognise him in this bold version? Yes, he knew she would because his figure hadn't changed all that much. And if she'd also been sent a copy she'd probably be ready to *neutralise* him, not to mention the equally *neutralising* effect if the picture were to appear on Twitter or Facebook. The number of colleagues coming to the office wearing silly white hats, for instance, could be legion. So naturally he rang his home number again. Again there was no answer.

He sat in his car in the almost empty basement car park. He bit the tip of his thumb. It was all a hell of a long time ago. Why was this kind of malicious, blackmailing and intimidating stuff being sent to him, Robert Simon Jermin? Why now? What possible relevance could it have to his present career in international insurance? And why involve Marsha? She had been his girlfriend before he went to Moscow, but he had done everything he could to hide this photo from her. It had done what it had been intended to do. It had destroyed him. Was it intended to destroy his marriage as well?

He switched on the engine. His card activated the gate to the basement car park and he drove up the ramp to street level. A light smattering of raindrops was instantly dispersed by the arcing wipers. He joined the traffic along Upper Thames Street and then along the Victoria Embankment where sponge-like trees in full leaf passed by one by one in the glow of his dipped headlights.

4

Raoul Cyrus Smithson flew into London Heathrow to find the installation of staging for the presidential arrival was already in progress. There would be an official welcome by royalty, a review of a guard of honour and then a short presidential statement for the media and members of a specially selected welcoming party. After that the president was scheduled to board a helicopter for the flight into central London.

The air of controlled panic round Heathrow made Smithson envious. The workmen at least seemed to know what they were doing. He was envious of them because he didn't have the faintest idea what *he* was doing. Covering Ed Kalthorst's back, right?

'Sure,' he said before going through immigration, 'this is it.' He said it to Arnie Cartwright, Special Branch, about the only Brit he knew at all well. He had worked with him once over a drug-related case involving smuggling via Moscow.

'This?'

'Sure. I brought this overnight bag. Nothing else.'

'And that bulge in your armpit?'

'Well-developed pectoral muscle, okay?'

'Look, I've got to vouch for you, R.C., *sir*. We have firearms laws, you know.'

He showed Arnie his handgun in its neat underarm holster. 'Is that all right, Arnie, *sir*.'

It was all right. Arnie Cartwright grinned kindly with his pale-blue eyes out of his round plain face, even if his lips scarcely moved. Smithson knew from the earlier occasion of working with him he could never be sure if Arnie were serious or not. It was a seriously awkward thing about working with Arnie.

'You'd like to freshen up, I imagine.' Arnie gave him a look as discreet as a rolled umbrella. 'These red-eyes can be hard graft. Oh, may I introduce the officer we've assigned to you? She'll be with you throughout your stay.

She? He was no sexist. But only three hours' sleep left him feeling spare.

A slim tall woman, thirty, say, blonde, in blue jacket and skirt, eyes bluer and brighter than Arnie's but with the same plain round features. She held out a hand, smiling. Both hands were ringless.

'Joan. Joan Boswell, Mr Smithson.'

'So you'll be bird-dogging me, will you?'

'I'm assigned to you, sir.'

'You know why I'm here?'

'To ensure the safety of the president of the United States, sir.'

'Okay, okay, so... Please call me R.C., if I may call you Joan.'

'Call me Joan,' she said.

He felt numb from the flight, numb from being driven down the Heathrow tunnel and to the M4. It was all strange even if sunny and windy as it could have been in Washington. Everything looked smaller, more crowded, more unnerving. Now more than ever he regretted having gone to see Ed Kalthorst.

The voice of Arnie came from the driver's seat in front.

'Officer Boswell will tell you what the situation is regarding your chap, Mr Kor-something.'

'Koursaros?'

'Yes.'

'If you've no objection, Mr, er, sorry, R.C.?' Officer Boswell said.

'None.'

'Then I'll debrief you *briefly*.' She had a high-pitched English voice. He found it hard at first to understand what she was saying. But he felt a rapport beginning. So she emphasised the '*briefly*' for good reason, because the Mr Koursaros who had been followed from St Pancras on arrival by Eurostar had booked into the Davenport Hotel in Parker Street off Kingsway under the name Kingman with an apparently authentic passport.

'Clickety-click!' Smithson snapped his fingers. 'That's it! All the Ks! Sounds like him.'

'If only things were that simple,' said Officer Boswell, making a face.

'You being funny?'

'I wish I were! No, just practical. He's not there any more. He's done a runner. We've lost him.'

It was as he'd suspected. This man he had been keeping under surveillance in one way or another for a dozen or more years had always left the letter K behind him as a kind of scent or spoor. It was the equivalent of a good luck charm, this initial letter K. Or just his way of sticking out his tongue.

'He booked a seat for a London theatre last night and did a runner afterwards. We've no reason to arrest him, you see.'

'Did he leave anything in the hotel?'

She shook her head. It made her well-cut hair swing bell-like either way. Plain she might be, but she was attractive and intelligent and he liked the shapes of her knees.

He did an Oscar-winning act of inhaling deeply and stretching the upper buttons of his waistcoat. Darlene had insisted he wore a waistcoat if he were to be in the presence of royalty. He exhaled slowly and looked round at Joan Boswell beside him on the rear seat. They were in the fast lane of the M4. It was disconcerting to be going fast in a right-hand lane. Like English names. Like her English voice. Like the swift, sympathetic look she shot him as he yawned. He tried to avert attention from his tiredness by patting his mouth and asking:

'So there's nothing else?'

'Oh, yes, we've got some stuff in the office I can show you. Surveillance shots,' Joan Boswell said. 'And some CCTV footage.

He nodded. He could do with the freshening-up Arnie had mentioned but duty called. The safety of the president of the United States came first.

As soon as they reached headquarters by Vauxhall Bridge Officer Boswell showed him the latest shots. There was no doubt about it being K. English-style sports jacket with open-necked shirt and checked trousers lent him a country-club smartness as he left the entrance of the hotel, stepped into a taxi, walked airily along Piccadilly. The pictures were a reminder that K had a chameleon quality despite his distinctively long face. He fitted into the mosaic of everyday London with a blandness matching its brickwork and cloudy skies.

'He'll have known, won't he?' Smithson observed.

'Yes, he knew he was being watched,' Officer Boswell agreed. 'The CCTV footage shows it, of course, but the shots our man took, practically all from the rear, show him glancing – here's one, look! – glancing round. There's more of interest from the Eurostar terminal. See, there he is, alighting with that girl behind him and the woman beside her, presumably her mother.' They both watched the monitor. 'Then there's this moment,' Officer Boswell pointed out. 'See? Your man's looked round just once. Who's he looking at? Is it that small man in the hat? Or is it the girl? It's not easy to tell, is it?'

'Reckon it's the girl.' Smithson grinned. 'Reckon so. And that wraps it up?'

'That wraps it up. It's all we have.'

She was honest, he thought. It was true candour. There was no evidence beyond suspicion that K was engaged in anything. There could be twenty other assassins hiding in the nooks and crannies of London who would be more likely to shoot the president and very likely had more reason to do so than this Mr Kingman. In any case, K had no history of terrorist activity in his past.

'We had him followed after he left the Eurostar terminal yesterday,' Officer Boswell explained, 'which was why we knew he'd booked into the Davenport and these shots are all from yesterday afternoon. As for losing him last night, we didn't really know what degree of strictness in surveillance we should observe. I'm very sorry.'

'Okay, so some you lose.'

'We're overstretched,' she said. 'Funding – you know.' Smithson acknowledged that he knew. 'As soon as I got the pictures I wondered if renewed close surveillance would be authorised, knowing you were coming. But it looks like we might not get it. There are so many other calls. All the priorities are given to the presidential visit. Unless you can persuade our Controller that you have good reason to believe K is a real danger. I know he's associated with this new People's Will party in Russia, isn't he, and it's their publicly stated policy to use political assassination as a weapon. I'm just so sorry we, er, lost sight of him.'

She was taking it personally and he liked that. 'All right, as I said, some you lose.' He yawned.

'R.C, you need some sleep. There's accommodation for you here,' said Arnie Cartwright.

More commitment to him. He liked it. 'Maybe if I hit the sack for coupla hours. I need to get oriented.'

'You certainly do.'

The accommodation was austere but adequate on the top floor of the building overlooking the Thames at Vauxhall Bridge. He stripped and used the shower. Perhaps he should have noted the soundproofing of the windows and the fact that the small bedroom had no clock. He drifted into sleep before he knew it was midday.

***

Robert Simon Jermin drove a familiar route once he had gone south of the Thames towards Wandsworth and beyond. Oncoming headlights of London-bound traffic flashed like pairs of eyes out of the rainy darkness and were changed by the screen wipers into melting, widening droplets of light and then vanished in the opposite direction as more eyes of headlights rose behind him, increased in brightness, filled his mirrors like a bursting super nova and exploded beside him with an audible swish of tyres and an arrogant overtaking flurry of red tail-lights.

He was not hurrying. He was keeping calm. He kept on telling himself I'm here now, I'm in England, I'm tired after a long day and I'm driving slowly. I'm driving home after having been halfway round the world and I'm now in my own quiet world of subdued dashboard lights and a smooth soundstream of soft music. Even if I were in outer space, would I think of that Russian girl in the white fur hat? Why would she always come back to remind me?

Yes, he told himself, 'Yes,' he said aloud to the sparkling dashboard. 'Yes, yes, yes, you started it all off, didn't you? Oh, yes, you did! I'd never have done what I did without you, you angel, you!'

Oh, stop talking to yourself, you old fool!

Anyhow she was a wicked little angel. The girl in the white fur hat, whose name he never knew, was a warning beacon in his life. He had often enough been warned about such attempts at seduction. They came, though, in different forms, as much from one side as another in the Cold War. There had been Grace Hampson, for example, whose eyes in the old Metropole Hotel on that first night had been no more understandable than the twin eyes of headlights in the opposite carriageway or those coming up behind him to rush past him like shooting stars.

Like the stars, the many years that intervened distanced him from what he was now. Now he had an insurance consultancy in the City of London, a wife, children who had already flown the nest and a reasonably good living. Of course, he could never escape from the normal qualms of wondering whether such happiness was really deserved, or whether the quiet desperation of the mass of men, in Thoreau's dictum, would eventually claim him. So long as he tried as best he could to feel the pulse of things in the insurance world, he could continue to reap a few rewards without becoming complacent. But as for Grace Hampson, to be reminded of her caused the recurrence of an old ache. It was part love, part excitement, part alcohol, part fear, part self-pity. The whole lot rolled into one quite literally set him shivering for a moment with a feeling of scalp-tingling terror, a feeling he had not had in more than three decades and crept icily through the roots of his hair.

No matter how real that was, more real emotionally was the sense of betrayal. To think of Grace, let alone to renew the emotions of that time, was to acknowledge the shame of disloyalty that hung in the air about her. Maybe that wasn't actually betrayal; it was Marsha's, his wife's, love and loyalty that would be betrayed by his very shame over that photograph.

Standing naked next to the naked girl in the white fur hat! However supposedly small that betrayal might be, it would never be small enough to rid him of the fear that his heart could always prove weak and fickle. That was what the girl in the white fur hat brought into his life. Grace had been the exciting sequel to that whole episode, but she had not been the start of it. What had started it was at the heart of his own past, his own heredity. It was the family connection.

If the mass of men led lives of quiet desperation, according to Henry David Thoreau, then a very large number of Russians, in Robert Jermin's experience, led lives of extraordinary family loyalty. True or false? Utterly true in his case, as he found out, since the devotion to family connections proved stronger than politics or ideology or religion when it came to his grandmother; and it was through his grandmother that he discovered the truth.

In her last years, in her small, but inevitably dwindling circle of exiles in Ladbroke Grove, his grandmother liked to be known as Lydia Grigorievna Musina-Pushkina. She flaunted the grand name despite having been married to a Colonel Earnest Thomas whom she had met in Arkhangelsk at the beginning of the civil war in 1919 or 1920 (she was always hopeless over dates). Ernie, as he was always known in the family, had helped her to escape from Russia. It was true love, she always insisted, marriage born of true love, but she had never lost touch with her Russian roots no matter how difficult had been the problems of communication, whether by the very occasional letter or - more difficult still - the occasional arrival of some distant family member or friend from the Soviet Union. Over fifty years, till she was in her late seventies, she maintained the tenuous connection. In the course of it, other members of her family, Robert Jermin's mother, for example, who anglicised herself so successfully she never mentioned her Russian heritage, tended to assume that Lydia's claims about her background were more myth than reality and really couldn't be taken seriously.

To a sensitive, adoring and perhaps rather gullible Bob Jermin, aged sixteen and upward, say, even into his mid twenties, she was the living equivalent of an icon – an awesome object of ageless, unique reverence. He believed in her. She liked to tell everyone she was the great-, great- (he had no idea how many generations actually separated her from such a distinguished forbear) granddaughter of the famous Musin-Pushkin who had allegedly 'discovered' the greatest supposed masterpiece of Russian medieval literature *The Song of Igor's Raid.* It was what entitled her to treat most of Russian literature as part of her family heritage. She frequently gave the impression of trailing in her wake endless progeny of various kinds with names like Alexander Sergeevich, Lev Nikolaevich, Anton Pavlovich, etc. She so confused Bob he actually thought for a while that Pushkin, Tolstoy, Chekhov, etc. were either closely related or at least had some ancestral connection. She assured him, with engaging dottiness and unassailable conviction, that 'my family used to know them, you know, all of them.'

It took him years to disentangle the fragile family lore from what passed for authentic fact. The family lore in her claims for it was always far more colourful than the fact. In knowing her he quickly learned it was wiser to accept his grandmother's version of Russian cultural history than attempt to challenge it.

She retired in her widowhood to a basement flat in Ladbroke Grove. She refused to divulge any of the circumstances of her pre-revolutionary background and Bob never discovered how she kept such apparent good contact with what remained of her family during the Cold War. All he knew for sure was that she lived on a small annuity. She did not need lots of money, she liked to claim, so long as she had all the riches of her Russian cultural heritage.

More than once he heard her say loudly as she bashed beetroot in the tiny, smelly kitchen preparatory to making her version of *borsch* – 'Pushkin not Russian, did you know? He African!' Bash! 'My great-grandmother said he had birthmark here,' pointing at the inside of her thigh embarrassingly close to her crotch. 'She knew because…' Bash! '…they were lovers. Pushkin was good lover, she said. He write poem for her: *Ia pomniu chudnoe mgnoven'e.* "I remember lovely moment." Oh, yes, he dedicate it to great-grandmother! She remember lovely moment too!' Bash! (Which Bob well knew was the most utter nonsense. The poem had been dedicated to Anna Kern.) Again a bash! Then:

'Have you had lovely moment yet, Robert?'

The third or fourth time she did this he stopped blushing, although he'd blushed initially. She'd said 'Oh, but you must! Every young man must!' Bash! Bash! Glancing sideways to see him grow as red as the pulped beetroot.

Until she was too frail herself to do much bashing any more she persistently wore bright red lipstick and a dab of rouge that made her look like one of Toulouse-Lautrec's *demi-mondaines*. Most of her vivid, darting gestures would have as their focus a strange, sequin-covered hat or headpiece that always seemed to be inseparably entangled with her grey hair and required constant putting to rights with small shoves and prinkings. He could hardly ever remember her without this rather unattractive, semi-decorative adornment. It was generally assumed she wore it because she refused to wear a wig – 'Oh, I look like Queen of Spades if I wear wig!' – but actually it was to hide the alopecia contracted as a girl in Petrograd. She liked to claim it was a Parisian-style turban made of silk and encrusted with black sequins. So legendary, not to say antique, was this crowning glory that only very occasionally did anyone venture to suggest it might be removed for cleaning. In fact, about once every couple of months she would stand under a shower to let it undergo a kind of ritual purification rather than actually remove it. Or that was what she claimed and Bob believed her.

He grew to love the confined world of that Ladbroke Grove flat. Once he had been instructed by his elders and betters in the Foreign Office to achieve fluency in the language of the

Soviets, it was to his grandmother that he turned. She was close to eighty. She explained quite candidly that her knowledge was rusty and possibly out-of-date. Old-fashioned or not, her Russian was so enlivened by outrageous reminiscence and wild improbabilities she could easily persuade a non-native speaker hers was the legitimate, pure, pre-Soviet Russian of the kind only spoken by the most educated members of the old cultural elite. So he spent almost three months visiting her basement flat in Ladbroke Grove before being posted to the diplomatic job in Moscow where he would meet the girl in the white fur hat.

Right, so he had driven home in the rain and was hungry and tired from globe-trotting, but the old fear returned more sharply the moment he let himself into the hallway through the front door and saw the damp reflection offered him by the long hall mirror. The mirrored image of his face told him it still retained enough facets of his youthful self for the naked Robert Jermin of the photograph to be fairly easily recognisable.

Simultaneously he recognised something else. Marsha, he realised, would be absent at a school meeting that evening. Tuesday, of course, there was always a meeting. He should have remembered that. He remembered it the moment he shed his raincoat. Staring at the raincoat, he noticed it was so dampened by rainfall during the brief dash from the car in the driveway to the porch that the shoulders were splodges of damp black cloth against the dove-grey of the rest of it. Like, he thought, his own reputation. He hung the thing up before trying to smarten his damp, matted hair

In addition to the hall light he saw there was a light in the sitting room. He peered into the room, calling out Marsha's name, even mildly alarmed she had not said anything on his arrival, only to see that the light came from the special illumination above the pictures she'd inherited from a wealthy uncle. Otherwise it was empty. Equally, of course, he told himself, Marsha probably wasn't there because she'd very likely received the grainy print and exiled him to a doghouse. There he was, then, looking at himself in the long mirror. Not naked, of course, but facially at least easily matching the features in the photograph despite a difference of some thirty years. Older, of course, the face less round, the delineation less exact, crows feet round the eyes and a lined forehead, but generally speaking the same save for the faint grin of pleasure at being beside the enticing naked charm of the girl in the white fur hat.

Had Marsha left a message somewhere? he wondered. Perhaps in his study? He opened the door to his study that was just by the hall mirror. The room was dark and his shadow extended across the carpeted floor in the rectangle of light from the hall. He had the strong sense that no one had been there since he had gone off to Tokyo. When he switched on his desk lamp this sense was confirmed by the sight of his desktop looking exactly as he had left it. Moreover, there was no note from Marsha. All that had changed was the flashing light on his phone indicating there had been calls. He pressed the replay button and lifted the receiver.

Two of the calls were routine adverts for solar panels and replacement windows. The final call was different. The voice speaking in his ear was female and American. It was terse. 'Hi! A message for Mr Robert Jermin. Someone we knew way, way back has suddenly re-emerged. I can't say much more than that right now. Just a friendly warning. I'll hope to catch you next time I call.'

No name, nothing! It was friendly, sure, but left no means of contacting whoever it was, no means of finding out who the "someone" referred to might be, let alone why the "someone" had "suddenly re-emerged." Although he tried to ascertain the source of the message, the caller's number had been withheld. It annoyed him. This absence of names reminded him of his own name and how his father had insisted on changing the spelling because he didn't want to be named after a street, meaning Jermyn Street. No, he was to be known as Jermin.

He deleted the message on the assumption that the promise of a new call justified it. That consideration became uppermost because at that very moment he heard the sound of the front door opening and Marsha's voice announcing:

'I'm home, Bob dear! Where are you? Oh, I see...'

She pushed aside the half-open study door and stood in front of him. Her yellow plastic raincoat gleamed with raindrops. She was holding a plastic bag and just releasing single-handedly the yellow raincoat hood from her hair. They kissed.

'You had a good trip?'

'How was your meeting?'

The over-eager, simultaneous questioning had the perverse effect of making both aware of the need for caution. His hands were damp from holding her round the waist. Silence held them still for several moments. As he felt in his trouser pocket for a handkerchief, his gaze encompassed her — Marsha, whom he loved, the smile on her face drawing the lips of her wide mouth slightly apart and emphasising the attractive straightness of her cheekbones. She was looking tired, no doubt after the meeting, but there was an added tension in her smile that he could not ignore. To his astonishment she turned and locked the study door behind her.

'Well, my dear,' she said a little curtly. 'what the hell *is* this?'

She placed the plastic bag on his desk and pulled the grainy photograph fully out of its envelope. Observed as a naked object in the brightness of his desk lamp, it was lurid in its blatant display of his scar and penis. He had his head turned and was apparently smiling at the naked girl in the white fur hat. The girl's face was shaded by the frame of her hair. She looked very young, the white fur hat barely reaching as high as his shoulder.

'It came in the post today.' Marsha spoke very intensely. 'This afternoon — well, you know how the post is now. It always comes late nowadays. Look, the address has been typed. Mrs M. Jermin. Why, Bob, dear? Why's this been sent to me?' She had been staring down at it as she spoke and now raised her gaze to his. 'It *is* you, isn't it? I mean, there's the scar.'

'Yes, it's me,' he answered after taking in a deep breath. 'I found the same thing in my office.'

'When was it taken?'

'Years ago.'

'Where?'

'In Moscow. When I was at the embassy.'

'In Moscow.' She appeared to taste the place name to know whether it was properly cooked. Licking her lips, she seemed dissatisfied. 'So this was what?'

'A set-up. It put an end to my career.

'The girl, who was she?'

'No, she wasn't what you might think. She wasn't a prostitute or at least not then. She said she was a dancer.' He had turned away from the bright oasis of light at his desk and moved a few steps towards the uncurtained bay window and the nearly total darkness of heavy rain. The brightwork on her car parked just outside the window shone vaguely back at him. There was a stretch of lawn vaguely visible and a distant silhouette of trees. The noise of rainfall was oddly cheerful. 'There was no sex.'

'I'm not wanting to pry, Bob dear, I was merely...'

'Yes, you were,' he interrupted. 'Anyone seeing this photograph would want to pry.'

'All right, all right. So who was she?'

'She wanted to learn English,' he said. 'She wanted to be a film star. I think she quite genuinely thought I could help her. She was a mixture of innocence and quite blatant seduction.

But there was no sex.' He turned and looked directly at Marsha. 'Believe it or not, it's the truth. No, she had another purpose, I think. In fact, I'm sure she had another purpose. She did what she had to do, that's what mattered.'

'Which was?'

'As I said, she put an end to my career.'

'So why's this come now?'

'Ah,' he said, 'I wish I knew that. I really wish I knew that.'

'But, Bob dear, you've never told me about this, have you? Doesn't this smack of, well, disloyalty or something like it. I've been worrying about it so much.'

He nodded. 'Of course it does. I know it does. But it's not that, not disloyalty. Please, dear, believe me.' He stepped back from the window and took Marsha in his arms. She resisted a moment and then let herself be held. 'Shame, that's what stopped me. I was ashamed.'

'But if it was so innocent,' she spoke over his shoulder, 'you could've explained it, couldn't you?'

'Explained it!' He gave a shudder of laughter. 'Oh, I did! Oh, I did, I really did! But if she wanted to shame me, she certainly succeeded!'

This was so undeniable that he released his hold and she stepped back from him. They looked at each other. She did not blink, but he did. Then she began taking off her plastic raincoat.

'So you explained what?' she asked a little sharply.

'I tried to explain how it happened.'

Instead, as he said this, he found himself doing a rapid re-run of the likely purposes. The most obvious one of course affected him most directly. Once his elders and betters saw the photograph, they recognised that it so compromised, neutralised and humiliated him he could no longer remain in Her Majesty's diplomatic service. That was obvious. But something else happened that made it inevitable. So within a matter of months his career came to an end.

He felt a twinge from an old wound in his leg. He then realised quite suddenly that there'd very probably been another purpose. Which was why the photograph had reappeared. Of course there'd been another purpose! The photograph was probably more connected with this second purpose than with the first, especially since it had been deliberately sent to Marsha. But what if it were tweeted or put on Facebook? No, he had to admit, that would be too public. This was intended as a private threat. They wanted to neutralise *him* once again, just *him*, that's why it had reappeared!

'But you weren't believed?'

'Oh, I was believed, but the photograph spoke louder than any explanation I might give. That's all I can say right now. Can you believe that?'

She shook the plastic raincoat. A spray of raindrops bespattered the carpet. 'Yes, Bob dear, I can believe that.' She gave him a tentative smile.

'Thank you,' he said.

'So how was Tokyo?'

'Tokyo was successful, very successful.'

5

What he knew most of all were the smells. With what sickly art Moscow tantalised and excited the organs of smell in the last years of the USSR! He grew to love the smelliness of Moscow more even than the rather half-hearted grandeur of its broad streets or the soulless expanses of its squares and boulevards. He was in love with the sea of smells into which he plunged daily. He could immerse himself in it like a pollutant freely re-entering the pollutant chain and enhancing its survival quotient. He loved to be in its poisoned intestine. He sought out the anonymity of its crowded sewer smells and merged with them as perfectly as a breath of corruption.

So perfect was the merger he did not at first realise he was both contaminant and contaminated. It was difficult for him to say precisely when it happened. Pushed and shoved with other germ-laden bacilli in the sewer system of the Metro he was not aware of the moment of viral attack. He was merely aware that he had somehow been contaminated.

He returned one day to his diplomatic apartment on the Sadovaia ring road, went to his bedroom and discovered something in his overcoat pocket that had not been there earlier. He stood by the double-glazed window with the little window known as a *fortochka* slightly open and saw four floors below him the snow-flecked backyard of a wooden house with a rusty metal roof. A young man was beating a carpet hung on a line. The strokes of the beating could be heard quite clearly. They were regular and deliberate.

As he stood in front of the window, he was surprised to feel the strange thing in his overcoat pocket. He pulled at it. To all appearances it was a copy of the humorous magazine *Krokodil*. Who the hell would shove something like that in his pocket? Unless, of course, it contained something disgusting. Cautiously he opened it. It didn't smell, there was nothing disgusting about it, except it wasn't the magazine itself, merely the outside pages. Inside were several sheets of carefully handwritten calculations and designs. It was therefore something undeniably very strange that he held in his hand.

The beating went on. It was so domestic and ordinary and the afternoon was just an ordinary afternoon filled with the distant sound of a cane whisk beating a carpet, but what he held in his hand was not ordinary at all. It was strange enough to change his whole life. He was sufficiently well versed in certain processes and procedures to realise that what he had received was akin to a Rosetta stone related to rocketry.

To hold it, let alone let anyone know he had it, involved such a risk his first inclination was to get rid of it at once. Burn it? Possibly. Dump it somewhere? Perhaps. Yet someone had risked a great deal already, he acknowledged with a churlish readiness to admit his own cowardice, by stuffing the thing in his overcoat pocket. Someone, that is to say, who must have deliberately chosen *him* as the recipient. But who would choose him and why?

He liked walking round Moscow, true. He liked being in the Moscow crowds. He liked the smell of the city. None of that explained why he, an English diplomat, should be chosen to receive something as potentially significant as this false copy of *Krokodil* containing page after page of handwritten material with drawings and lengthy calculations. Unless, of course, this really was what he supposed it might be: details of new Soviet research into rocket guidance systems, the sort of thing that would be top secret at the best of times and would never, never, never be allowed to fall into the hands of the West, let alone into the overcoat pocket of an English diplomat walking round Moscow. The likely provenance of it, therefore, could supposedly endow it with a certain respect. It needed to be kept protected and hidden.

Of Finnish manufacture, the desk in his bedroom contained one small, apparently secret compartment. It was only accessible if one drawer were pulled fully out, which could only be done by pressure on a catch situated within the kneehole section of the desk. If the *Krokodil* magazine and its contents were rolled up tight, it could be fitted into this secret compartment. So that's where it went, although Bob Jermin knew that anyone familiar with that particular design of desk would have no trouble accessing it. He had to assume and hope that neither the Russian maid, Sophie, nor his flatmate, Charles Evesham, had that knowledge. But it could only be temporary because the administrator of the block of flats often exercised his right to poke around. Bob knew he had tried to open the desk more than once.

Then came the incident with his angel. To encounter an angel on the wide tarmac area outside the Metropole Hotel two days later in the centre of Moscow was something he never expected. Oh, yes, he expected the mica gleam of old snow in the gutters and trolleybuses hissing and trundling their way past like shoeboxes on wheels and the usual pedestrian crowds... but an angel? It was an early lesson in life: Never imagine you will never meet an angel!

She was a serious-looking girl with a pale, sensitive face. He was first conscious of her three or four paces ahead of him. She was clearly coming towards him. He took the only possible evading action – he buffeted someone on his left-hand side to make way for her. What he could not avoid was the almost childlike face in which eyes shone as if pinned into the soft cushion of the complexion. They made her look attractively tired. The smile-lines of a slightly knowing child puckered their edges and lent a kind of radiance to the fixed, pale-blue gaze of the eyes themselves. Quite unsubtly and directly they seemed to solicit him as they looked straight at him.

She was wearing the normal Muscovite uniform of black overcoat with shiny buttons, the fashion, it seemed, for that season, but the fur hat that topped the ensemble was white and looked expensive. Her blond hair fell down conspicuously either side of her face, curling inwards at its tips and looking a bit like little fingers stroking her chin. The effect was innocently coquettish. She seemed to wear no make-up, not even lipstick.

Coming straight up to him, she said in English with all the seriousness of a child:

'You are English, sir. Please help me.'

It was so charming he could not resist it. To make her point more obvious she thrust her arm through his and propelled him towards the Metropole Hotel. Resistance seemed ungracious, even churlish. On the contrary, he felt flattered by being recognised as English and challenged by the naïve directness of her approach. Angels, he felt quite unselfconsciously, would probably behave like this.

'You have money?' she asked as she drew him into the hotel foyer.

The query immediately put him on his guard. If she asked about money, no matter how artlessly and childishly, he had to downgrade her at once from angel to prostitute.

'No dollars?'

She was persistent.

'No dollars.'

'Deutschmarks?'

'No.'

'So I have money,' she announced with surprising candour

and pride as if she were alluding to the colour of her hair. 'You like me, yes?'

'Well, yes, you're very attractive, but, you know, I don't think this is…'

'It is what?'

'I don't think it is right.'

She pouted at this. 'What is not right?'

'This meeting, your question about money. How did you know I was English?'

'You look like English. You will help, yes?'

'What kind of help?'

'Help me to speak English.'

'But you already speak English.'

'Good,' she insisted. 'Good English.'

The request, for all its oddness, intrigued him sufficiently to let him be drawn into the Metropole. The foyer was crammed with luggage and noisy visitors. A great deal of loud, mostly drunken talk and laughter was coming from the bar-room on the right. At the end of the foyer a couple of Intourist women were overseeing shabby porters as they tossed suitcases into one of the lifts while the other lift disgorged well-dressed American sightseers. She propelled him up the stairs.

'You are visitor, yes?' she asked.

'No,' he said.

'Businessman?'

'No.'

She stopped on a kind of half-landing and looked at him sideways. A group of busily talking Americans came down the stairs between them before she had time to ask whether he was a student.

'No, no. I am living here in Moscow.'

He had no intention of telling her he was attached to the

British embassy, let alone of discussing the matter midway up the staircase. A fierce moral debate preoccupied him. Should he go on following her or stop now? Should he politely disengage himself or see how things worked out? He could believe all he had been told about the dangers of becoming ensnared.

'Where are you taking me?' he asked somewhat ridiculously, knowing it could only be a bedroom.

'For talk. We talk.'

'In a bedroom? Why not downstairs in the restaurant?'

'Very loud. People not nice. I know peaceful place.'

So she knew a peaceful bedroom, he told himself. 'Right,' he said.

'I want English conversation,' she said. 'That is why you come here. Please not to talk now,'

She propelled him even faster but in total silence. He could not help being delighted by the strong and determined way she pressed herself against him and moved him along in a swift balletic movement up a further flight of stairs. A chemically deodorising atmosphere persisted here, mingling with tobacco smoke. Just by the lifts, where the corridors formed a T-junction, sat the usual elderly lady, resident keyholder and female equivalent of Cerberus at the entrance to her own Hades. She looked up aggressively as they approached but recognised the girl at once and broke into a smile and greetings.

'English conversation,' the girl explained.

The elderly woman nodded several times and handed her a key. The girl's response was a slightly disdainful toss of her head. She marched Bob a short way down the right-hand corridor. A door was unlocked to reveal a shabby little bedroom immured in the gloom of partly drawn curtains. He made out a worn Turkey carpet in the entrance-way next a small bathroom, a high metal bedstead with a patchwork quilt coverlet and a long spotted mirror on the front of a large decrepit-looking wardrobe. The generally jaded appearance of the room was compounded by a sound of continually running water from the bathroom.

'Please,' she said.

He entered and she immediately locked the door behind him.

'I want you talk,' she said. 'Please sit.'

She patted the bed.

'About what?'

She untied a scarf from round her neck and took off her coat. This was followed by the expert removal of a woollen jumper over her head without disturbing the white fur hat. She then smoothed her simple print frock round her hips and stood in front of him with folded arms.

It was impossible to deny she was slim and shapely, although seeing her close-to he realised she was older than she'd looked at first glance. This was no child. She was probably in her mid-twenties but thinned and neatened by her ballet training. She looked up at him very solemnly. Her long fair hair framed and slightly shaded her features as it fell loosely from the coronet of her white fur hat. The bedroom suddenly seemed to him exceedingly hot. He drew off his own fur hat and unbuttoned his coat.

'Please tell me about Marlon,' she said.

'Marlon?'

'Yes, about Marlon Brando.'

'You mean about his films.'

'No, about him as man, as person.'

'I don't know him personally.'

'You are liar.'

'Excuse me,' he said, 'but I am not a liar. I simply do not know Marlon Brando personally.'

'You know film stars, yes?'

'I thought you wanted English conversation.'

'Oh, yes. Please talk. You like me, yes?'

'Yes, of course I do. I said so. You are most attractive.'

'That is good, yes?'

'Very good.'

'I feel hot. Do you feel hot?'

'It is very hot in here, yes.'

'Help me, please.'

She stuck out one of her feet for him to remove an ankle-length boot

'I really think I should go, you know,' he said.

'Please,' she said. He pulled. She said thank you and offered her other foot. 'Now you.'

She knelt and quickly unlaced his shoes. 'You love Simone Signoret?' she asked. 'You like her?'

'Yes.'

'I like her very much. She is sexy, yes?'

'Yes.'

'I look like her, yes?'

'No.'

'Help me,' she said. She had turned her back to him and was indicating that she wanted him to undo the buttons at the back of her dress.

'I think I must go,' he said.

'I am attractive,' she said. 'Why you must go?'

'Look, I will pay you whatever you want.'

'Oh, money, pooh! You like Brigitte Bardot?'

'Yes.'

'I look like Brigitte Bardot?'

He admitted she did look like Brigitte Bardot, only much younger.

'Ah!' She suddenly flung her arms round his neck and kissed him on the lips. 'I love you, Englishman! You love me, yes?'

He could not be sure whether she really wanted to be reassured or was simply employing the patter she normally used.

'Look, if you really want the money, here take this.' He took out his wallet and showed her a small wad of hundred-rouble notes. He knew it was risky, but things had gone too far. No doubt this was not a one-girl operation. Somewhere in the vicinity was either the KGB or a pimp, not to mention the hotel staff, and he could anticipate at any moment the door suddenly being unlocked and flung open to admit a photographer or one of the followers.

'Capitalist!' she said scornfully.

'Please,' he said. 'I've told you you are attractive. Please take what you want and let me go.'

She fingered the notes in the wallet and gently extracted four. To him, at his favoured rate of exchange, it would hardly have been a king's ransom, let alone a pimp's backhander. She folded the banknotes up neatly and stuffed them into some secret place in her white fur hat.

'Please unlock the door,' he said.

'You look like Laurence Olivier. See. Key in door.'

He was relieved and perhaps flattered. 'So I look like Laurence Olivier. I know you wanted to talk about films and film stars, but you don't know anything about me and I could be...'

'You English. You talk like Englishman. I wish to talk like English lady.'

'Why?'

She came up with a story at this point about apparently

looking like Audrey Hepburn. If she could learn to speak English like Audrey Hepburn she would be able to star in Hollywood films.

'You have no idea,' he protested, 'how difficult that is,' knowing as he spoke how ridiculously priggish he sounded.

'Please.' She offered her back again and pointed to the buttons on her dress. 'I wish to go to America.'

Her whole approach lacked any professionalism, or was so calculatingly unprofessional it perhaps fooled him.

'I can go to England first. Then to America,' she said calmly, lifting the hair from the nape of her neck. 'Please.'

'No, I am not going to help you undress. I can't get you to America or England.'

He was sure at this point she would mention marriage. She lowered her hands from behind the back of her head and looked at him.

'No?'

'No,' he said.

Did he read disappointment in her eyes? He knew she was challenging him with her oddly unprofessional kind of seduction. Or did he misread her completely?

'Look,' he said and tried to explain. He used the simplest possible English words to make it clear he had no intention of marrying.

'Marry?' She bubbled with laughter. 'Why I marry?'

It was so candid and made him seem so crude he felt completely at her mercy.

'I want to learn good English,' she insisted. 'Good English. Please.'

She turned her back towards him again. He rose to his feet and began rather nervously fingering the topmost button of her dress. It served him right for being such a prig. What is more, the delightful feel of her back and the modest scent of lavender as she held up her hair for him spurred him to join in her fun.

'You like my hair, yes?'

'I do like your hair.'

'Yes?'

'Yes.'

'I am dancer, you know.'

'Really.'

'I talk good English, yes?'

'You speak well.' He managed to undo six buttons.

'Take off,' she said.

She turned round towards him, letting her hair fall back in place and gently, but dramatically, made a motion with her hands as if she were throwing open a casement window. It indicated that she wanted him to remove his overcoat and jacket and every other item of clothing, so far as he could tell.

'Take off. *Snimai*. No need.'

'I, er...'

Already she was again absorbed in her own film star fantasy. 'I look like Audrey Hepburn, yes?'

'No. Your hair is blond.'

He shed his overcoat and jacket.

'Yes, but my face, yes?'

There was a resemblance and he admitted it. Quite quickly he found himself divesting himself of his shirt and vest, as if rivalling her in the rush to undress, and then his trousers and pants were off. The discarded clothes were spread over the coverlet of the bed. She smiled charmingly at him.

There comes a time, of course, in any such encounter when discretion, if that is the best way of describing it, is swept aside in a torrent of unstoppable desires. If they talked about the impish charms of Audrey Hepburn or the magnificent sensuality of Marilyn Monroe, this, he concluded, was her game, her delight in myth, and what delighted him was to find that it merely served as an *aperitif*, a taster, for the afternoon's main feature. The auditorium was already darkened, of course. In the strangely jaded atmosphere of the little bedroom the silver screen of Hollywood at its most alluring was summoned into being. It was possible to imagine the vulgarly changing tints of subdued lighting playing over the pleats of the curtains before they slowly drew aside to reveal the screen itself. Pale gold to yellow to pink to pastel shades of green and blue darkening to mauve and purple.

So the buttons were undone and with a little shimmer, soundlessly, the cotton dress dropped to her ankles. She neatly removed woollen tights. With a light flick her vest and bra were removed. Then her knickers came off. The main feature was beginning. Her nakedness glimmered without any glamour. She did not turn to him at first but stood in front of the long dim wardrobe mirror and studied herself. Tentatively, with a childlike lack of narcissism, she cupped her hands below her breasts and lifted them. She saw presumably her own beauty in the token silver screen of the mirror, but seen from behind the slim, almost immature line of her thin shoulders and back looked so defenceless, he thought, and in need of loving that it was a surprise, almost shocking, to see how maturely the spine tapered to her firm hips and the dark, womanly cleft between the soft white rounds of her buttocks.

But that was not even the moment when the curtains swung aside and the silver screen lit up. That moment came when she turned towards him, her hands at her sides, and a girlish, contented smile drew her wide lips apart. She had every right to be proud. She still wore the white fur hat like a crown from which her fair hair draped almost to her shoulders above her forward-thrusting, firm white breasts with the pink nipples and she looked queenly, as romantic as a superstar and somehow as frostily still and untouchable as a screen goddess in the hot bedroom.

'I want to go to America,' she said. 'You will take me, yes?'

He took in a deep breath because she forestalled his answer by letting her eyes travel down his body. They studied the long scar of the bicycle accident running across the lower part of his abdomen. She stooped, almost as if she were doing a medical inspection, and looked more closely. He reddened and tried to cover his private parts, but she gave a brief laugh, flicked the tip of his penis with the tip of her finger and immediately swung herself round so they were both facing the wardrobe mirror. It was then she stamped her foot down on the carpet and there was a flash of light.

'Oh, my God!' he cried. 'What's that?'

But he knew. He knew at once. They had been photographed. Practically instantly she seized all her clothes and dashed away into the bathroom, bolting the door loudly behind her and calling out in a kind of sing-song:

'We go to America, yes?' Then she broke into peels of laughter.

The laugh of course was on him. No, we don't, he thought; we don't go to America. We try to find out where the camera is, and the first thing he did was to try to open the wardrobe doors, but they had obviously been fastened tight in some way. The flashlight, he noticed, had been fixed to the top of the wardrobe. Seeing his naked reflection close-to in the mirror instantly changed his mind. The scar was as livid as ever. All romance had vanished. There he was naked facing the mirror wearing nothing except his black socks. It was ridiculous.

Ashamed at the sight, he instantly revived the skill he had learned at school for dressing quickly after games and within a couple of minutes had pulled everything on. All that remained were his shoes. He thrust his feet into them without lacing them, desperate to escape the taunts and laughter coming from the bathroom and quite unable to shout anything back. It seemed both ridiculous and demeaning to offer any kind of retort to this wicked little angel.

Actually, as he realised much later, she had been both good and bad. It didn't take a moment's thought to accept that he had been very expertly trapped. The photograph was to prove humiliating, of course; she, though, despite all her skilful entrapment, was to take him to America in a quite different sense. And for that he was grateful even if it eventually meant he got badly hurt, both physically and emotionally. For one thing, at that very moment, he blessed her, the girl in the white fur hat, for having left the key in the door lock. Without a word he unlocked it and went out into the corridor. By sheer good luck he found himself almost at once swept along in a crowd of evidently holidaying hotel guests, all speaking Russian very loudly and boisterously, who didn't give a damn about having to give up door keys to the female Cerberus at the top of the stairs. In an instant he was descending to the next level and then down to the foyer. Though trailing a little behind the party he was directed at once into the restaurant and the deafening noise of a balalaika orchestra.

***

'Hey, you, you're English, aren't you? I feel at home among you English, you know. May I?'

Bob turned on his bar-side metal seat and faced her. Her features, her hair, her dress, not to mention her accent, were as un-English as Times Square. First, she was tall. Oh, dammit, he didn't want to itemise, but she was tall, about his own height, he noticed as he slipped awkwardly off his seat out of English politeness. 'Of course,' he was muttering, her coppery hair giving her maybe a couple of inches on him so that the upper gold rim of her spectacles was near the level of his eyebrows and her cobalt eyes just below the level of his. She looked at him with that fresh sunrise glow on a blue sea that made him sure American women specialised in having eyes like that. Then her wide mouth and sculpted lips drew apart in a perfectly natural, welcoming smile with the required touch of nudity showing in the whiteness of her teeth. Her slim neck repeated the nude display but decency was preserved with a pearl necklace. A brown jacket and neat, almost military skirt falling below the knee made her seem power dressed to the perfection of milled steel.

'I'm having a little drink,' he explained unnecessarily. He had had half a carafe-full of vodka. 'For my health. How do you know I'm English?'

'I saw you at your embassy party for our new ambassador. We didn't meet, but I asked who you were. Mister German, isn't it?'

'I am, er, yes, Jermin, Bob Jermin, Robert Jermin.' He spelled out the name. 'It sounds the same.'

'Oh, well, sure. My name's Grace Hampson.'

It was the last thing to have expected after the encounter with his wicked little angel. Most guests in this extension to the bar-room of the Metropole hotel were half- or three-quarters drunk, but it was a modest enough escape hole from the noisy restaurant next door. He took her outstretched hand and shook it. She introduced herself as Personal Assistant to Mr Thoreau.

'Who?' he asked somewhat rudely.

If he was going to be entrapped again, he wanted to have a few quotable names to offer after the blatant anonymity of what had just happened to him. His reputation, including his career, being mostly dead in the water, he had been trying to kill off what remained in the alcoholic suicide of vodka. This Grace Hampson was interrupting the process by bringing him back to life.

'Mr Thoreau is a friend of the ambassador. He wants to

obtain an insight into what the Russians really think. It's a crucial time. Hey, your necktie's not right. Let me fix it.'

'What they really think. Yeah, that's crucial. Thank you, but you needn't, you know.' But she was already tightening the knot of his tie, her blue eyes now so close he could only stare at them open-mouthed. 'I've just had – thank you, thank you – a bit of a shock. I'm in shock. But I'm happy, really happy.'

'I'm the one who's happy,' she was saying. 'There. You're looking one neat happy man.' She stepped back. 'Because, Robert, you can help me. That would really make me happy. I'd like to introduce you.'

'Introduce me?'

'To Mr Thoreau.' She gave a light laugh and studied him as he stood rather unsteadily in front of her. 'We need to cooperate, I think, don't we?'

'Why?'

'We fish for contacts, isn't that right? I'm out here with Mr Thoreau and we have to make contacts with as many people as possible. You Brits, the Soviets, all the people who know something. Do I sound typically American and naïve?'

'Yes.' In a sense he wanted her to take offence. She responded with a blandly courteous smile. 'Okay, so I am. I'm new. Help me, Robert.'

'Just smile,' he said. 'And look as much like apple pie as you can. And stop calling me Robert, call me Bob.'

'That's all?'

'Oh, and perhaps you ought to stop using that perfume.'

They stood face to face in the crowded bar-room and he felt as if they were already on terms of almost indecent intimacy. The vodka had made him light-headed. She at least did him the honour of blushing very slightly. The pinkness made her seem charmingly, healthily juvenile.

'Hey, that's enough.'

The bar-seat next his was suddenly vacated. Spontaneously they both sat down side-by-side. She wrong-footed him by adding: 'And I think you could use some deodorant.'

'*Touché.*' He knew she was right. The bath in the apartment he shared with Charles Evesham had been full of rolls of film undergoing processing. He'd not been able to have a bath for a week. 'I smell because the first lesson for anyone who wants to make contacts in Moscow is to smell right. If I smell of deodorant, then I won't be smelling right. Now let's have a drink.' He seized a small vodka glass and poured her a drink from his carafe. '*Za vashe zdorovye*! Tell me, what brings you to the Metropole?'

'I'm here with Mr Thoreau. We were dining. You know I've never had vodka before.'

'Knock it back!' He swallowed his own small fiery glassful and she followed suit more carefully and delicately, saying 'Oh, holy cow, that's strong!' and gasping.

'Another?'

'No, no, thank you.' A flutter of hands. 'I'm just not used to strong spirits.'

'It makes for contacts round here.'

'So, okay, it's what we want.' She wiped her mouth with a small handkerchief. 'I just want your help to find out what's going on round here.' She very earnestly leaned forward and whispered. 'You know we're in the middle of a Cold War and we've got to help each other. I want you to put me in touch, involve me, get me into the Moscow scene – you know what I mean. Mr Thoreau says he wants a hot line right into the heart of the Russian people, so we can know what they're really thinking. It'll give us an insight into what the mood is.'

He knew he must be drunk, or she clearly wasn't drunk enough to realise how what she was saying sounded in all probability like Mr Thoreau's own words uttered after a few stiffening vodkas to an afternoon session of the appropriate Senate vetting committee.

'Are you really serious?'

'Of course I am.'

'And what do I get in return?'

'CIA co-operation.'

'I thought we had that already.'

'It could be closer.'

'How much closer?'

He never found out. A loud American voice exploded above their whisperings, even above all the surrounding loud drunken talk of the bar-room.

'Hey, Grace Hampson, so you're here! I've been looking for you all over!'

There were no introductions. Grace sprang up instantly and followed the speaker's broad back out into the foyer of the Metropole Hotel.

6

Officer Joan Boswell had a bad conscience. An official inquiry could reveal a shameful degree of cock-up in the surveillance deployed for this K. He should never have been allowed to do a runner, meaning she and Arnie would never have been placed in the embarrassing position of having to apologise. But her conscience told her that a report from MI5 about a Mr Silber might be relevant.

The Controller admitted over the phone that it was a national disgrace. Yes, he'd received a complaint from the U.S. embassy and something needed to be done 'pretty bloody quick.' But wasn't Silber something of a long shot? It was their only lead, she pointed out. He authorised her to do a recce but at all costs to ensure it was inconspicuous.

The address was in one of those up-market suburban roads in south-west London with detached houses of the era of Peter Pan set behind walls and tall gates. Surveillance, if it were to be at all discreet, could only be conducted at a distance. Earlier periodic surveillance had related to people trafficking and had offered no firm evidence. One fact alone in the brief report on it had impressed Officer Boswell: the residence seemed to be only accessible through the front entrance for it backed onto other property and had no sideway.

Officer Boswell parked in one of the few curbside spaces available that gave an oblique view of the house. It was a spacious Edwardian mansion with overhanging eaves and needlessly tall chimneys. She immediately used her new smartphone to take several shots of the house from her oblique viewpoint within her car. Once she had stepped out, she continued her apparently casual recce by glancing through the wrought-iron gates as she strolled past. She saw a curve of red tarmac-ed driveway, a gleaming silver BMW, recently mown lawn, clipped shrubbery, cupressus, roses.

The whole set-up spoke of respectability, as did the adjoining dozen or so houses whose front gates and gardens she strolled past under the shade of plane trees. It was the time of afternoon when children were being collected from school. In this sort of neighbourhood this meant mother or au pairs bringing them back in cars. Only a few older kids cycled. A couple of girls in dark-green blazers aged, say, ten or eleven, were the only pedestrians. A housepainter up a ladder had a radio going at one house. Outside another a BT engineer was working at wires in an inspection pit. Otherwise the momentarily sunlit front gardens and facades of houses, all with conspicuous burglar alarms, looked smart and respectable and defiantly private.

She strolled into an adjacent road, similarly tree-lined. A short walk farther on she joined a road running roughly parallel to Silber's road. There was more traffic. Thick cloud hid the sun at that moment. She counted off the houses one by one until she reckoned she had reached the property backing on to Silber's. It was a gaunt Victorian house converted into flats and looked sinister against the suddenly dark sky. Tall poplars, not to mention a line of garages, obscured the view at the back. She could not even see the wall surrounding Silber's, let alone the house itself.

What caught her eye were balloons in various colours tied to an adjacent gate-post. She heard the cries of children and thought it must be a party. Pity if it started to rain. The thought occurred no more than a couple of seconds before she caught sight of a figure some half-dozen plane trees away coming towards her. The long face was raised to the sky. She was certain it must be Kingman. He was of medium height, just as in the CCTV footage and the covert shots, in a sports jacket, but at that moment he was struggling into a thin nylon raincoat, one arm raised into a sleeve. A siren broke the quiet of the afternoon in the same instant. A police car came fast down the road with roof-lights flashing.

It alerted him as it alerted her and other passers-by. Maybe she wasn't quick enough. On the spur of the moment, as the police car disappeared down another road and its siren quietened, she turned into the gateway where the balloons were and walked briskly, almost at a run, along concrete driveway towards garage doors and a back garden. A boy came running out holding a large ball with red stripes. Seeing her, he ran back into the back garden again and she followed him. What could be more natural, she felt, than a mother coming to join in the fun of a children's party?

About a dozen children aged between three and five were there, supervised by three women. Most were busy on a stretch of lawn playing some game. The boy, though, was apparently playing by himself. She asked him for the ball and he handed it to her solemnly. She asked him his name.

'Listair.'

She threw the ball for him to catch. Instead he kicked it. It bounced against a garden urn and ran out into the driveway. She and the boy ran after it. As she bent down to pick it up she saw the raincoated figure at the gateway looking down the length of the concrete driveway towards her. Their eyes very obviously met. She could have sworn she felt the shock of his gaze like a stream of electricity.

'Alistair!'

The shrill woman's voice came from the garden. Officer Boswell threw the striped red ball for the boy. He again kicked it. This time it struck the garage door obliquely and bounced back onto the tiled patio of the back garden right to the feet of a woman about Joan Boswell's age who came running up repeating the boy's name.

'Alistair, I said you shouldn't! Alistair! Oh, who...who are you?'

'I am looking for a Mr Silber,' said Officer Boswell.

'Who?'

She repeated the name. She felt shaky from the sight of Kingman's eyes. The boy's mother was looking at her suspiciously.

'There's no one here of that name. You can see, can't you? It's a children's party.'

'Yes, I can see that. Do you know if a Mr Silber lives anywhere near here?'

Alistair's mother hustled the little boy away from the patio area, nudging his shoulders gently ahead of her. 'No, I don't. Ask Connie over there.'

Connie turned out to be the hostess for the children's party. She approached with eyebrows raised and fingers playing with the sleeves of a cardigan she had obviously put on recently.

'I think it's going to rain. They said it would. We'll have to get the children indoors. Yes, what is it?'

Officer Boswell repeated her question and was conscious of receiving a more sympathetic hearing. Connie said she thought there was someone with a name like that living in a house backing onto the adjacent garden. There were garages over there, she pointed out.

'I was told,' said Officer Boswell with all the authority of a white lie, 'Mr Silber did repairs at the back.'

Connie gave a wry smile. 'I think you've been misinformed.' She began waving the children towards the house. 'Come on!' she called. 'It's going to rain! Everyone indoors!' She lowered her voice to a stage-whisper. 'You'll find he doesn't like visitors. He's got *cam-er-as!*' Then she looked away. 'Come on!' she called. 'Everyone indoors!'

Cameras! Officer Boswell thanked her and walked briskly out onto the concrete driveway. She walked past the balloons and retraced her steps to the front of the tall Victorian house. Kingman had vanished. Maybe he'd gone up the stone steps into the house and into one of what appeared to be flats, judging by the bank of buttons and little name-plates by the front door. Or perhaps he'd gone down the tarmac-ed driveway to the line of garages at the back where she glimpsed cars parked. Wheelie bins with roughly painted numbers stood against the house to one side of this driveway. Bits of newspaper and empty crisp packets blew about in a sudden breeze. She strolled down the driveway towards the back of the house.

The only movement apart from the rubbish blowing about was the surging motion of the poplars as they felt the wind push against them and their leaves responded with a deep, tremulous hissing. The sound made her conscious of the noise of her footsteps in the echo-chamber between the garages and the house. She looked round her. Parked cars, shut garages and a wall topped by metal struts supporting barbed wire.

It hardly seemed likely that Kingman could have come this way. She studied the garage doors. Most were up-and-over but two had doors with vertical side-hinges and one in particular had an ordinary door set within the main door. She pushed it. A bright interior light shone at her. It showed a small van parked inside and at least one surveillance camera. She closed the door at once but not soon enough. She could smell tobacco.

'Was there something?'

A man opened the door practically the instant she had closed it. He peered at her. She might have expected overalls and an oil rag. Instead he was smartly dressed in jeans and black leather jacket with a white sheepskin collar. He looked about twenty-five and very muscular.

'Do you do repairs?' she asked. 'I was told someone round here did repairs.'

A frown. He took a puff at a cigarette and then flung it on the concrete floor and stepped on it.

'Nope.'

He shut the door without giving her another glance. Her recce was becoming too conspicuous, she felt. A loud bolting of the door from the inside told her she had perhaps seen too much. She turned and walked away from the garages.

The first heavy drops of squally rain were beginning to darken the tarmac as she started to run. It would have been sensible to have sheltered somewhere but she decided to get wet. She needed the security of her car more than anything at that moment because she thought she knew where Kingman was and security for communication by mobile phone could only be ensured if she used the system installed in her car.

The rain grew heavier as she ran under the plane trees. All pedestrians had vanished. Traffic swished by and she felt wetter and wetter and the residential roads seemed cold and unfriendly. Finally her car came in sight. She slipped into it but as she did so the vehicle parked immediately in front of her reversed and she found herself boxed in.

Hey, why?

It was a van in front of her with British Telecom markings. She recalled seeing the man working in the inspection pit. Busy trying to catch her breath, she wondered whether to get out again and protest until she saw the gates of the Silber residence had opened. The van had reversed in readiness to leave the curb but had been stopped from going farther by the emergence of the BMW.

She switched on her engine and the wipers automatically swept to and fro. It seemed too good to be true. She had not only found where R.C.'s Kingman might be but could possibly identify the registration number of Silber's vehicle. She did. Within thirty seconds she had spelt out the letters and digits to the Vauxhall Bridge headquarters.

'Who was the driver, did you say?' the voice at the other end asked.

'I didn't,' Officer Boswell said. 'Just tell the American agent R.C. that I've seen him.'

'Seen who?'

'Just tell him. If he's awake.'

She reported to the Controller at once on returning to the office. He was sceptical.

Three hours later Raoul Cyrus Smithson awoke. His digital wristwatch, like the darkness outside, told him it was 20.47 and he simply could not believe it.

***

The next morning, as soon as Officer Boswell was in the office, she downloaded her shots from her smartphone and printed them. They lay on her desk. She couldn't remember taking so many. To her surprise, her magnifying glass showed her a face staring from an upper window in the bland façade of the Silber residence. If it were blown-up, might it offer further evidence?

Arnie leant over her shoulder and looked intently at the monitor once the pics had been set up again. 'You want Mike to see what he can do with it?'

'Yes.'

Mike was their expert with pixels. 'Give me time, give me time.' It was his mantra. He perched himself in Officer Boswell's chair at her desk, pushed his spectacles back, did what seemed to her was a whole Bach fugue on her computer with the fingers of his right hand and up sprang a fairly clear image.

'That's a new one you got?' he inquired. She said she'd bought her smartphone only the previous week.

'They make'em better now.' Mike conceded the point a little reluctantly. 'This is the best I can do. Okay?'

She thanked him and set up the printing process. Printed, regardless of the rash of dots, a set of features emerged. She had apparently taken three rapid shots of that section of the second floor of the façade containing bedroom windows. One of them framed the staring face but now sufficiently enlarged three different times for some kind of identification. It was apparently male, oval, unshaven, the brows straight above clearly pouched eyes, the mouth generous but unsmiling and a sharp chin giving the contour of the whole face a neat, firm outline. Dark hair colour, true, but little in the way of tints to complexion or eyes save for a pale red for the lips. Near vertical lines in the cheeks naturally suggested age and experience, features converging with deep lines on the temples. Somehow it was not, Officer Boswell thought, an Anglo-Saxon face, though she was not sure why.

Raoul Cyrus Smithson sloped into the office, giving a not too apologetic smile and excusing himself for tardiness. 'I haven't slept like that for weeks. So, Joan, forgive me if I'm too familiar, what is it you have here?'

She told him what had been found. She told him she was sure she'd seen the man called K and now she'd just downloaded and printed an image of a face visible in a bedroom window of the Silber residence. He whistled through his teeth.

'You say you're sure about seeing K?'

'I saw him and he saw me.'

'All this was in my big sleep, right?'

'Late yesterday afternoon, yes.'

'And this is?'

'It looks like the man who was with K at St Pancras. I can probably get an enlargement if you like.'

'No need, I reckon.' He pursed his lips. 'I think I know this face.'

Could it be James Pinckney? Could it be the living dead? Could it be Mrs Van Straubenzee's hunch? Could it even be the face of the Soviet maidservant he and Ed Kalthorst had interrogated in the Moscow embassy thirty, forty years ago? Why did something in the face ring so many bells for him?

'Let's compare,' he said. She called up the shots and CCTV footage from the arrival at St Pancras at R.C.'s bidding. 'I would say what you've got here is pretty damn right-on. There's no better shot of *him*, is there... No, okay, I know you'd been asked to concentrate on the one who calls himself Kingman. But there's a connection, isn't there? Perhaps it's intended. Suppose we're supposed to know Koursaros, calling himself Kingman, has come to London, and suppose we begin to wonder who's with him. If he's Pinckney, that seems very unlikely. We're bound to be puzzled, though, we're bound to be doubtful. According to what we know, Pinckney's dead. He's somewhere in Forest Lawns. Therefore he's not Pinckney and yet maybe he *is* Pinckney or someone looking like him. Do you get my meaning?'

'No, R.C., I don't.'

Officer Boswell was more than a little bored by his ramblings. R.C. picked up instantly on her reaction and bellowed with laughter.

'Right! You're right! Let's think who.'

'Who?'

'Who else is there?'

'R.C., I'm at a loss.'

'*At a loss*! Boy, aren't we all at a loss! I mean let's think who else could possibly… possibly know. I don't like sending it to Ed. And he wouldn't want it sent. The White House now vets very carefully all in-coming data. How secure are you here?'

'We have an internal system that's not let us down yet. Outside that there's no guarantee.'

R.C. smiled his best cynical smile, nodded and studied the image of Pinckney more closely. Then he snapped his fingers. 'What was that name? Germ, no, not German, but Jermin! Jermin!' He spelled the name. 'He was in your embassy in Moscow. Is he accessible here in London? He knew this guy we renamed Pinckney. He knew him better'n anyone.'

Jermyn Street was her thought, but that wasn't much help. She called Arnie away from what he was doing peering at his monitor. He had often been successful in identifying hitherto unknown names and had an encyclopaedic memory for them. This one, though, sounded so fake and suspiciously made-up that she doubted it from the start.

'Who?'

'Jermin.' She spelt it.

'Connected with?'

'Moscow. The embassy.'

'Yes, there was a Jermin. But…'

Arnie had leaned right back in his revolving chair, his neck stretched back, his head resting on the topmost cushion of the leather upholstery. What he stared at apart from neon lighting seemed utterly without meaning and could hardly explain why he was smiling.

'So but what?' Joan asked a little curtly.

'From what I recall, he was dismissed. There was a scandal. A velvet trap. But he'd been shot.'

'Shot? Who shot him?'

Joan's question led to Arnie looking inquiringly for a

moment at R.C. 'I think it was outside the American embassy, wasn't it?'

'Oh, yeah, right!' R.C. declared. 'I remember now! That's our man! He *was* shot, sure. Of course, of course, I got my young assistant to get me up to speed... One moment.' He tapped into his cellphone. The data came up almost at once. 'Robert Simon Jermin – yes, here he is. One *bolshaia shishka*, as the Russians say. He runs an insurance consultancy, IIC, that means International Insurance Consultancy. Oh, very grand! Very, very grand! And where would that be, I wonder?'

'Hell, I don't know!' Arnie cried. 'In the city somewhere, I imagine.'

'Yes, he was shot, I remember that,' R.C said calmly, a little unsettled by Arnie's sharpness. 'He was with Pinckney then. He'd be able to identify him. *If*, of course, we can find him.'

In fact, as Arnie pointed out, it took less than a minute to find him via Google and his insurance consultancy. Naturally enough there was an address and phone number.

'You call him,' R.C said to Joan. 'A smart English voice'll sound better than my CIA stars and stripes. Okay?'

She obeyed. A young female PA voice responded to her inquiry with news that Mr Jermin was in a conference, but when the name Raoul Cyrus Smithson of the CIA was mentioned, there was a pause. Shortly afterwards she came back with agreement to a meeting in Mr Jermin's office that morning at midday, especially in view of the fact that it concerned the forthcoming visit by the president of the United States.

***

The white of his beard, carefully trimmed to the shape of his chin and cheeks and almost matching the whiteness of his open shirt, emphasised by contrast the smart moist redness of his lips as he spoke and somehow lent an authority to the words that they hardly deserved. He had been speaking about his decision to 'go native' in his retirement, as he put it. Bob had not been surprised to find him in his office that very morning. He had been waiting for the conference to finish, but when Bob actually confronted Wilbur Oldfield he could not help instantly wondering how many years it had been since he had seen the old man. Nothing reminds you more of your own age than seeing the changes that age has wrought in friends. Except Wilbur was not, strictly speaking, a friend. He was a business acquaintance from another way of life, or that's how he thought of him, older than him by a decade or more, but very well-informed. It was the need for information that brought them together.

'I've always liked being here in the UK,' Wilbur Oldfield said, 'which is why I bought a home right here in London, in Fulham, when I retired, but I can't stand your winters, so I go back to California each fall. So what's the information you were asking about?'

'Thank you for coming in here this morning. Knowing how careful you have to be about information on your own staff, as we have to be too, I wanted,' Bob said, 'to ask you whether you can recall any woman on your staff here, in the firm, who may have had some connection with *us* – you know what I mean, MI5, MI6 or some other agency this side of the pond – because I had a very strange phone call last evening, a woman's voice, American, and my first thought was if anyone knew you would. As you can understand, I couldn't mention this in a phone call to you or by email, but you were over here so long you've become a sort of tribal memory, which is a most respected office to hold. Do you remember any woman who was here thirty years ago and might have known me because I can't think who it might be. And it's been very worrying.'

'Hey, I might be a tribal memory, but you're not giving me much to work on.'

'You were attached to the embassy, weren't you?'

'I suppose officially, yes, but I was no diplomat, as you know. I had what your people used to call a roving brief, principally to do with Soviet rocketry. That's how we met, remember? There were no female personnel, though. The representation comprised myself and an administrative assistant. The assistant rotated annually, I stayed. We relied on your people mostly and I got to know some of your people pretty well, like I got to know you. Not a woman, though. What was she calling you about?'

'It seemed to be about someone we'd both known in the past. Anyhow the caller's number was withheld.'

Wilbur Oldfield raised one eyebrow and shook his head. 'Not promising.'

'And now,' Bob said, 'while I was in conference a call came in from a police officer.' He consulted his PA's note. 'PC Joan Boswell. She's apparently working with someone I once knew, oh a hundred years ago, Raoul Cyrus Smithson. Know him?'

'Of course I know him! Or *knew* him!' Wilbur Oldfield fingered his beard. 'What the hell's he doing over here?'

'It's to do with the president's arrival tomorrow.'

'White House suspicions, I bet,' said the American. 'He was always referred to as R.C.'

'Oh, of course!' Bob exclaimed. 'R.C., yes. I remember him.'

'Very competent and much respected. Someone said he was on the verge of retirement, so I can't understand why he'd be over here right now. It doesn't make a lot of sense.'

It didn't make a lot of sense to either men until a minute or so later when the tall figure of R.C. entered the office and Bob shook his hand. Officer Boswell was immediately introduced along with R.C.'s exuberant greeting on catching sight of Wilbur Oldfield.

'Hey, what's it been – years and years, eh? It was right here in London, wasn't it, when you, sir,' R.C. had turned to Bob, 'were recovering from a leg wound and Mr Oldfield here had to deal with what we all called his "cargo", right?'

'Right,' Wilbur agreed. He remained seated while R.C. and Officer Boswell had chairs offered them and R.C. began a short explanation of the need for speed by saying: 'Well, he might be back again, that's why we're here. Joan here'll show you.'

And the grainy enlargement of a face in a window was produced for all four faces in the office to look at. What Bob saw were the thin, ascetic features of a man in his late fifties or early sixties. Distanced and blurred by the rigid contours of the window frame, he appeared in near silhouette as if he were almost looking at something in the room but was more likely peering at something outside, though the picture itself had been so sharply guillotined that the visible location amounted to little more than a couple of upper-story windows, which were presumably bedroom windows. The whole purpose was obviously to concentrate on the face. He had to study it very carefully and quietly despite Wilbur Oldfield's rather noisy denial of any knowledge of the man's identity.

'Mr Jermin, sir,' R.C. asked, 'does it remind you of anyone?'

Bob narrowed his eyes. He gave a gesture indicating the need for quiet. The narrower his vision became and the less sure the silhouette looked there emerged a face like a dark cloud in which all the emphasis fell on the line of the forehead and nose and lips and, strangely, the whole image seemed more youthful, if only for a moment, more recognisable. A name flashed into his mind.

'Great Peter,' he said.

'Who the hell?' exclaimed Wilbur.

'That's right!' R.C. pondered something a moment. 'It's

right! There *was* some name like that. He was James Pinckney for us.'

'I don't know,' Bob added. Because doubts began to cloud his recollection, let alone reinforce certainty. 'I thought your people said he'd died.'

'Right again,' said R.C. and snapped his fingers. 'But apparently he's been on Athos, Mount Athos, in Greece.' The statement was greeted by a short silence. 'And apparently he's right here in London right as of this very morning. And brought here by or accompanied by a politically ambitious Russian oligarch travelling here with the passport name of Kingman, that's right, isn't it, Joan?' Joan Boswell agreed. 'And we have reason to believe, despite it sounding more like something out of a Hollywood movie, that this Mr Kingman poses a threat to the life of the present incumbent of the White House. Which is why he's here on the eve of the eve of the present incumbent's arrival tomorrow, having brought his assassin with him.'

Bob blinked. There was something gigantically outrageous about the implication of this. 'You mean Great Peter or James Pinckney, if that is who we're looking at, wants to kill the president? What makes you think that?'

'Kingman has publicly said as much.'

Bob stared at R.C. 'If he's been on Mount Athos…'

'He's been declared dead,' said R.C. calmly. 'He's perfect, he's unknown, he's the ideal assassin. But you're not sure, isn't that what you're saying?'

'I *am* saying that, yes!' Bob looked again at the face in silhouette. 'Thirty, forty years is a long, long time. There *is* a resemblance, a sort of resemblance, but I don't think I would swear to recognise him if I were asked to identify him in a court of law. In any case, if he's been a monk on Mount Athos, he would hardly seem to be the obvious candidate as an assassin, let alone an assassin of the president of the United States.'

Am I lying? He was suddenly thinking. Or am I pretending?

What was that description he used? What was it he said he was? *A Dagger of God*? Yes, that's what he said he would be: a Dagger of God! So I'm wrong. I'm lying, I'm lying...

R.C. flicked his fingers again. 'Right, absolutely right. So maybe he's not your "Great Peter." But if he's with Kingman, alias Koursaros, and he's here right now, he must have some purpose for being here, on the eve of the president's arrival.'

7

R.C. said, looking ruefully at Officer Boswell: 'You reckon you saw him?'

'It looked like him, yes.'

'What am I doing here if I don't check on such a witness statement? Okay?'

'Well, we'll need warrants, won't we?'

'Did I hear you say okay, Officer Boswell?'

'No, R.C., I don't think you did.'

'Right. Suppose I say we pay a friendly visit? So I can verify?'

'Verify?'

'Verify a very reliable witness statement. Agreed?'

'Agreed. If you think...'

'Yes, let me do the thinking. I'd like to do the thinking on this one. As a matter of fact, I've just had an idea.' He had a small bag with him and extracted something. 'Look,' he said, 'you take this. Keep it out of sight until it becomes necessary.'

'What is it?'

'It's a facemask. For medical purposes. Just keep it out of sight.'

She accepted the unusual gift more in wonderment at R.C.'s ingenuity or sheer masculine charisma. If her claim to have seen K – or whatever his name was – could be proved, then she would do whatever R.C. suggested. So she drove him to the Silber suburb and the house with the tall chimneys. The only parking space was some way off the wrought-iron front gates. They had to walk under the plane trees past other seemingly shut, impregnable-looking houses of the same vintage before catching a glimpse of the curved driveway, this time devoid of any parked BMW. R.C. recognised at once what Officer Boswell had said about the place: it gave such an appearance of up-market probity and respectability it looked too good to be true. The gates were locked. Mail, etc., had to be delivered through a letterbox fixed in one of the brick gateposts adjacent to a brass plaque with buttons and microphone for access.

'Maybe we'd best not,' he muttered and turned away immediately to follow his companion's directions to what she thought might be the back of the property.

'I think it might be the way in,' she said.

The trouble was Officer Boswell couldn't be sure. Their footsteps down the tarmac-ed driveway beside the tall Victorian house were even louder than hers had been the previous day. This time, though, there was no sign of rain. Bright sunlight shone on the black plastic wheelie bins and lent their crudely painted white numbers an air of rough dignity. Several cars were parked opposite the shut garages, but it astonished her to see that the one she had approached yesterday was wide open, its interior quite empty except for the young man in jeans and smart leather jacket with the white sheepskin collar sitting smoking. He did exactly what he'd done when first seeing her. He stamped out his cigarette on the concrete floor.

'Young man,' R.C. commanded, 'does a Mr Silber live round here?'

He received one curt glance but not a word. The young man's reaction was to spring to his feet and begin closing the garage door. R.C didn't like this kind of behaviour.

'Hey, cool it! I asked you a question. Politely.'

'Who's asking?'

'I wish to meet with Mr Silber. We have matters to discuss.'

'No one meets Mr Silber. I get told when he's here.'

'Mr Silber has guests, doesn't he?'

'So you're a guest?'

'Maybe that's what I am. And this lady here is a guest who would like to see Mr Silber. Miss Boswell here.'

Officer Boswell tried to smile as amiably as possible, but the smart leather jacket merely scowled and reached under his jacket for what emerged as a mobile phone that R.C. almost instantly seized from him and sent skittering across the garage floor. He then brought the half-closed garage door banging shut and told Officer Boswell to lock it along with the smaller integral door.

'Now you take us to see Mr Silber,' he said quietly. 'Please. And no fuss, no fuss. We are visitors.' He ensured compliance by seizing the young man's left arm and pinning it sharply behind his back despite his protesting expletives. 'Very nasty language, mister. Enough. Enough.'

But the smart leather jacket proved a great deal stronger than R.C. anticipated, or rather it surprised and annoyed R.C. that he wasn't as strong as he had been when younger, and quick as lightning the young man freed himself and dashed through an inner door into what looked like a kind of workshop. R.C. pressed his lips together and shook his head. 'My!'

Officer Boswell, having locked the garage doors, was on the point of warning against going any further with what she could only think was an invasion of privacy, knowing full well that both she and R.C. would be instantly recognisable from the CCTV cameras. She couldn't help herself, however, because R.C. had gone into the workshop and was already through another door into a large greenhouse. She had to follow.

'R.C., please, we mustn't!' she implored.

He shot her a faintly congenial smile. They were already out of doors again, in an obviously well-kept area of kitchen garden. The young man was running along a path to one side and disappeared almost instantly behind shrubbery set among a line of poplars.

'Just be calm,' R.C. said. 'We're guests. We're visiting to make sure Mr, er, Kingman is in good health.'

Officer Boswell couldn't help admiring the chutzpah. Whatever his background, no Mr Kingman figured in any file of persons regarded as suspicious or a threat to security that she had come across, but she had put her trust in R.C.'s knowledge, so she followed him round the edge of the kitchen garden and along the path through the shrubbery into an area of lawn. It was here that the first stabs of alarm bit into her for a moment. The rear of the house came into view. Most conspicuous were French windows facing onto a patio. The sun struck the windows momentarily with a flash of light. It hardly took an instant for her to realise that the flash was due to one of the windows opening. Across a distance of newly mown lawn they were being confronted by a woman standing silhouetted in the full-length rectangle of the opened window, a hand raised to shade her eyes against the sun's brightness. Beside her was the young man. He was pointing to the visitors and obviously speaking about them.

R.C. gave a kind of welcoming salute as he strolled across the lawn, his manner one of friendly authority. The young man stopped speaking as he approached and greeted him with a hostile glare.

'Hi,' came R.C.'s American voice, 'my name's Smithson.' It was so casual, he might have been a relative or close friend. 'Dr Raoul Smithson. Nice to meet you, ma'am.' No hand was proffered, but the greeting at least elicited a response.

'I am Anne Sutherland, Dr Smithson.'

'Nice to meet you, Anne.' He merely made a chewing motion with his lips. 'Is Mr Silber home?'

The woman called Anne revealed herself as middle-aged. She wore the dark blue jacket and matching skirt of someone used to being professionally in charge, not exactly a policewoman, more possibly a nurse, or so she seemed to Officer Boswell, but at that moment the issue was irrelevant because R.C was already introducing her as his assistant.

'My young associate here is more qualified than I am. How is Mr Silber?'

'He is not here. Who are you?'

'They're not friends!' the young man shouted. 'They're intruders! I told you!'

'Really, Nick,' she scolded, 'please, not so loud! Tell me – who *are* you?'

The repetition of the question was uttered without harshness but officiously. She had a resonant, determined voice that was used to being obeyed, but R.C. must have caught some covert signal that made him adopt a different attitude.

'We're from the agency,' he announced in a confidential manner of the kind that might well be suited to exchanges between professional people. 'If Mr Silber is absent, that is a pity, but we are acting on orders to see if one of his guests, a Mr Kingman, is here. The agency has been informed of illness. Am I right?'

'What agency is that?'

There was the faintest suggestion in her question that she disbelieved the whole thing. R.C. seemed undeterred. He flipped open a small wallet and showed her a card.

'He arrived from abroad, didn't he?'

'I think he came by Eurostar,' she admitted and then almost immediately said disapprovingly: 'This is American' as she studied what was being shown.

'Right, ma'am, it's medical insurance.' R.C. closed up the wallet and thrust it into his jacket pocket. 'You see the agency has reason to believe he may be seriously ill. You have heard of diphtheria, I imagine?'

'Of course.' She looked shocked, took in a deep breath and narrowed her eyes. 'You can't imagine I don't know about diphtheria, but are you suggesting one of Mr Silber's guests has it? He may have a cold, I know that, but he's not likely to have… Look, it's rare now, diphtheria is.' What had been a rather fierce rebuttal began to lose its impetus. 'No, he's not got diphtheria, I'm sure he hasn't.'

'So Mr Silber's guest has a cold? He's here and he has a cold?'

'Yes.'

The admission opened floodgates. 'Then we must see him,' R.C. insisted and strode intently forward towards the open French window. 'Where is he? In a bedroom? Show me!'

The young man called Nick began to protest. 'I tell you they're fucking pigs, they're cops! Don't let 'em in!'

He barred the way for an instant, but R.C. pushed past him so roughly Nick lost his balance and staggered backwards rather awkwardly through the French window. He collapsed into a nearby armchair. Before he had time to recover the woman called Anne had entered and was telling him to get back to where he should be.

'You know you're not meant to be in the house,' she was saying. 'And I don't want to hear that sort of language from anyone! Now off with you!'

She shoved him complainingly out through the French windows and turned the key in the lock. He was left for several moments staring through the diamond leaded panes and shouting.

'Please,' she said, offering the word more as an apology than an invitation, and gestured for them to follow her across what was obviously a sitting room into a spacious hall. 'He has a bedroom upstairs, but he is a law unto himself, so I can't be sure he'll be there. Mr Silber is very generous with his guests. He allows them to...Ah!'

Her exclamation was justified. Standing half way down a straight flight of stairs and looking down at them over dark-stained banisters was an elderly man with white hair. He was neatly dressed in a sports jacket and necktie, clothes that gave him an oddly out-of-date, rather theatrical look. He was just wiping his nose when R.C.'s strongly accented voice pronounced an overenthusiastic greeting:

'Hi, Mr Pavel Ivanovich! Mr Kingman, isn't it? Or is it Mr Koursaros? How are you?'

'Do I know you?' The handkerchief was lowered and the handsome, elderly face was slightly lifted in disgust.

'Are you well, sir? Your voice is husky. My assistant will be preparing herself for a modest inspection if you will permit it.'

Indeed Officer Boswell had already begun donning the facemask and was just at that moment looping the fasteners round her ears. Half her face was already obscured by the time R.C. smirked, looking up at the stairs and saying:

'Smithson? Remember?'

The elderly man frowned. 'What name?'

'Smithson.'

'No.'

'Your voice is very husky, sir. Do you have a sore throat?'

There was no immediate answer because a little fountain of tinny sound suddenly filled the hall and the woman called Anne had a phone to her ear. She was saying 'Yes, sir, of course. No, it's that boy, Nick. Yes, well, there are visitors here... I know, I know,' and then in a stage whisper, one hand obscuring the phone for an instant and leaning towards R.C., she explained it was Mr Silber and quickly disappeared through an adjacent door to continue the conversation out of earshot.

R.C. resumed his apparently urgent concern for the elderly man's health. This time he spoke so confidentially his voice had none of its previous energy. It was as if the hall were little larger than a small bedroom.

'Sir, I have to inform you that three cases of what is thought to be a form of diphtheria have been identified among passengers who arrived in London yesterday by the same Eurostar service as you did. I and my assistant here have been given privileged advance information about this. We have been instructed to contact you as early as possible to arrange treatment with an antitoxin and/or penicillin if necessary. You see your symptoms, sir, make it highly likely you may have caught the infection. Maybe also the companion accompanying you. I believe he may be a certain Mr Pinckney, also referred to in Russian as *velikii Piotr* or Great Peter. Am I right, sir? He will be in as much danger as you, my dear Pavel Ivanovich. And we must contact him. It is very urgent.'

The elderly man's response took even R.C. a little by surprise. He wiped his nose once again, shook his head slowly up and down in a kind of acknowledgement of what he had just heard and emitted a short bellow of laughter. This was followed by a second bellow of laughter.

In a tone of some annoyance R.C. broke in with: 'A laughing matter, that's what you think it is!' but the remark sounded rather silly. Pavel Ivanovich stopped laughing and resumed his slow, apparently bewildered shaking of his head, this time from left to right.

'I have no companion. Mr Pinckney? Who is Mr Pinckney? Who is *velikii Piotr*? And you say I am sick man. I am not sick man! You are American agent! I remember you now!'

'Right,' said R.C. 'So you remember my name — Smithson?'

'You are fool, Mr Smittson!'

'Yes,' R.C. conceded, 'maybe I am. Fool enough to know you, Pavel Ivanovich or Mr Kingman or whoever you are.'

A half-smile, not quite a grin, drew the line of his lips together as he looked up at his adversary on the stairs. For an appreciable moment, lasting perhaps as long as ten seconds, the two men stood silently looking at each other. Then the elderly man blinked and leant forward over the banister rail. He spoke in a quiet voice.

'Your president will die.'

'Sir, that is one big claim.'

'It is fact. Your president will die.'

'Why do you say that?'

'I know it, Mr Smittson.'

'You know it because you are involved, is that what you're saying?'

'No, no, I say it to warn you.'

'You know who it is, the person who will kill?'

'No, no. I know your president will die. I warn you.'

'Thank you for the warning,' R.C. said. 'And I must warn you that you may have contracted diphtheria, *difteriia – ponimaite?- difteriia.*'

The elderly man sneezed and once again flourished his handkerchief but did not speak. Instead, after briefly wiping his nose, he resumed the slow to-and-fro headshakes he had been making previously.

'Okay, have it your way,' R.C. said. 'We know where you are. The agency will be informed.'

Still sustaining his authoritative manner, he directed Officer Boswell to follow him and rapidly strode out of the hall and back into the sitting room. It took little effort to unlock the French windows onto the patio. The young man called Nick was nowhere to be seen. Bright sunshine as ever flooded the lawn area. As R.C. led the way across it, impressing Officer Boswell with his calmly authoritative manner, she quickly removed the facemask and simultaneously pressed the little alarm button on her smartphone. She felt the time had come to assume that departure from the Silber residence could be a lot more difficult than arrival, no matter how great R.C.'s chutzpah.

By the time they reached the large conservatory, there was no doubt other staff had been alerted. A teenage boy in a white vest and yellow shorts, presumably connected with the garden, barred the way to the workshop and began saying he'd been told not to let anyone through. The police, he said, had been summoned.

'Good,' said R.C., learning this had been done on the insistence of 'Mr Nick.' 'Because, you see, we are the police. My assistant, Officer Boswell, will show you.' Which of course she did. The boy looked at the document and seemed genuinely confounded by it.

'You see I don't know, I've never seen one of these before.'

R.C. clapped him on the shoulder. 'Good boy. Make sure you don't see 'em often. Now just stand aside.'

He did. They entered the workshop only to find the door to the garage was locked. This, Officer Boswell supposed, was the only possible exit from the Silber property. As R.C. tried to budge it, she phoned HQ and learned a patrol car nearby would shortly be arriving. At least fifteen minutes, she thought.

What happened next shocked her. R.C. had his revolver out. The door had bolts on the side facing him. She saw he must have assumed there were unlikely to be bolts on the other side when he fired twice at the key lock and the cheap metal casing flew away. The door swung open. This might be justifiable in the United States, she was about to say, oh, but not here in London, England. Nick, she assumed, had unlocked the garage doors, because she saw him momentarily holding one of the them open, only for all her thoughts to become concentrated on the virtually simultaneous arrival of a large saloon car, probably a BMW. It could be seen to enter slowly like a train drawing to a halt. In equally stately fashion the car doors opened practically the moment it stopped. A uniformed chauffeur burst out at the front and a well-dressed man in a black suit from the rear door. What struck Officer Boswell at that instant more than the man himself was the high gloss shine of his black shoes as he stepped out of the car.

R.C. rather casually re-inserted the revolver into its armpit holster before briefly waving aside a small residue of smoke. 'Gentlemen,' he said in quiet greeting, 'my apologies for damaging your property,' but the words may have gone largely unheard in the ensuing noise of car doors banging and men shouting. The revolver, however, had been noted.

'What the bloody hell!' shouted the black suit in the highly polished shoes as he confronted R.C. 'Mr Silber wants to know what you're doing here.'

'What I'm doing is, well...'

The explanation tapered into nothing because a man emerged from the far side of the car. He was sixty-ish, dark-haired, bespectacled with thin, lined features and an evident stoop that meant only the upper part of his face was clearly visible over the car roof, but Officer Boswell recognised him at once as the Gustav Silber, known familiarly as George R Silver, or 'Slippery Silver,' who featured in the people-trafficking files she had studied at HQ. He walked with a stick, it seemed, and came slowly round the back of the car with a broad smile on his impish face.

'Good morning, good morning,' he was saying, 'who has been visiting me this fine day, eh?'

'They're intruders,' proclaimed Nick, who had been pressing himself up against the side of the garage as the car entered. 'And he's got a gun. I told you when I called you - they're intruders! They're bloody pigs!'

Mr Silber had by this time made his way round the back of the car. R.C., confronted as he was by both the black suit and the uniformed chauffeur, adopted an air of somewhat aggrieved desperation.

'Urgent medical attention is needed,' he announced. 'One of the residents of your house, sir, has possibly contracted a diphtheria-like illness.'

'So you shoot your way out of my property, yes? You damage my property?' Mr Silber, still smiling, indicated with his stick the door to the workshop. He looked up at R.C. and the smile slowly withdrew from his face. Instead he issued orders. 'If you have a gun, please surrender it to my employee, Mr Stanley, here.' He indicated the highly polished black shoes. 'I do not allow people to carry lethal weapons on my property. Nor does anyone on my property have diphtheria or anything like diphtheria. Who are you, black man?'

'I am a black man, sir, working for a United States medical insurance business. They have an agency right here in London. No, sir, I will not surrender my gun.'

Officer Boswell broke in at this point. 'Mr Silber, Interpol has informed us that you are known to harbour illegal immigrants...'

'Utter nonsense!' Silber interjected.

'So naturally,' Officer Boswell continued, 'a U.S. representative would be entitled to carry...'

'Entitled! Listen to her!'

'Entitled to carry a weapon in the light of this knowledge as he would be entitled in the United States.'

'Oh, would he, indeed! Oh, what gung-ho nonsense! Who are *you*, young lady, to talk about entitlements?'

She had had no need to answer. All normal morning sounds were suddenly obliterated by the siren of an approaching police car. It came at speed down the access road beside the wheelie bins and ground to a stop within a few feet of the garage entrance. Officer Boswell recognised Arnie as the driver. It was his companion, though, who jumped out of the car, clapped his peaked hat on his head and strode in policeman-like efficiency out of bright sunlight into the shady garage doorway.

'Officer Joan Boswell? Ah, yes.' Recognition brought a sharpening of the tone. 'And a Mr Smithson? Right, sir?' He was consulting with equipment attached to his collar. 'That was the name, wasn't it?'

At this Mr Silber started to protest, wielding his stick in a shooing motion directed as much at the newcomer as at his own employees, who almost immediately assumed he was indicating they should be off and on their way, meaning into the workshop. He started shouting as best he could that it was all illegal, he was being defamed, he'd never heard such nonsense, it was police harassment, the tirade pursuing R.C. and Officer Boswell like so much blue smoke as they hurriedly stepped into the car's rear seat while the peaked cap slipped into the front. Arnie immediately reversed the car smartly out of the garage area and up past the wheelie bins. It was only when they reached the street and had joined traffic that he announced loudly and irritably:

'You bloody well shouldn't have been there!'

'Oh, yes, we should!' R.C. responded.

'No, you shouldn't! We've been running a covert operation on that man. You could've ruined it!'

R.C. shared a glance with Officer Boswell, seated as they

were side by side on the rear seat. She held the glance long enough to acknowledge a degree of guilt.

'Who authorised you to go there?' Arnie asked.

'The Controller yesterday,' Officer Boswell answered a little shakily.

'That was a recce. He didn't authorise this lark, did he?'

'I was the authority,' R.C. broke in. 'I authorised it. And Officer Boswell can bear witness that she has heard, as I have heard, an explicit threat that the president's life is in danger, a threat made by that Mr Kingman, whom I know as Pavel Ivanovich Koursaros, now resident in Mr Silber's house. I am authorised by the White House to ensure the safety of president of the United States during the visit to this country. Goddam it, that's why I'm here! That's enough authority for you!'

'Okay, R.C.!' Arnie cried in retort. 'I accept that.'

'Good.'

'If so, then case closed. Unless we get a complaint from Mr Silber.'

'Dare you say what the operation is you just mentioned, that maybe is going to be ruined?'

'I said covert.'

'You sure did say covert.'

'Then it's covert. Case closed.'

'Right.'

R.C. stared out of the car window at pedestrians, cyclists, parked vehicles and plane trees going by one after another in the bright London sunshine.

PART II

8

Spring in Moscow can be as short-lived as a firework. Over in an instant, it strikes sparks from metal roofs, glints in the gold leaf of cupolas, flashes like molten silver in waters sparkling in gutters, glitters among the fountains of new emerald leaf on trees naked all winter, bursts into flame on windows just clear of frost, splashes sunlight down streets and squares in lunatic, gilded abandon.

Huge transparent gravestones of shadow adjacent to tall buildings may still contain dead bodies of snow for several weeks, but the boulevards, parks and open spaces are filled with soft, half-heard words, a murmuration of early breezes, the faintest quiver of angels' wings, the quietest of prayers spoken out of an earth still aching from the torture of winter.

Lit by the same firework, the sky unfurls itself to reveal a light blue dome fringed with cloud. It fingers the world at first with a chill brightness, then quickly enough with a gathering warmth. In scarcely more than a week it is caressing passionately, embracing all life in its sensual urge to please and hinting already at its deeper, engulfing love, which is the burning stove-mouth heat of summer.

***

Bob knew his flatmate Charles Evesham was a loner. At heart Charles knew this was true and Charles himself knew he would never be any different. But to have admitted his feelings would have been to imperil the *personnalité sociale* which he sought to create in the thoughts of others.

He could not say why he was as he was. There was no need to blame life for any unfairness towards him. He was vaguely homosexual but he did nothing about it because he had never been sufficiently fond of anyone to warrant any kind of relationship. He loved his mother and was a devoted son and somewhat unimaginatively anticipated he would end up married because his mother, like the aristocratic world on whose fringes he belonged, expected him to be married. Basically he was in love with himself. He also loved his work because it was out of the ordinary and gave him boundless opportunities to feel self-important.

To be fair to him, as Bob Jermin would have been the first to concede, he was astonishingly competent. He was a first-class photographer. He was also 'good with his hands', as they say, in technical matters, in devising all sorts of security gadgets, in repair and maintenance of television, for example and in the more domestic functions of cooking and keeping his clothes clean and tidy. In short, he was remarkably self-sufficient. A wife might have found herself superfluous. He was, needless to say, a mine of abstruse information on intelligence matters.

He fed his self-importance by cultivating an exceedingly polite social manner. This earned him brownie points in Western embassies on the Moscow diplomatic scene. It also made his *personnalité sociale* particularly attractive to women. He had acquired a completely factitious and shallow reputation as a ladies' man. It amused him to be a good guest at an ambassadorial dinner or cocktail party and amuse his hostess with light-hearted small talk. It amused him because it was an act of concealment on a social level that more or less paralleled the need for secrecy in his professional and private life.

Because he found himself continually under close scrutiny in Moscow, the last thing Charles Evesham wanted was to give the faintest suspicion he might be prone to nobbling by some

Russian rent boy with a ballet dancer's physique. Spotlessness was therefore his watchword. The apartment he shared with Bob Jermin epitomised such spotlessness. Like thousands of other Moscow apartments, it was cramped, but it offered all that was necessary: kitchen, bathroom, sitting room and two small bedrooms. The major difference in the case of this apartment was that Charles Evesham's tastes ruled supreme. His were the decorative Russian objects such as scarves as wall-hangings and other display objects such as wooden spoons, small wooden carvings or one or two Socialist Realist pictures of earnest-looking workers happily engaged in socialist construction, not to mention a couple of painted side-tables on spindly legs that were prone to fall over at the slightest touch. His was the bedroom always locked and his was the insistence, at which Sophie the maid willingly connived, that all the rather elderly furniture should be spotlessly clean, the parquet floor brightly polished, the rugs regularly beaten out, all surfaces dusted.

Bob Jermin's sole contribution to the adornments of the apartment was a photograph in a silver frame of his girl friend Marsha Parkinson. He insisted that it should be conspicuously sited on the sideboard in the sitting room, but it suffered a little from having to compete with a slightly larger portrait of Charles's mother seated in a Tatler-style pose in Tatler-style surroundings ('The Hon. Caroline Evesham,' ran the text, 'in the drawing-room of her lovely home in Kensington'). However, the smiling image of nineteen-year-old Marsha competed well, so much so that Sophie always treated her portrait with the reverence of an icon.

Charles Evesham was nominally a third secretary in the embassy's chancery, but his function as an expert on military intelligence was largely to take 'trips'. Officially he was in search of medieval churches and archeological sites in Northern Russia and the Ukraine. Naturally a lot of his photographs succeeded in including uniformed troops next to old churches or army vehicles with prominently displayed markings parked next to examples of more recent ecclesiastical architecture, since it was forbidden to photograph bridges or railway stations, let alone barracks or airfields; and he was extremely zealous in respecting these rules while at the same time managing covertly to photograph an extraordinary amount of prohibited items.

On the other hand, his zeal had an unsocial consequence. It turned the cramped bathroom of the apartment into a photographic lab whenever he returned to Moscow. There was a routine for such purposes that involved both men. They would work in a darkroom dimness, using sign language to indicate their needs as each roll of 35 mm film was unloaded and set going on its journey from negative to positive. They usually worked late into the night. By morning and certainly by the time Sophie let herself into the apartment nothing would remain of their activities save traces of deodorant intended to mask the chemical smells. What it meant, though, was that the bath could not be used for bathing on such occasions. Both men came to be known for their modestly enhanced body odour that mattered little in the general ambience of Moscow living.

Sophie of course knew what went on. She informed on both men and went through their things when they were away, which was the principal reason why Charles Evesham did his best to keep his bedroom locked and Bob Jermin locked as much as he could into the supposedly secret compartment in his desk. But she never stole. She was part of the atmosphere of surveillance surrounding them, though she spoke no English and candidly admitted that her ideological armour had serious gaps in it. To her credit, she was ridiculously house-proud, incurably sentimental and utterly devoted. Each day, when they returned from the embassy at lunchtime or in the evening, having been transported by embassy car or minibus in each direction, her 'Mister Charles' and 'Mister Bob' would be greeted with broad smiles and a kind of motherly muttering addressed more to herself than to them. She was certain, among other things, that they were homesick. In Bob's case, this certainly led him to catch her more than once in the act of picking up the silver-framed photograph of Marsha Parkinson and kissing it to an accompaniment of sighs, head-shakings and murmurs of wonder at the smiling face.

Understandably she preferred to spend more time in the apartment than in her actual home, a corner of a room shared with her trolley driver husband in a nearby tenement which was so shamefully small she could hardly ever bring herself to mention it. She would arrive at half-past eight in the morning and was often still in the apartment at half-past eight at night. She was a reasonably good cook, provided regular meals, would do washing and ironing for a fee and was never drunk.

She proved much later to be a sacrificial help at an opportune moment in Bob's involvement with intelligence, for which he remained eternally grateful. On the other hand, Charles Evesham himself proved a more valuable guide when it came to the practical matter of what to do about the material that had appeared in the pocket of Bob's overcoat. Of course he had become marked. He had traded on the simple likelihood that the less conspicuous his clothes, the more invisible he would be in Moscow in those last years of the Soviet regime. After all, part of his remit at the embassy was to 'sniff the air,' as it were, of the state of things in Moscow at a time when rumour after rumour suggested that dissidence was not confined to Solzhenitsyn but was as endemic to ordinary life as the pervasive miasma, both economic and political. He did what he could, aware that he should not have 'contacts', for that could easily make him *persona non grata*. Nonetheless he was marked. The very fact of having been singled out to receive all the material concealed within the covers of the *Krokodil* magazine was proof enough. Having concealed it however insecurely in the secret compartment in his desk, he felt ashamed of it because he could not help feeling it had some connection with this encounter with the girl in the white fur hat. And at the back of his mind, fatuous though it might seem, he sensed it was all very private. He sensed it was all connected with his grandmother. Somehow or other he could not escape the feeling that she was responsible.

Charles Evesham had his own little wheeze for masking any conversation if it involved sensitive matters that were best not overheard by listening devices. Two record players would be set up, each of which contained summer garden sounds ('I love listening to them,' he would say) – birdsong, a light plashing of water, the occasional noise of cattle, a passing aircraft, a church bell, all within a murmuration of softly buzzing insects. He called it 'being outside'. 'A little time outside, it so reminds me of summer holidays,' would be the whispered justification and the whispering would be prolonged as long as the garden sounds continued. He was certain the arrangement ensured secrecy but Bob doubted it; and when he decided to reveal the material from his overcoat pocket there was very little to be whispered about. Charles Evesham's initial reaction was more like a low whistle than a whisper.

'All these calculations, what the hell are they?'

Bob offered the obvious whispered conclusion. 'They're all to do with rocketry. They must be.'

'Hmmm.'

'Look at the diagrams.'

Charles Evesham nodded. 'Yes, I see them. I see it's all handwritten. And you've no idea who supplied this?'

'None.'

'And it could be a hoax, couldn't it?'

'Yes.'

Charles Evesham sighed. 'Awfully tricky, this sort of stuff. Do you want London to see it?'

'I don't know. Do you think I should?'

The material was riffled through once more. 'What's this?' he asked, pointing to one of the sheets.

'They're instructions. At least I think that's what they are.'

'*Zapretnaia zona*. You're being asked to go into a *forbidden zone*, that's what it says. Well, well. Are you going to try it?'

'If I'm caught,' Bob answered, 'that's the end, isn't it? No more career.'

'Of course. So?'

'So I do it for Her Majesty?'

'No, Robert, you do it for yourself.'

Charles's Evesham's emphasis was right. The garden sounds murmured very satisfactorily. His whisper had the requisite stage impact to drive home his meaning.

'You've been chosen,' he added very quietly. 'It's up to you. No, I'm not going to let London know about this. And I'm not going to tell anyone. It's your choice. I know you've shown it me as a matter of trust and I'm very grateful to you for letting me see it. But I warn you, if it's a hoax, you'll simply be declared *persona non grata*. And you know how many places round Moscow are forbidden zones. Go anywhere without permission and they'll declare it a forbidden zone.'

The advice was partly as Bob had expected. He locked the material back in its supposedly secret place and never spoke of it again. It was referred to only once by Charles Evesham when he inquired casually whether Bob was thinking of going where he shouldn't.

'Going to hell, you mean?'

'No, just going outside.'

'No, Charles, I have another plan,' Bob answered. Which was perfectly true, as it turned out.

9

The new American ambassador's friend, Mr Thoreau, was not someone who would say 'Hi, call me Chuck!' He followed rules. They were gentlemanly after their fashion, courteous, shrewd and self-serving. Bonhomie, well-met-ness, good 'ole fellow-ness were their attractive packaging. Similarly his voice had a magisterial, drawling earnestness suggesting the need to convey a heavy load of words over considerable tracts of meaning. The need had indeed impregnated both his way of thinking and his features, tanned as they were to an immaculate Californian poolside hue.

Rectangular rather than oval, his face was dominated by eyes shaped like portholes giving glimpses of a blue tropical sea. Small lines of sixty-year-old youthfulness radiated warmly from these eyes and usually endowed his pliable, well-shaped lips with an aura of 'Have a nice day' contentment, but like portholes they were mostly so fixed in their gaze a smile would take them by surprise. Then the multitude of small lines round them would squeeze themselves into tight wrinkles of faintly juvenile wonderment.

He liked to remind people he was a Californian born and bred. His watchword was thoroughness. He had not earned the nickname 'Thorough Thoreau' for nothing. Thoroughness had brought him wealth through speculating in Californian real estate and it had enabled him to become politically active in Republican Party circles. He had made a particular name for himself with his anti-Soviet rhetoric, in which connection he had been thorough in his reading, his consultation with Harvard Kremlinologists, his boning up on economic statistics and his learning of the language. That was why he had been invited to join the newly appointed ambassador as a member of staff at the United States Moscow embassy.

He applied the same rule to his diplomatic activities as he did to his dealings in real estate. 'Start at the bottom' was his rule. In other words, if you want to discover the real value of a property, go and consult the people at the bottom, as it were, those who last lived and worked there, those who lived closest nearby a tract of land, speak to their children if necessary and make sure you have a thorough picture of what the property meant to them. It might take time, but in the end it almost always paid off. Once you had bribed, cajoled or browbeaten what you wanted out of those at the bottom, you could almost invariably negotiate a better deal with those at the top.

He applied the same rule to his role as 'observer' at the United States embassy, privileged as he was through his friendship with the new ambassador. He would start at the bottom of the diplomatic pile in Moscow and Bob Jermin turned out to be as near the bottom of the pile as anyone. So as Grace Hampson had promised, he was invited to visit the embassy to meet him. It was she who met him in the embassy foyer.

'Hi, good to see you. May I call you Bob?'

He smiled. 'I'll call you what?' he asked.

She uttered her name, almost swallowing it in the ensuing confidential whisper as they crossed the foyer: 'Mr Thoreau likes to be known as "Thorough Thoreau"...' The combination of vowel and fricative had the susurrating thrill of nylon stockings brushed sexily together. 'But for short we know him as TT.' The tit-bit was graced with a delicious smile. 'This way, please,' and she pressed an elevator button.

TT's office in the enormous edifice of the United States

embassy was adjacent to the ambassador's and reached by a private elevator. It hissed Grace and Bob calmly up its steel tower. To his surprise, leaving him barely time to straighten his tie, the doors opened onto a deeply carpeted corridor which led into what appeared to be an elegantly furnished small office. A large mahogany desk sported a desk lamp with a dark-green lampshade, behind which was TT himself seated in a tall-backed revolving leather armchair. Prominent on the wall behind him was a huge wooden carving of the American eagle. It glowered to one side through half-open blinds towards a vista of colourless Moscow rooftops.

'Why, Mr German, how good of you to come.' TT lifted himself out of the armchair to offer a hard-skinned, muscular handshake and accompanied the gesture with a neat compression of his smile lines. He was jacketless, but wore a tie with a palm tree on it. 'Please take a seat, Mr German.'

Bob sank into a well-upholstered armchair, slightly stunned by the office and its occupant. He noticed that Grace had seated herself in an upright wooden chair to one side. A Miss Frost was mentioned as a secretary, but she was apparently in a small adjacent room next door, from which came the distant rattle of a typewriter. Polite initial small talk was temporarily postponed in favour of business, it seemed.

'You know my Administrative Executive, of course, Miss Hampson,' TT said. 'First off, may I ask whether you have any objection to her taking notes of our little chat? General notes, you know, on the topics. No details. Just so we can refer to them later to refresh our memories. Any objections?'

Bob said he had no objections.

'Mind you — may I call you Robert? Thank you. Just address me as TT, everybody round here does — mind you, I am not sure of the protocol in these matters. It may be your British Foreign Office has some objection to this kind of direct approach? Do you think there is?'

'I am not sure what you mean, sir?'

'I mean.' TT laughed in a series of tut-tuts, as if the matter were too indecent to discuss. 'I mean I don't want your people thinking I am poaching you and your knowledge. I want us to be open to each other. My office here has been declared absolutely secure, I can assure you, so you can say whatever you like. The point is, isn't it? that we're both on the same side in this Cold War and we should share and share alike in our approach to the Soviets. Don't you agree with that?'

Bob agreed.

'Right,' said TT. 'If that's settled, then we can...'

Grace had already anticipated his nods and discreet hand waves and complied. The period of small talk began. Cups of coffee were distributed. As they drank they discussed the weather, the need to wear galoshes in the spring thaw, the price of meat in the kolkhoz market, the domestic problems facing TT and his wife during renovations to their apartment in a nearby diplomatic block and the strange fact that no one played golf in the Soviet Union. 'Why, it's an ideal place for golf, Robert, don't you think? Undulant,' TT conceded in developing his real estate patter, 'verdant, so spacious, you could build the best golf course in the world out here. Isn't that right, Grace?' Grace of course agreed.

TT finished his coffee, rested his elbows on the desk and, leaning forward, declared in a solemn drawl, speaking over his clasped fingers that were occasionally unclasped to fiddle with his shirt cuffs:

'We have a cunning and determined adversary out there, you know, Robert. Putting aside the ideology, the Marxist, anti-capitalist rhetoric and anti-Western propaganda, I believe there is a simple human element on which we have to focus. I want to make that our priority. We mustn't allow ourselves to fritter away our priorities through lack of understanding of this human need. Robert, I want to put it to you – if you saw a house on fire and heard a woman shouting for help, would you pass by on the other side? You would not. You would defy the flames and smoke and rush into the house and rescue that woman even if she were screaming her head off that you were a lapdog of the bourgeois West. You are the sort of person who would do that, I believe. Well, I hear Liberty herself crying out from the upper window of the Soviet Union and she needs intrepid, determined people like you and me to defy the flames and smoke and come to her rescue. Now Grace here tells me you have put out feelers, as it were. You have been trying to blend into Moscow life. It's not easy, of course, for diplomats from the West to do this kind of thing. But I'd like to create a network of sorts that would give us an insight into how Mr and Mrs Average live here in Moscow. Do you know what I mean?'

Bob shook his head. About to stem the flow of preposterous rhetoric, he was forestalled by TT continuing with his drawl.

'I don't mean intelligence. Mr and Mrs Average don't concern themselves with matters of that kind. No, I mean we need to establish some kind of human relationship, even a channel of communication with ordinary decent citizens of Moscow who have no access to the West, who have a view of us much distorted by constant propaganda against the West, brain-washed people, for sure, but anxious, you know, to get at the truth. I want to know about the difficulties they encounter in daily life, their real feelings about things, their hopes and so on. Okay, so I know the objections. We can be accused of meddling. We can be accused of espionage. We can all be classed as representatives of the capitalist encirclement, of capitalist imperialism. These are risks we have to take. But if you can hear the voice of Liberty crying out, as I can, and see the smoke billowing out of the windows, risks have to be taken. Which is why I would like you, Robert, and Grace here to co-operate as closely as you can in making contacts here in Moscow, so we can begin to establish a reliable network that will give an insider's picture of the Moscow scene in what many of us consider to be the final years of the present, the Soviet, administration. Do I make myself clear?'

TT made himself abundantly clear. Bob could see how easy it must have been to clinch lucrative real estate deals in California once such groundwork had been done. The notion that Moscow could be so easily suborned, even supposing that a Mr and Mrs Average existed and were actually ready to be networked, was Disneyland fantasy. He was about to speak when Grace said:

'It will have to be long-term, TT.'

'Oh, most assuredly.'

'And we will have to be very cautious, I think, to start with.'

'Oh, very, very cautious.'

'So Robert and I will have a lot to discuss. We don't want to prejudice our diplomatic immunity.'

'Oh, no, that's right. It must be done officially unofficially,' said TT, accompanying the remark with a laugh. 'Always within protocol. I'm sure you both understand that.'

An intercom buzzer sounded on his desk and he pressed a button. Grace put aside her note pad and pencil and sprang towards him as if in defence of her boss's reputation and spoke quickly, softly, with intentness, into a desk receiver. It transpired that some urgent business had to take priority.

'Oh,' said TT, 'I'm so very sorry. I had especially arranged for this niche time in my morning schedule. Grace will look after you, Robert. It's been good to have you visit with us. We must do this again.' Again came the slight lifting of his body, his right hand outstretched for the handshake and an accumulation of wrinkles as the smile gathered and the eyes shone. 'Thank you for coming. But examine the possibility, as I was saying. See what you can do about creating a network, so we can really help Liberty escape from her burning house, right here in Moscow, okay?'

There was no need for an answer. The interview was over. Grace led him out of the office as TT lifted a receiver and began saying into a phone: 'Hi, Chuck, good of you to hold. How can I help?' He was clearly in converse with the new U.S. ambassador, who, as Bob knew well knew, liked to be addressed as Chuck.

But Bob also knew that Grace was almost as alarmed by her boss's naivety as he was. Glad as he was to be free of TT's slightly intimidating presence, he was relieved that she was more concerned with her boss's position than her own.

'You won't mention you've been to see TT, will you?' she whispered as she strode ahead of him away from the carpeted corridor into a glass-walled passageway between offices.

'No, of course not.'

'No kiss and tell to your own folk.'

'Well, I don't know,' he muttered.

She showed him the whites of her eyes as she glanced in his direction. 'I'm glad we didn't have time to get into any detail,' she whispered. 'It would have been so, so embarrassing.'

She was not the Grace Hampson with the milled-steel glitter about her now. Her neat outfit of loose grey cardigan, smart white shirt and embroidered collar with a cameo broach at the neck and shirt with knife-sharp pleats was worn as if brandishing the wish to be taken seriously, but it was not an armour strapped on to ward off all male attention.

'Don't pretend you weren't about to explode!' A grin curled her lips. 'You know you were!' She gave a graphic demonstration of a volcano exploding. 'You were just bursting to protest! He's not as naïve as you think.'

He said he didn't think anything of the kind. She disregarded the disclaimer.

'You've got to remember he's new at the job. He doesn't understand how things work here in Moscow, but he'll learn. I think he's a quick learner. And he doesn't give up easily. He's a stayer.'

Her defence of her boss impressed him. Perhaps it was TT's appeal to women that partly accounted for his success. He said:

'Doesn't he realise we're all watched, we're all listened to? None of us is a free agent here.'

She opened a door in the glass wall labelled 'Grace Hampson, Administrative Executive' and showed him in. 'I know.' She followed his eyes as he glanced round her office at the light fittings or whatever else might contain listening devices. 'All right. I know what you mean. It's all been checked out. Do sit down. We ought to talk through what we're going to do.'

He nodded towards the window. Impolite though it might be to imply that the United States of America had not developed means to combat recent developments in listening surveillance technology, he saw that she took the hint and instantly closed the Venetian blinds. The neon glare from strip lighting in the ceiling made her coppery hair shine brightly. He looked round at the usual office furniture of desk, filing cabinets and upholstered metal chairs and noted the homely touch of a row of plants on the windowsill and a green fabric dragon with a long tail perched on her desk.

'It's serious, Bob, it really is. Sit down.' She swept the dragon to one side. 'I talk to him when I'm feeling down. He's Brutus. I've had him since my seventh birthday.' Jerking open a drawer in a filing cabinet, she thrust Brutus out of sight. 'TT's right about one thing. Our way of life is under threat, you know that as well as I do, and we're here right at the very heart of Communism, which is where we could make a real change. We could create a network as TT says.'

'No, we couldn't,' he said bluntly. 'We're here to represent our country. We're not spies. We have to work through official channels, with due respect for the laws of the country and the traditional protocols as accredited diplomats.'

'Oh, Bob, how stuffy that sounds!'

'Stuffy it may be, but it's true.'

She sat down in a swivel chair on the other side of her desk and for the first time their eyes met as she slowly swivelled from side to side. He was puzzled by her inconsistencies. There was her smartness and outward display of her professionalism; and there was the endearingly juvenile way she had so quickly thrust Brutus out of sight. None of such inconsistency showed in her eyes as they gazed at him steadily through the lenses of her smart, gold enhanced spectacles. They made him uncomfortably certain she was assessing him for his worth as a collaborator.

'Look, you heard what TT said and we've got to talk it through,' she said. 'Maybe you don't think we ought to do anything?' Her gaze moved away from him. She picked up a pencil and began playing with it.

'What makes you imagine that you and I, two junior diplomats, add up to a hill of beans in this crazy world?' he said. 'After all, I have to think of them.'

'Them?'

'The people you and I make contact with. They wouldn't trust us at all, the – what did he call them? "The Mr and Mrs Average Moscow citizen" – well, something like that, the average Moscow citizen, they wouldn't trust us at all if they felt we were putting them in any danger. Or putting ourselves in danger, for that matter. I mean I'm followed almost everywhere. Aren't you?'

'Okay.' She threw down the pencil. 'Be stuffy and English!'

'Grace' – it was the first time he had used her name – 'what do you want me to do? Put yourself in my position.'

'Oh, no, no, you're right. You're right, Bob, we just can't do it.' She leaned back in the swivel chair. Almost in profile to him, he noticed how attractive her lips were and how firmly her breasts pushed out the material of her white shirt. 'I know we'd put both our careers on the line. They'd declare us *persona non grata*! I'd have a desk job back in Washington. It's just that, career-wise, you know, coming out here is such a big deal. I'd thought it would give such opportunities to do something about the situation. To build up friendships, get a fresh angle on what's going on, how strong Communism is, all that sort of thing. It's why TT was appointed, you know. The Cold War's got to stop some time and maybe a lot sooner than we all think, and TT feels we can really do something. Oh, God...' She ran fingers through her hair before giving it a shake '...I so wanted to help him get the whole thing started!'

He forced himself not to smile. It was not her naivety, not her sincerity. That he took for granted. What mattered was the purity of it, the ideal notion that human beings were precious and deserved to know more about each other, that they were not to be classified and segregated and perhaps exterminated on grounds of class, social worth, racial theory, political expediency or religious hatred and enmity.

'He must know the Soviet Union is a para-military state governed by Communist Party edict, doesn't he?' he said rather stuffily.

'Oh, of course he does! He knows the dangers, he said so, didn't he. It may seem so politically incorrect and silly that no one should try it. All TT wants is to find a way of getting to know what Mr Average in Moscow is thinking and feeling and doing. It doesn't need more than a dozen or so contacts. They mustn't be bribed or given any inducement. Just so we can meet with them or they can report to us. So long as it's not a repeat of *Pravda*. He wants the truth, so our policies can be framed within the parameters, you know, of what is... Oh, God! Shit! Sorry, I didn't mean...'

She picked up the pencil and again dropped it and he simultaneously grinned and bit his lip.

'Parameters!' she cried, looking up despairingly at the ceiling.

'Configuration!' he offered as consolation.

'Capitalist encirclement!' She blew it towards him like a kiss.

'Bourgeois objectivist!' he flashed back at her.

'Marx-Engels-Leninist!' she countered.

'Peaceful co-existence!' he said solemnly.

'Okay, okay, in true *Pravda*-ese – within bourgeois objectivist parameters of Marx-Engels-Leninist peaceful co-existence, that's what I mean,' she said. 'Phew!'

'That's beautiful,' he said. 'That is incredibly beautiful!'

'Oh shut up!' She laughed sarcastically. 'It's the trouble with you English, you don't take any of it seriously enough.'

'Perhaps you and I should have a talk with your Brutus,' he suggested.

'Oh, you're just being catty! No, Bob, I can see it won't work! We'd better forget we ever had that meeting with TT or that I ever got you into this. Okay?'

'Not okay,' he said. 'Not okay at all. Because I can see this developing into a beautiful friendship.'

She glanced at him with her lips attractively parted. 'You can?'

'Yes, Grace, I can. On one condition.'

'What condition?'

'That we do what all diplomats are supposed to do – lie abroad for our country.' He lowered his voice to a whisper. 'I mean we can just sit on it for a while and then feed him bits. Who's going to know? Is TT going to? Are you going to rush to him and say, Look, TT, we're thinking up some bits to tell you? Am I going to tell our ambassador?'

'Clev-*er*!' She tapped the pencil against her pouting lips. 'Oh, but shit, we can't!'

'Oh, but shit, we can! Who's going to know?'

'Bob! Robert German, Jermin, you are one sly person! How can we though?'

'By insisting we can't name names since that would endanger our contacts, our informants.'

'Right. I can see why it must be secret.'

'Of course it must be secret. And you know as well as I do…' He indicated with several gesticulations that caution should be their watchword. She grasped what he meant.

'You mean *they*?' She pointed to the phone, the walls, the ceiling lighting.

'I certainly do mean *they*!

'So where do we meet?' she whispered.

He wrote on a pad. 'Your place? I've got CE in mine.'

She looked at it and frowned. She mimed 'What is CE?' and he wrote 'flatmate.' Immediately afterwards he tore the sheet into the smallest possible fragments and dropped them in a metal ashtray. She fished a lighter out of a handbag. The fragments were quickly burned to ash.

10

No, they could not meet at the American embassy, not during the week, in any case. As for TT's plan, they both knew it was a dead duck. They could no more establish a network of contacts without suspicion than walk naked across Red Square. Which is why, some two weeks later, on a warm spring afternoon, Robert Jermin stepped out of a taxi outside the National Hotel. He knew he was being followed. A belted raincoat appeared in the foyer after he had already surrendered his coat to the cloakroom attendants and made a point of finding a seat by one of the potted palms to read *Pravda*. He fixed his eyes on the hotel's revolving doors and waited. Whatever the belted raincoat did was no concern of his.

He had to wait nearly fifteen minutes before Grace arrived. Her entrance in what looked like a sable coat of Gloria Swanson variety had a brief show-stopping effect. It caused the sort of adulation usually devoted in Moscow to astronauts or Kremlin leaders. There were no wolf-whistles, only a certain amount of bowing and scraping from hotel staff and cow-eyed gaping from bystanders. She carried it off expertly. With a throwaway smile, in a little-girl American accent, she fended off the attentions of the cloakroom ladies wishing to seize her coat and, allowing Bob to take it, accepted his role as her guide. He led the way with pride into the restaurant and to a table by a window.

'Here? You're sure?'

'Quite sure.'

The coat was draped over the back of her chair. Napkins flicked over chair seats and table cloth and adjustments made to the rather horrible red plastic shade of a central table light were signs that waiters admired her and were ready to be attentive. She received their services with another smile. Smoothing the dark blue skirt beneath her with a scooping movement of both hands, she sat down. It was plain that her navy-blue jacket and *lapis lazuli* brooch at the neck were designed as much for a business occasion as for entertainment. She looked round her.

'You really are sure?'

'I am really sure.'

Bob intended this late-afternoon restaurant dinner to be a time for planning. It was, after all, somewhere in Moscow where they would not be overheard, even though to all appearances the military uniforms at other tables and their big-bosomed women were usually a lions' den of pricked-up ears and predatory eyes dedicated to peering at as many people as possible. He tried to calm her doubts with a movement of his hand held vertical as if window-cleaning the air.

Suddenly, along with this gesture, a six-piece orchestra seated on a dais struck up. The murderously ear-splitting first chords almost instantly summoned the *jeunesse dorée* of Moscow to vacate their tables. In competing droves they packed the dance floor. At first self-consciously decorous, the men held the girls at arms length and tried to emulate formal ballet steps. Then the pace quickened. A gathering exuberance quickly accompanied changes of tune. Shortly it became a competition to see who could dance quicker and with more twirls and flourishes. The excitement evidently infected the waiters, who danced their way between tables holding aloft trays filled with tinkling bottles and glasses. When the music reached a crescendo and stopped there was furious applause and the dancers returned to their tables pouring with sweat. A cacophony of talk, laughter and raised glasses naturally followed.

This ritual was repeated every few minutes. The noise wrapped itself round Robert Jermin and Grace Hampson in a kind of protective auditory shell that ensured their privacy. She sat there opposite him smiling a little uncertainly both at him and the antics of the dancers. He ran a finger round the inside of his shirt collar and tried to keep his mouth from breaking into an idiotic smile. He knew he was falling in love with Grace. He recognised the fact while trying to pretend he wasn't, even though he knew well enough she filled his thoughts night and day.

She perhaps knew the effect she was causing. He supposed she was practised in this feminine art and would never surrender the outwardly poised, professional, smartly dressed administrative look she projected so assiduously through her gold-rimmed spectacles. Or maybe the showy Gloria Swanson creation on the back of her chair meant something else? He was dying to ask her. Instead he handed her a piece of paper and watched her eyes travel down the page. It delighted him to be able to study for an instant the porcelain brilliance of her complexion and the sheer touchability of her open lips. She raised her eyes to his.

'Who are all these?'

'Our contacts.'

'You mean your contacts?'

'No, no, our contacts.'

'How did you get to know them?'

'I chose them from a collection of Chekhov stories.'

'Chekhov!'

'Yes.' He was whispering now. 'TT wanted examples of Mr Average, isn't that right?'

'Right.'

'Well, I don't think there are any more average people in Russian literature than those in Chekhov's stories.'

'But we can't! I mean they're not real!'

'So what?'

'We've go to have *real* contacts, Bob.'

'You know perfectly well,' he objected, 'that you're not going to make what you call *real* contacts, *average* contacts, here in this restaurant, are you? What your boss wanted was a network, didn't he? You agreed we could create a network of names, or simply use initials. Here's a beginning.'

She kept her mouth open and slowly shook her head to and fro. 'Bob, that is so crummy it is almost very good. So you really think we can invent it all?'

'Sssh, walls have ears! I mean we agreed, didn't we? All we have to do is try some creative thinking. Have you got any better ideas?'

She frowned. 'It's so risky.'

'It's not as risky as trying to do it in reality. Anyhow, how is anyone going to check?'

She considered this, pouted slightly, said 'Phew!' and then nodded. It made him suspect she thought he wasn't taking it seriously. He anticipated her objections by adding:

'If questions are asked, we can always say we are not prepared to endanger the confidentiality of our sources. Right?'

'Right.' She nodded again but without conviction.

He smiled in response to her rather doubtful, apprehensive look. He had thought so much about her likely reaction that even to receive this much approval was sufficient reward. So he struck while the anvil seemed hot.

'Fifty-fifty,' he said.

'Fifty-fifty what?'

'You invent half, Grace, and I invent the other half.'

'You mean I do the woman's point of view?'

'You do the woman's point of view and I do the man's. Creative thinking at its most creative.'

'Oh, God,' she cried, 'this is just too neat!' Her smile squeezed her long lips a mile wide. Moving her head in a slow, amazed to-and-fro movement, she raised her little vodka glass and sipped its contents before offering a much more serious thought: 'So what if I invent a Miss L who works as a secretary? Say, she's twenty-eight years old. She's not a Party member, hates the Soviet system because her grandfather or some relative disappeared in the purges, has a boyfriend who's a drunkard...'

'Make it a husband,'

'Right... Has a husband who's a drunkard, shares one room in an apartment with an elderly mother and is fed up with the system. That's it – she's fed up with the system! Anything would be better for her than her present life here in Moscow! So what's she think?' She held a finger against slightly open lips. 'Maybe she thinks she'd like to go to America, what about that?'

'No, she hates America,' he said. 'She doesn't like foreigners. She wants Russia for the Russians.'

'Okay, so she's very patriotic. Mostly, though, she wants better clothes. She wants to be able to dress better. And she'd like to get her mother somewhere else, you know, somewhere different, somewhere...

'You have a mother problem, do you?'

She gazed at him for several moments and then gave a short laugh. 'A parent problem, that's what I've got'

'You want to get them off your hands?'

'Not really. I love them both. The trouble is my father always beats up on my mother. Beats her, too, as a matter of fact. Always criticises. Basically they hate each other but are addicted to each other. That's really why I'm out here. I had to give myself some space from it all. So when TT asked me to come with him out here, I said yes.'

'And now you're not so sure?'

She ran the tines of a fork along the white tablecloth, leaving miniature ski tracks. 'I thought it would be smarter, know what I mean? There's no class about it.'

'You like class?'

'I like everything classy, don't you? You know…' She looks round her '…it could be classy, all this. It's nice when you live in a classy place and feel right. But this is all so dirty. Don't you think Moscow is dirty?'

'Sssh!'

'Well, I think it's dirty and run-down, say what you like. I didn't think it would be so common. That's what you English say, isn't it? You call things common. I think this is really common. Sometime I think it's just the pits.'

'Okay, it's the pits!'

They went on whispering to each other as if they were in bed and he became more inquisitive.

'You talk about us English? Is there some connection?'

'English cousins.'

'Literally?'

'Literally. They live in London. It's called… Oh, what *is* it? Putney, is that right? Yes, in Putney. Half-cousins. By my mother's first marriage.' She told of what he recognised as a fairly ordinary suburban family whom she has clearly romanticised. He suspected she had fallen slightly in love with the eldest boy. 'John's got this lovely smile. I've never seen anyone smile like that. And then there's the accent. Your English accent just makes my skin go all, you know, *goosey*.' She shuddered. 'I love it.'

Her skin may have erupted in goose pimples but she was having a catastrophic effect on him. Apart from causing a faster pulse rate and a high state of nervous excitement, she made him laugh. They seemed to have the same funny bone. Partly due to an *aperitif* of small servings of caviar accompanied by several vodkas tossed quickly back along with pieces of rye bread, her complexion began to shine as warmly as her eyes and they laughed at the silliest things.

It was only a prelude. The meal was long and slow. It saw daylight fade beyond the windows facing on to Marx Square and the distant Kremlin walls. Street-lighting came on against a still pale sky and vehicle headlights rushed in shoals over the undulant tarmac. He thought their distant firefly glitter in the dark window mirroring Grace and himself was an omen of excitement, as if he could see his future life unfold itself out of the depths of a magic crystal. They began talking with such ease and candour it seemed they had known each other for years.

She was, he discovered, an only child, though both her parents had been married previously. Her father had a possessive streak that meant she was brought up very strictly. Educated mostly at religious schools in California, where she learned about morality, the dangers of blind dating, table decoration, deportment, *nouvelle cuisine*, the European novel and a range of the usual academic subjects, she claimed to have spent one memorable term at a school in England. Memorable? Because she had more fun during those three months than in all the other ten years of her education. Then she had gone to Stanford.

'Daddy's rich, you know. That's how TT came into the picture. When it was likely TT would get the Moscow assignment, I went back to school at UCLA Slavic Studies and did a crash course. I liked it, but I won't bore you with the details.' She pointed out that if there hadn't been a Republican win the previous November she wouldn't be sitting here in the National Hotel. God bless the Republican Party, he said, suppressing the desire to ask what criteria were used by the Republican administration for selecting their Soviet experts.

They moved on to the main course and she told him about Pacific Palisades.

'It overlooks the ocean, you know. Our home has a view far out towards Catalina Island. That means not much smog. Usually it's fret off the ocean.'

'Fret off the ocean?'

'It comes in like a fog. The temperature can be in the nineties one moment and then a bank of ocean fret comes in and it's dropped to near freezing. I've lain out on our patio by the pool very often and been sunbathing. Suddenly there's this chill damp air all round you, just like a white cloud. It's eerie. You've got to pull on warm things at once or get chilled to the bone.'

Judging from what she was saying, all of which fascinated him, he found Grace Hampson's twenty-four-year-old life had very little more serious in it than this ocean fret. She worried that she was short-sighted and had to wear glasses, but it seemed that in other respects she was endowed with perfect health and an attractive figure. She seemed on the surface the most self-assured person he had ever known.

Periodically they joined the migrations to the dance floor. Her self-assurance showed itself in a delightful mix of firmness and suppleness. He felt the pressure of her spine against his hand as he held her and enjoyed the electricity of her body moving against his. She accepted this pressure and returned it with a soft, embracing energy.

Twirling her lightly in a series of exuberant, rather old-fashioned dances, he found himself on a carousel of spinning chandeliers and other dancers' faces. They went round and round, all the time their own eyes locking into each other at some point in the whirling movement. It was an ecstasy in which their two bodies melded softly and seemed totally at one.

'You know,' she said back at their table, gasping, 'no one told me about the restaurant in the National Hotel. Do you come here often?'

They drank mineral water. No, he said, he had only been here once or twice.

'With a girl?'

He admitted quite honestly it had never been with anyone as pretty as her. She got the picture.

'So it's never been one to one before?'

'Never.'

He felt her fingers touch the back of his hand as he replaced his glass. There was such a sexual overture in that slight touch he tried to seize her fingers but they slipped away. It was not that she seemed to be evading him. Rather it was as if she expected him to respond differently.

'You're my first date here, you know,' she said. It was a candour that invited an equivalent candour from him. And suddenly she caught a changed look in his face. 'There is someone, isn't there?'

He was thinking of Marsha. 'I'm sort of engaged,' he admitted.

'Sort of?'

'I am. I made a promise.' It sounded utterly silly. The engagement had never been announced. It was merely an agreement between Robert Jermin and Marsha Parkinson that they were in love and were an 'item.' So he quickly began telling about his grandmother and the Ladbroke Grove flat. A smile gathered on Grace's face and the long lips gently drew apart to reveal glittering white teeth.

'So you've made a promise.' She reached for a compact which she snapped open. After briefly looking at herself, she slipped it back in a clutch bag. 'I respect that, Bob, I really do. I was engaged to someone from Stanford. We even made marriage plans. I met his parents and found they were like my parents, so on the surface it all seemed dandy. Then – I don't know – I was twenty-two, maybe a bit selfish, I wanted out. He was nice. I don't want to spoil anything.'

He was about to say she wouldn't be spoiling anything and knew he would be lying. The small orchestra struck up again with a shellburst of brass and drums. Ironically he was grateful to it for interrupting. It was not that he had a bad conscience about Marsha, more a question of nerves, something endemic, he thought, to life in Moscow and confirmed for him by the fact that his hair, damp from the exertion of dancing, had become cold as ice, as had the dampness round his collar.

'Perhaps we ought to re-invent ourselves,' he suggested, knowing the vodka was talking. 'We don't have to obey the rules. We are planning to invent some much else, aren't we? I'm not talking about betrayal.'

'Oh, yes, you are!' She gave him an intent look.

He knew he was being silly. 'I think,' he said, 'your feelings ought to guide you. The heart speaks its own language, you know.' His nerves were taking control, he knew, in saying such things, hopeful that the increasing orchestral noise and the clatter of people rising from their seats to dance would blot out his words. What his heart told him, though, was that he was under Grace Hampson's spell. 'When you meet someone,' he went on dizzily, 'don't you sometimes have an intuitive sense – maybe it's just through what the eyes say, do you know what I mean? – that you know that person. There's a silent shout of hurrah. Do you know what I mean?'

'Oh, you're a romantic, Bob!' The long lips smiled again. 'Of course I know. And I've learned to mistrust it. Mostly it's sweet talk. A silent shout of hurrah – listen to yourself!' He was about to redden with embarrassment when she spread out both arms. 'But I love it! I love it! Don't get me wrong! I love the way you say things like that.'

'I'm not meaning Chekhov now!' he blurted out.

'No, no,' she said, 'this isn't Chekhov! Chekhov is for real!'

At that moment his eye was caught by something. A man was swaying towards them. He came up the aisle between the tables and loomed above Grace. His sweaty, pockmarked, blue-veined features had a sinister menace when highlit from below through the plastic cone of the table lamp. He leant down, showing signs of black stubble on the jaws, and had the fixed, idiot look of someone very drunk.

'Izvol'te, inostranka! Davaite! Iantsuite so mnoi!'

He was malodorous and Grace craned her neck away. She waved him off agitatedly.

'Odin tanets!' he muttered aggressively. He looked from her to Bob and back to her, his eyes making an effort to focus and his whole body shaking in angry disbelief at rejection.

Her cry of 'Bob!' was hardly necessary. He was on his feet and confronting the drunkard at once. But the man turned to him. Bob knew he was no match for the other's size and potential strength. A half-formed gulp of fright filled his throat and almost stopped him breathing. He tried to push the man away. For his pains he received a full-frontal blast of the man's bad breath, followed by a couple of shoves that insulted him. They suggested he was little more than a lump of garbage, which in fact he was at that moment because he crashed backwards against a neighbouring table and caused a commotion of breaking glass and crockery that vied in sheer noisiness with the raucous orchestra.

Incensed more by the indignity of it than the insult, he retaliated by scrambling to his feet and swinging his right fist at the man's face. It connected. But not enough to deter. Probably a cheekbone. He saw the man grimace and his eyes narrowed. The man had his fists up and suddenly there was a blow to the side of Bob's jaw that made him stagger. He began to feel sick as he simultaneously knew his tear ducts were filling and had a taste of blood in his mouth. Blinking madly as his head wobbled, he regained enough self-control to swing his fist again. This time a sharp pain in his knuckles shot right up his arm. He knew he had connected.

The man took a step back. Holding his nose and shaking his head, blood dripped onto his shirt and jacket and quickly became a smeared crimson mask over half his face. It seemed to redouble his menace as he prepared to lunge again. Bob could do no more than stand there in front of him holding his damaged right hand. He was preparing for the worst when his assailant was quickly seized by a couple of waiters and hustled protestingly out of sight.

In seconds the dinner with Grace Hampson was over. It happened so abruptly there was hardly time for Bob to realise he had blood trickling out of one corner of his mouth and he could not close his lips. He wondered if a tooth might have been loosened.

***

'Bob, that was… that was…' Grace leant back against the plasticky rear seat of the taxi and burst out laughing. It was all over. Bob had been wondering how he could apologise for what had happened, except he had a handkerchief pressed to his mouth. He tried to laugh with her but found it too painful.

'Oh, hell,' he murmured very softly, unable to move his mouth. The taxi bounced up Gorki Street. He felt very, very sick and very, very unfunny.

'Hey, don't be an idiot, it wasn't your fault! The way you went at him – boy, that was something!' She planted a kiss on his undamaged cheek. 'I've never been on a date like this before! I've never had anyone fight over me before!'

He could not tell whether he should be proud of this or not. All he could tell was that he wanted to smile and the pain of his torn lip made the whole of one side of his face seemed stiff and rigid as if after a local anaesthetic. He shook his head feebly.

'Robert Jermin,' she said, 'you acted like a real hero. Am I grateful! I am just one hundred percent grateful!'

11

A week or so later Bob was accompanied by Grace
Hampton past the uniformed security guards in the foyer
of the new American embassy and into the elevator. She had
invited him to see her new accommodation on the top floor,
grandly described as Penthouse Suite A. Previously she had
been accommodated in a noisy room above the American
entertainment centre known as America House.

Limp hand waves towards light fittings, skirting boards and
plasterwork were designed to indicate where bugs had been
found. 'They were all over, can you believe it? There and there
and there... All done during the building work.' One raised
eyebrow and a light shrug of the shoulders. 'Don't ask why. The
workers stuck them in right under the noses of the CIA men
sent out to supervise. How they did that, I don't know. It was
designed as ambassadorial accommodation, including a kind of
ballroom or place for movies, but that was all abandoned when
they found so many bugs. Now it's been divided into four
small suites. Probably there'll be some more made.'

She showed him her en-suite bathroom with gold-plated
taps, gold-plated handgrips in the bath, gold-plated fittings in
the shower. Her comment 'Isn't it just real neat?' matched the
different lighting modes – green, pink, azure – that could be
obtained in the bedroom as well. However amazing the initial
impression of Penthouse Suite A might be, it was evidently
composed of contrasts, of the sumptuous and the makeshift,
the expansive and the cramped. Grace's high heels went rat-

tat-tat on the marble flooring of the bathroom. In her bedroom by contrast the deep pile carpet emitted no sound at all as she showed him the walk-in closet almost as spacious as the bedroom itself and a fancy, oriental type screen standing in one corner. A mirror fixed to the closet door matched the mirrors of her dressing table and the mirror-fronted built-in furniture occupying most of the partitioning between her apartment and the one next door. To Bob his reflection reminded him how dowdy he looked in his dark-blue suit and tie beside the glowing copper of Grace's hair and her smart striped jacket and skirt with razor-sharp pleats.

It amused him to see that Brutus, the fabric dragon, had been promoted from office mascot to bedtime companion. He was seated on the pale-pink artificial silk bedcover leaning against the padded bed-head and gazing speculatively with one large green eye at the narrowness of the bed itself.

'Cute?'

'Cute,' Bob agreed, though he didn't look cute himself as he found his full-length image repeating itself a little jumpily in mirror after mirror as they re-crossed the room to return to the parlour. Momentarily he wondered whether Brutus and his green eye were just waiting there to be supplanted or whether it was a sign of special favour that her bedroom had been shown to him at all. In the parlour she began a slightly uncertain explanation:

'So, Bob, that's what my apartment is. I know you may think it's a bit of a rush job. I mean, it's better than where I was, but it's dark, isn't it?'

'A bit, yes.'

'Oh, I miss California! Never thought I'd do that but I do! I miss the sun pouring in, know what I mean?'

In fact, the penthouse suite was warm and rather airless, but of course it was deprived of sunlight. Having only one window in the bedroom and one hardly larger in the parlour, electric light, in all its different modes, was essential. Being at the top of the embassy building, it was also open to overhead noises. A helicopter flew over and it sounded as loud as thunder just above their heads. On the other hand, city noises were muffled and partly lessened by the continuous low humming of a generator. It was only drowned out by a modest shuddering as one of the elevators rose from time to time to the top floor and the doors opened on the adjacent landing.

'So we start, do we?'

It was a question Bob grew to associate with Penthouse Suite A of the new American embassy building. It became their meeting place for several discussions of the plan they had hatched. Naturally it became a place of tryst in due course, although initially their priority had to be the network designed to please TT. This meant that everything had to be talked about in the lowest of low voices. Despite the reconstruction work needed to get rid of the listening bugs and replace them with 'clean' walls, light fittings and so on, Grace insisted that her penthouse might still be vulnerable. As a result, Scott Joplin, Ella Fitzgerald, Sinatra, the Beatles, the Beach Boys and a number of Californian groups Bob had never heard of provided what she considered an effective enough sound baffle. To this accompaniment they had to 'start' – in other words, they had to study with great care the products of each other's creative thinking about membership of their network.

Bob's suggestion was a journalist, a member of the Union of Soviet Writers, who wrote under the pseudonym Trigorin and specialised in visiting collective farms. He was likely to be a keen member of the proposed network, with the added cachet of being in close contact with rural opinion. Unfortunately he had marital and drink problems that could make him unreliable. Grace had not been idle. She had invented a ballerina, Nadia Arkardina, who resented never being given lead roles. She had special value as a network contact because she claimed to have slept with Leonid Brezhnev and other members of the

Communist leadership. Her ideas on Soviet defence policy were a bit haywire, sure, but they were '*from the horse's mouth*', so Grace claimed she claimed. Grace also claimed she said she was often invited to be in attendance at certain more intimate Kremlin functions. In one respect she was an ideal networker: she was quite sure the Soviet Union would soon break up into little pieces.

Bob insisted no one would buy this, let alone TT.

'And why not?' whispered Grace, hurt.

'She'll be bound to be a KGB plant. She'll have been planted in the network.'

'Okay, so she's disenchanted. She's just a disenchanted person. Disillusioned with life. You know.'

He thought this fine, but if she'd had access to as many beds as Grace supposed she'd be under surveillance day and night.

'Not at night, surely!' Grace released an arpeggio of giggles.

'Not when she's with the comrades, obviously.' Bob knew the game had to be played seriously if anyone were to believe it, but the effort of suspending disbelief did not seem to come naturally to her. 'Okay, so she'll be followed, like we're all followed, won't she? So how's she going to contact you without being followed, how does she manage that?'

'TT's not going to know,' Grace insisted in a whisper, 'is he? If we feed him information that sounds sort of, you know, reliable, he's not going to ask how we got it.' She sniffed as if she could smell the falsehood in all this. 'Anyhow,' she added, 'she's a bit kooky. But she's a real Deep Throat.'

'So she does it for money! That's worse still!'

'No I don't mean *that*! I do not mean *that*! I mean she's disillusioned. She wants to *tell*. Don't you see what I mean?'

He was prepared to concede that much, except he spoiled

it by putting a different gloss on it. 'It sounds like she's a kind of Mata Hari.'

'Hell, no, she's not a spy! She feels she's being used. And she wants out. She wants to kiss and tell.'

'Then why don't we have a networker who's actually from the KGB? That would make it all right, wouldn't it? What if he's her lover?'

Clearly there were possibilities in this. Except, in Bob's view, to have Arkardina and Trigorin as pseudonyms for their networkers smacked of plagiarism, assuming of course that TT or anyone else who might read their reports knew Chekhov's *The Seagull*, but Grace felt this didn't matter. Quite blatantly she plumped for *Three Sisters* and another Chekhovian name for the proposed 'lover': Vershinin.

'He's an idealist. She's an idealist. Anyhow I like the name. It's sort of superior.'

'It is *superior*,' he agreed.

It was so ridiculously superior and so obviously unbelievable that he found himself beginning to enjoy all the fairy-tale nonsense they were devising.

'So networker V,' he whispered, 'an idealistic KGB officer, is in love with networker Miss N.A., a minor ballerina, who sleeps with maybe half-a-dozen top Kremlin leaders and has haywire ideas about Soviet defence policy. And both of them are only too glad to let Washington know all about their grievances. It's a start, I suppose.'

'Yes, it is, Robert, it is,' and she gave him a warm smile, apparently ignoring his intended irony.

Her endorsement sounded a tad too enthusiastic and authoritative. Their whispering brought them close to each other and had a mutually inspiring effect. It led them quickly to build up a wider membership to this particular network involving a disillusioned Party member, a ballet teacher, a son-in-law who was a metal worker and his young wife Ania with two small children, their parents-in-law and resident *babushka*, a daughter who was a nurse and a brother in the army, not to mention a younger brother who was a Young Octobrist. Yet it was agreed this seemed too elaborate.

Bob's Trigorin was meanwhile kitted out with two ex-wives, problems with accommodation, a drink problem, a problem with an elderly mother and aunt (both collective farm workers) and several incipient problems with rival members of the Union of Writers and a Party bureaucrat who accused him of serious 'deviationism', including the most heinous of such deviations, which was a marked lack of 'Partyness'. But he enjoyed the protection of another Party faction within the Union. All this tended to make him a valued networker. After all, he could access blue-collar, grass-roots opinion and Washington would be delighted by that.

It was agreed between them after lengthy discussion that, at least to start with, just two or three active networkers would be more useful as conduits for the opinions of Mr and Mrs Average Moscow than dozens of them. For one thing, Robert Jermin and Grace Hampson would have to be seen actively nurturing their network. That is to say, they would have to be conspicuous in Moscow restaurants – in, say, the restaurants of the National Hotel, the Metropole Hotel, the Moscow Hotel or in the Aragva Restaurant and several others where, by covert but unspecified means, they would make contact with their networkers. The networkers of course would never actually *meet* either Bob or Grace, since they would naturally not wish to be identified as having contacts with Westerners, let alone with diplomats accredited to the American and British embassies.

No, it all had to be secret. Material would be thrust secretly into pockets, concealed in newspapers and magazines, stuffed into matchboxes, etc., etc., but it was essential that all such exchanges should occur in public places, no matter how supposedly covertly. What is more, each of the networkers, despite their many domestic and other problems, should be well-informed, sensitive to trends, deeply aware of current political attitudes, able to tap into sources of opinion from most spheres of life because they were 'well-sited at axial points in the median cultural infrastructure of Soviet life and society' (so Grace explained in the first report she submitted to TT who instantly responded with 'Boy, does that get a finger on the pulse, I reckon!'). Apparently it was likely to get such a finger on the social pulse that TT also asserted (so Grace asserted) that their first report would become essential to policy-making in Washington.

'TT reckons,' Grace told Bob, 'it's just what they need. A direct line to Mr and Mrs Average Moscow. It's better even than a whole spy network. And it's costing peanuts. Isn't that something?'

This was about a month later when they were drinking Bourbon and Coke, her favourite, not his. Sitting side-by-side on a sofa in the dimly lit parlour of Penthouse Suite A after she had submitted their first report to TT and a Heavy Metal group from somewhere or other ring-fenced them with thudding drumbeats, he knew the drink and the noise were fuelling a frantic inner debate. What he knew mostly was that he had fallen in love with Grace Hampson. He also knew their project was silly and likely to endanger both their careers. If it collapsed, as it surely would the moment anyone asked serious questions about their fictitious networkers, maybe it would take their relationship with it. How could he focus on this? How could he penetrate through the haze of drink and drumbeats to reach an answer? How could he summon up the courage to tell Grace he was in love with her and not spoil it all for TT and her trust in TT and the cause of Liberty?

These were really big, complex questions. She banished them almost on the instant they forced themselves on him by leaning forward and touching the corner of his mouth.

'I was wondering, you know...'

He flinched in surprise at her touch. She gave an uncertain, slightly embarrassed half-laugh.

'I was wondering how it was now.'

'It's better.' He knew what she was referring to. 'For a couple of weeks I've not felt any pain.'

She grinned. 'I didn't think you were serious, you know, before that. To get hurt like that and for my sake! That was one interesting guy, I thought! When I saw you in the taxi, leaning back against the seat the way you did, with the handkerchief to your mouth, I thought Hey, this may work out! This may be it!!' The grin elongated itself into a broad smile.

If there were messages in smiles, he smiled back at the likelihood that this was a crucial one. He was stirred by her spontaneous gesture of touching him on the mouth more deeply than by any of the polite, fleeting kisses exchanged between them on greeting and parting. He knew it was largely because he scented on her finger the perfume she had been wearing at their first meeting.

It spoke of her body heat. Suddenly they were kissing passionately. It was not clear exactly how things had managed to change so rapidly from politeness to passion, but they had. Over the weeks spent dining out in different places, sometimes together, sometimes separately or with others, and over the time spent preparing the nonsense for TT they had grown very used to each other, very close to each other, and yet it still surprised him a little that as they kissed now he received a message from somewhere in outer space that said 'I've waited for this, waited and waited...,' a message of such hunger for contact that she reinforced it by moving her hand to the nape of his neck and pressing his mouth firmly against hers.

Equally spontaneously and naturally he felt the swift uncurling of desire, an engorged arousal so urgent it had the force of a comet striking the moon. She laughed and lightly pushed him away.

'Please, just, you know...'

'What?'

'No, you don't know.' Grinning, she undid two of his shirt buttons in a leisurely, tentative fashion. 'You don't know anything, Mr Robert German, sorry Jermin, or however you pronounce it, do you? You haven't really shown me what your feelings are. What do you really feel?'

He quickly completed what she had started and undid his tie and collar button. He was not foolish enough to push his luck any further, though he knew he could well have misinterpreted her intentions. She flipped the ends of his undone tie in his face.

'That is *so* rude! It is *so* rude!' She studied him as if expecting him to say something, but he couldn't help keeping his mouth shut, consumed as he was by embarrassment at the pressure in his crotch. He smiled at her like an idiot. She leant forward and kissed him on the lips. 'I think you really ought to go now.'

Then she patted the back of his hand, jumped up and disappeared into her bedroom.

'Move over, Buster!' he heard her say loudly. She was obviously talking to Brutus.

He knew he had to make a decision. *To do or not to do, that was the question? Whether 'twere nobler...*

He followed her into the bedroom. It was a Shakespearean moment that demanded a suitably theatrical performance. He supposed she had turned the lighting to a dull misty red glow, hardly illuminating very much save for the bed itself and a couple of bedside tables but making it obvious that Buster had been flung on a chair. Grace herself, he assumed, was using the en-suite bathroom. He licked his lips and tasted as much her Bourbon and Coke as his own. He felt maddened enough by that taste to throw off propriety as readily as throwing off clothes. The strange sexy exoticism of the red glow acquired depth through being reflected so darkly in the mirrors and seemed to invite him to act. After all he was not going to be fooled again as he had been by the girl in the white fur hat. This time he kicked off shoes, flung his jacket, shirt, trousers and pants on the chair with Buster and was in the bed before Grace came out of the bathroom.

She altered the light phasing, or it altered itself, and turned from red to pink, ending in a faint yellow glow. Seeing him in her bed, she simply expressed her surprise by repeating her earlier remark.

'I thought I asked you to go. So what's this?'

His clothes on the chair and his bare shoulders above the pale-pink bed cover were all the evidence she needed. She seized the cover and drew it back so quickly he didn't have time to catch hold. All he did was cry out. His bare chest and stomach were revealed, try as he did to pull some of the bedclothes back over him, but suddenly it didn't matter. She wasn't looking at his penis. She stared down at the scar running diagonally across his stomach almost from thigh to thigh.

'What?' she cried. 'What *is* it?'

He began to explain about his cycling accident. 'Oh, boy!' she said.

Then that suddenly didn't seem to matter. She disappeared behind the oriental screen he'd seen when first shown the bedroom, calling out: 'Okay, stay where you are! You're a lot more rude than I thought! I can show you something too.'

It didn't take a moment for her to quell his offer to get dressed, supposing as he did that the sight of his scar had upset her, though equally sure despite everything that this was not the first time the screen had played a useful role of concealment prior to intimacy. So it surprised him a little to find the lighting had assumed a new, dark-blue atmosphere entirely of its own accord as she emerged from behind the screen and said:

'Promise me.'

'What?'

She slipped into the bed beside him. In its nakedness her body was smooth, voluptuous, warm and soft. It pressed firmly against his.

'Not, you know, the whole way.'

He looked at her, close as she was in the narrow bed. Her eyes glowed. He knew she must feel the growing pressure from his crotch.

'Boy, you're hot! Not sex,' she whispered. 'Please.'

It came as a slight shock. Not that he had expected sex as a specific outcome, but it had been a prominent impulse.

'Does it disappoint you?'

'I, er...' He supposed she was menstruating. In which case, of course, he would behave like a perfect English gentleman.

'It's not what you might think.'

'I see.'

'You don't see actually.'

'Don't I?'

'No, it's...'

These exchanges were having a wilting effect. 'What don't I see?'

'I just want us to be very close friends. I just want you to feel how I am. Like this,' she pressed herself even closer. 'Can't we love each other without having sex?'

'Of course.'

It was puzzling and of course frustrating but he presumed it was a preliminary stage. He respected it, even though the instant he said "of course" she pressed her lips so firmly to his he almost slipped out of the narrow bed.

'Please, Bob, close friends, that's all. Just not the whole way. I'd like to take it slowly.' She yawned.

There was in this much celibacy a tender voluptuousness

155

of its own. Their bodies fitted very neatly against each other. Her head on his shoulder, his arm holding the hollow of her back, the very softness of the physical meeting, of one skin, one nakedness against another, his warmth against hers, induced a deepening calm between them, a fresh honesty of feeling. Over a short time a gradual normalcy occurred. It seemed utterly natural that they should be in bed together, holding each other.

'I love you,' he whispered. He thought he said it at least loud enough for her to hear. Or did he?

He wasn't sure. He was astonished to find she had fallen asleep. Her slightly sweet breath came in absorbed, child-like, regular puffs against his cheek.

***

Perhaps he fell asleep as well because he found himself suddenly hearing the shriek of a doorbell. It penetrated the thud-thud of the Heavy Metal still doing its thing in the parlour and the sense of shock caused a Niagara of adrenalin. Grace stirred beside him as he stiffened.

'Shit!' she cried, springing from the bed as the doorbell gave a second electric shriek.

He caught sight of her nude back and her shapely, cushiony white buttocks. Unlike the rest of her body and her legs, they had not been so warmly caressed by the Californian sun and given a smooth, ubiquitous burnish. They were white and beautiful and apparently – maybe his eyes deceived him in what was now a faint, leaf-green haze of lighting – deeply creased by the way she had been lying. He couldn't be sure. She pulled on a bathrobe, slipped feet into slippers and skipped out of the bedroom. A moment later he heard voices in the parlour.

The thudding continued and made the voices inaudible enough to obscure all meaning though not enough to obscure the fact that the visitor was female and Grace seemed to be in the visitor's debt in some way. He debated quickly whether to get dressed but not quickly enough. She returned with an explanation.

'The girl from next door.' She made a throwaway gesture. 'Julie, remember? I'd been keeping some provisions for her. I'd forgotten she might come, but I'd put them by the front door. Of course she had a good peek at the parlour table with the two glasses and all our stuff. Maybe she won't pick up on anything. You didn't leave anything there, did you?' He denied it at once and pointed to his clothes heaped higgledy-piggledy on the chair next the green shape of Brutus. '...Yeah, well, maybe she won't.'

He could guess what was going through her mind at that moment. 'You want me to go?'

'No, no...'

He raised himself up on one elbow. This time he reached out a hand to her. She stood beside the bed and looked down at him before slipping off her bathrobe and taking his hand and yielding herself to him. With a little laugh she let herself be drawn into the bed. He held her round the waist in a loose embrace.

This time they said nothing to each other. They kissed gently, a long, sensual kiss. He knew he couldn't suppress the instantaneous erection pushing urgently upwards against her. As they drew slightly apart he saw she was smiling at him and nodding as if scolding.

'Okay, so I know what you want. Do you really love me?'

'I really love you.'

'Come on, then.'

They were her words, or he assumed they were, spoken as if to the dragon but extremely softly, without embarrassment, with invitation and fond challenge. He rose to it. Excessively masculine in his initial thrusting purpose, he quickly softened the movement. It grew smoother and smoother as soon as he could feel her willing reaction to it. Then an exquisite quickening followed, the first mild tenseness dissolving into a shared rhythm that had a beat closely matching the drumbeats from the parlour. The pitch, though, quickened further. They were wild towards each other, passion-driven. The sexual imperative had a leaping, maddening determination that increased and mounted higher and higher and became a sheer raging incontinence of thrusting pelvis to pelvis. Her increasing gasps turned gradually into cries. He climaxed into her and she quivered with him.

No sooner had he withdrawn than she astonished him by reaching out to her bedside table and grabbing a wad of tissues. The practicality of this seemed to extinguish all ecstasy. He flopped down beside her. Again, though, to his amazement, she leaned across and kissed him while he felt only the onset of exhaustion. The necessary clean-up brought such a sense of anti-climax he wondered if he had done something shameful. Had he? There was an impulse to spring out of the bed and go to the bathroom. Instead he found himself imprisoned by the weight of her hand resting on his chest.

She nuzzled against his shoulder. Her eyes shone lovingly at him through the loops of her fine coppery hair, now in charming disarray and free of course of the spectacles and its usual smart coiffeur, so that he tried to gently move some of the coils from her face and she responded by lightly seizing his fingers and entwining them with her own. They lay tightly side-by-side. She gazed at him very intently.

'Tell me you saw,' she whispered.

'Saw what?'

'The first time. When I got out of bed.'

'What?'

'When Julie was at the door.'

'Julie?'

'I thought I told you. It was Julie, Julie Frost. TT's secretary. She lives next door.'

'Oh.'

'Did you see?'

'What?'

'When I got up. Oh, have a long look.'

He could not understand what she was talking about. To his surprise, sliding her fingers away from his hand, she turned over on her elbows and showed him her naked back.

There was the neat line of Californian suntan running across the small of her back almost from hip to hip and repeated at the back of her thighs where the suntan stopped and the whiteness began. Across the upper curve of both pinky-white buttocks ran another faint blue-white line of scar tissue.

'Why?' The sight was not pretty but it was not really offensive either. It was hard for him to react. 'I mean, how did it happen?'

She did not reply immediately. Her face was buried in the pillow, having deliberately turned away from him. It took a moment for him to see she was crying. The sight disarmed him. He felt such a surge of pity and love for her he began drawing her towards him. He kissed her shoulder and her arm and then her face as she turned towards him and tasted the saltiness of her tears and she literally smiled at him through her tears in return for his kisses and started laughing softly and succumbed at once to his arms as they seized her and embraced her and held her fiercely close.

'Oh, God, you don't mind?'

'Why should I mind?'

'There was, you know, the boy at Stanford. He minded. It turned him off.'

'You've seen my scar, haven't you. Does that?'

'No, no, Bob dear, it doesn't, of course it doesn't! But if I tell you how it happened...'

'You don't have to...'

'Maybe if I tell you, it *will* turn you off.'

'It won't.'

'Oh, shit, I've got to. It's something I... Look, I've just got to!'

And she told him what he had already guessed but had no wish to know for certain, how her dear daddy had beaten her. It was pitiful but understandable. He respected and loved her all the more for her courage and candour.

Why, though? Why? Why? Why?

Oh, she said, he would pick on her. It started when she was thirteen and he thought she was becoming too interested in boys and sex. In fact, whether interested or not, she had little chance of doing much about either, he being so strict and her school having such strict rules. Best of all, though, she had learned to stand up to him and now pitied him for someone who couldn't express his fondness except through such sternly vicious behaviour. In a crazy way she understood, she said, and forgave. And seeing Bob's scar somehow endeared, even excited and made a lure for her to want sex. Was that shameful?

No, he said. But she said it had left her with a legacy, it really did. It was as if he had beaten sex into her and made it enjoyable. She would want it, but she would have to stop herself. So she would be smart towards the world, equal to anything, so tough beneath the well-shaped lips of her pretty mouth and the light powdering of freckles on her cheeks and the attractive, clear gleam of cobalt eyes behind the lenses of her spectacles that no one would ever try to break her will as her dear daddy had tried.

That, thought Bob, was where the milled-steel look came from! He held her close and said:

'Grace Hampson, I love you! I'm crazy about you! And I say God bless the Republican Party and TT and the Cold War and the Soviet Union! Because without them you and I'd never have... never have...'

She pressed her fingers over his mouth.

'Not so loud! Bugs! Ssshh!'

12

It was so unwise, the way his grandmother, Lydia Grigorievna, would insist on writing in Russian.

She had told him in the Ladbroke Grove flat that she would.

'It is my native tongue, Robert. I write what I like. No Lenin will ever stop me, no Stalin. I write to you in my native tongue, Robert. *Dovol'no!*' The black sequin-covered turban was given a little shove. 'But you say I must use what?'

'The diplomatic bag.'

'Dip-lom-at-ic.' She wagged a finger at him. '*Ty bolshaia shishka!*'

***

Bob Jermin had even, on one occasion, standing for the second or third time by an inverted metal cone ashtray or spittoon in the crowded subway at Arbatskaia (as instructed, naturally) caught sight of the courier or whoever he was. In a fur hat and long black leather coat – if, of course, it *was* his contact (the weather still changeable enough for frosts, true) because in the swirl of humanity filling the subway who could be sure? – *if* it was, then he could not help feeling, as he had felt before, that he was being played for a sucker. The KGB would wear a fur hat and long black leather coat. It lacked only a smoking bomb, dark glasses and fedora to be the real thing. Bob was sure he was living in a caricature world. Until, that is, he had the fourth letter from Lydia Grigorievna.

She had loved playing the game of secrets. She loved it because it was inevitably better to pretend the half-truth than endure the unvarnished fact. Through her he had learned how, as émigrés, they had communicated with those 'at home' by using certain masterpieces of Russian literature to achieve a Gnostic awareness. Six lines of a poem by Pushkin could be the Rosetta stone, a paragraph from Turgenev, a page from Chekhov. Once the references were known, all the rest fitted. This time there was no caricature. All he had to do was destroy the letter and make a careful note of a dozen lines from Pushkin's *Eugene Onegin*.

Because he was being instructed to attend a rendezvous in a forbidden zone, that was what it was all about. It was a test, of course, of his courage and trustworthiness. If he failed it, there would be no more passing of material and very likely no further contact. The date was specified, the train time, the address and the password. Lydia Grigorievna would have no idea about certain zones being forbidden to Western diplomats. He was a *shishka* to her, a *bolshaia shishka* even, a 'big wheel' and he could go anywhere in what, for her, was a Russia of the imagination so vast it was inconceivable that anyone could be prevented from going wherever they wished. As for Grace, when he explained he was busy that weekend, she asked, one eyebrow raised:

'Who is it, Bob?'

'It's no one. Honestly. Embassy work.'

He knew she disbelieved him, but there was never any doubt that 'embassy work' came first. It was only a little odd, though, that this particular weekend was a public holiday and embassy work would not normally occur on a public holiday.

From early morning hot sunlight poured down on Moscow and its environs. The heat turned the train journey into a Dantean hell of sticky intimacy. There was only standing room in Bob's carriage. He quickly learned the shape of the middle-aged woman's navel whose round stomach thrust itself into the hollow of his back. Every contour of the musculature of the teenage boy whose naked chest was pressed right up against his shirtfront imprinted itself on his skin. They were stuck so close to each other the contact amounted almost to a sharing of the same arteries and the same blood.

The train's motion crushed them even tighter. No eye-contact, not a word exchanged alleviated the sense of it being a struggle for survival. The only consoling feature of the journey was that at the end of each bout of mutual torment during the station stops a renewal of the train's slow swaying motion brought a stream of cool air flowing through windows and roof ventilators.

He could not help thinking of Grace Hampson. Why he had denied himself the pleasure of her softness to experience this torment he could not imagine. If it had not been for his grandmother he would never have done it. The contrast being so great, on alighting from the train at the final stop he shut all thought of Grace out of his mind.

The militiamen at the station exit, indolent in their white shirts under a canvas awning, leaned on the wooden railing outside their guard post and merely fanned their faces with their peaked caps as the crowds surged past. They were no more than bored onlookers at the holiday spectacle. He was no concern of theirs, Bob felt. So he followed the crowds in going down a long meandering track leading down from the station towards woodland and the promised lake. Inconspicuous during the journey, now he knew it was imperative to disappear. It was not that his tattered baseball cap and sunglasses, not to mention the old linen jacket he now slung over his shoulder, made him conspicuous. It was the fact that he carried no vodka bottle, lugged no crate as did many others, did not stagger drunk from a train ride's heavy drinking, did not sing and was not shrieked at by groups of equally drunk girls who flocked round the men. In the baking heat of the sun he quite simply felt sick and a little dizzy.

At last the track entered woodland. A chasm of shade formed by tall silver birches became the instantaneous pretext for people to slip away and relieve themselves. It was the moment he had waited for. He had been instructed to enter the trees and follow a northerly path. Maybe he guessed right, maybe he didn't. The tall trees formed a vast arboreal cathedral. He discarded sunglasses in the gloom and put on his jacket against the sudden sunless chill. Soon he was quite alone. The crowds had gone off to the lake and he found himself treading his way through an undergrowth of leaf mould speckled with spikes of ankle-high grass and small-leafed plants, soft and slightly moist, darkened of course by the height of the trees. Odd little dots of sunlight showed him vaguely what appeared to be a narrow path of grasses beaten down by previous footfalls. It wound in and out, in and out of tree trunks, mostly on a rising incline. The odd leaf would smack him softly or a stray branch suddenly whip him in the face. Gradually he was penetrated by a sense of panic as solid as the rock-hard, twilit stillness surrounding him.

He could not be sure he was not being followed. He would move forward along what he took to be the path and stop suddenly at what he supposed was a footfall behind him, only to hear all around him nothing but the stirring of branches in the high canopy and the very faint accompanying hush of the woodland at ground level. If he thought he caught a glimpse of a human silhouette among the trees behind him, then he could not really suppose the figure was following him. He was after all entering a forbidden zone. He was behaving oddly. It was more than likely he was being followed. Nevertheless he pressed on.

Larger splashes of sunlight broke through the high foliage at various points. They clearly showed what looked like a narrow pathway through the trees. He stepped out onto this pathway. It wound among tree trunks but somehow seemed more purposeful than the track he had followed previously. He was able in fact to jog rather than walk and he jogged quickly along this path, keys and coins jingling softly in his trouser pocket. He traversed what seemed to be an upward sloping area of woodland leading towards an exterior brightness. The light shone brighter and brighter through the trees. It was all that mattered. Though there came with it another sound, he thought at first it was simply a louder breeze from the treetops. Then he quickly realised it was water.

The instructions mentioned a bridge over a stream. So far the instructions had worked well, so he jogged quickly along the path and came out abruptly into fiercely bright sunlight, only to find too late that the path ended where there might have been a wooden bridge but was no more. He slithered feet first into a narrow channel of fast-flowing water and in an instant was striking out wildly. The water came up to his neck, the jacket almost torn from his armpits in the fast flow.

It might have been a torrent of spring, but it had the sharp, paralysing cold of recent winter in it. He gulped madly at its freezing, engulfing race. Spun by it first against one bank, then the other, he barely stayed upright and saved himself only by seizing hold of the root of a bush. It steadied him while simultaneously toppling him off his feet. He spun round and found himself facing upstream with his arms outstretched ahead of him clinging to the root. He had been swept sideways. There was a loud dinning of water nearby. Desperately he clung to the root. Just as his fingers began to loosen, his knees felt what seemed to be silt. He was able to raise himself to a kneeling position. From there he struggled upwards, using whatever branches he could find to scramble free of the water and heave himself with panic-driven urgency up the steep bank through a thick tangle of undergrowth and trees.

He had never imagined he would find the strength to do such a thing. His clothes clung to him limpet-like, but worse was the shock. It turned him into a sodden, quivering, teeth-chattering mass of nerves, especially as at that moment another terror struck. He glimpsed a figure upstream on the opposite bank, just where the path had ended. One of his followers! Fear stabbed at the nape of his neck. There was a rushing in his ears.

Through foliage he saw the figure was a man, athletic, in loose trousers and gym vest. He had a shaved head. It shone nakedly white against the dark trees. He was jogging at a standstill and looking round him, shading his eyes against the sun. He seemed to be studying the bank where Bob crouched, looking first left and then right, up- and down-stream. His jogging continued intently. It was obvious he was debating what to do. He peered downstream. Bob saw him purse his lips.

Suddenly he turned his head away and revealed a deeply sunburned neck. A voice seemed to have summoned him from behind. It was acknowledged by a nod, a final hand-shaded scrutiny of the bank opposite and a reluctant heel-spin of the jogging feet. He turned and ran back into the obscurity of the silver birches.

Bob drew in a deep breath of relief. He could not stop himself from shivering but he managed to relax slightly. Two things had become clear. The sheer volume of noise in his ears came from the water spilling over a waterfall farther downstream before presumably tumbling into the lake. The second was that most of the bank on his side was in deep shade. Maybe these two things had saved him. His follower, though, would be back. And he had to follow the path through the rest of the woodland, bridge or no bridge.

Until, that is, he took a look behind him. Something glistened in the tree-shade. He blinked and took a second look. What he saw was a chain-link fence topped by barbed wire. Its mesh stood fair and square between him and the woodland on that side of the stream. It was new, of course.

The earth disturbed at the base of the wooden posts was still comparatively fresh. *Niet-niet-niet*! it said. *Niet-niet-niet*! And it told him why his follower had turned away.

So that was that! The instructions had been a total let-down: no bridge, no way forward, now way back, no way anywhere... Lydia Grigorievna would have cackled with laughter! 'Another fine mess you've got me into,' Bob thought.

It took a minute or so to sort things out. Here he was stuck squatting among bushes and trees in sodden clothes, every muscle straining to prevent himself sliding back down the steep bank, faced by the impregnable fence above him and an icy stream below. A rock and a hard place had nothing on it! So I go back, do I? I give up?

Then something caught his eye.

Just above him the soil looked as if it had been disturbed. A fox? Maybe some other animal? He scrambled a few steps farther up and saw it was a track or what looked like a track with tree roots acting as hand-grips. It ran down the steep bank towards what looked like stepping stones upstream of where the bridge had been. All right, no bridge, he thought, but human ingenuity springs eternal and if there is a track... Sure enough, just by the base of one of the posts lay a large bush, its fresh leaves already dying. It concealed something. He looked more closely and saw it concealed a hole in the fencing through which others had obviously crawled.

It required only to push the bush aside, which he did gingerly, and crawl on all fours. Two lengths of plank had been thoughtfully placed there. He drew the bush back into place behind him after crawling beneath the wire and looked round him at a continuation of the same twilit cathedral of silver birches. He rose slowly to his feet once he had made sure he was far enough away from the fence not to be seen from the other side.

He shook himself down. Water still dripped from the

bottom hem of the linen jacket but his light summer trousers, though clinging, were not as grippingly damp as his underpants. Quickly squeezing out as much moisture as he could, he started running. He had a hard-headed sense his luck might not hold much longer.

His shoes went squelch-squelch and his damp clothing bit into his skin. Fortunately his worn old cap had remained firmly on his head, but he did not need to remind himself he could hardly look less like a diplomat of HMG in such clothes. If he were caught, he would have all hell to pay. Plead diplomatic immunity though he might, he doubted if it would do much good.

The instructions had seemed explicit: he had to follow the path until he came to a track, a village, a junction, there he would turn right and his destination would be the second dacha on the right. All this he had committed to memory and he knew he might have misinterpreted or forgotten some essential part – perhaps the absence of a bridge, the presence of a fence. What else? As he ran along the woodland path with his teeth still chattering he cursed himself for a bloody idiot. He should never have let himself get involved in this hare-brained business dreamt up by his dotty grandmother.

And for what purpose exactly? The only certainty was a codeword and a name. The codeword was no problem. As for the name, Lydia Grigorievna had referred to someone called 'Great Peter.' Surely she meant 'Peter the Great'? No. A firm shake of the head and a flash of sequins. 'In my family he is Great Peter, *velikii Piotr*.' Bob did not argue. He was too much in thrall to the family mythology to raise a query, let alone an objection. If he was known as 'Great Peter,' Great Peter he would be. Some ancient sage, he assumed, elderly, bearded, round-faced, round-eyed, like one of the eminent nineteenth-century Russian worthies celebrated in portraits in the Ladbroke Grove flat and always described as 'family friends'.

The path ran on and on and he was soon out of breath. Diplomatic life in Moscow had left him in poor shape. Too many late nights, too many drinks, too many restaurant meals. He slowed to a walk. Then suddenly he was flat on his face. Parallel to him through the trees, although partly hidden by a rise in the ground, he saw the peaked caps of militiamen. They were talking quite loudly and one of them was laughing. The noise they made probably concealed the sound of his plunge into the leaf-mould, grassy floor of the woodland. A patrol? Looking for him? More likely, he thought, a party of them on their way down to the lake. But he lay with his face pressed down into a patch of grass and slowly their voices and laughter died away.

He raised his head and looked round him anxiously, saw no sign of movement – everywhere just trees, trees and more trees – climbed warily to his feet and started walking again. So it was an area under strict control. Not only forbidden to people like himself, he supposed, but as with everything in the Soviet Union always controlled and constrained and always penetrated by surreptitious little holes like those in the fence. They were what made life humanly tolerable. Frightened though he was by knowing he was an intruder in this forbidden area, as he walked he came across more and more evidence of human untidiness. Discarded cigarette wrappings, cigarette stubs, scraps of paper showing faded newsprint, all sorts of rubbish lay scattered in the undergrowth. It seemed to him all evidence of freedom in keeping with the fact that he was no longer so imprisoned by trees. What is more, the sun streamed down in full force.

And then he heard a noise he hadn't heard for months. It was the familiar rural sound of a tractor. He stepped out of the shade of the trees onto a deeply grooved track and saw the tractor at work some distance away beyond open scrubland. A little cloud of dust rose in its wake and its noise came in waves through the heat of the morning.

Soon he felt he was in a sauna. The heat began to bake him. His clothes stuck to him now less from the damp of immersion and more from his own sweat. Knowing he had no chance of concealing himself, he walked boldly on and tried to look relaxed. The ferocious dazzle of the sun burst on him in a series of flashes through trackside shade, but once that protection was gone he was naked to an ultramarine sky from which waves of heat scorched through his linen jacket and struck hammer blows against his skull despite his cap. The sense of dizziness returned.

It seemed the landscape rocked from side to side. On the horizon was a line of pylons. Immediately ahead above the undulating land was what? He focussed as hard as he could. A pitched roof? Yes, and an observation tower. And not far from it the round gold cupola of a church.

He swayed on down the track. He supposed it led to the village. Decrepit palisade fencing, a patch of cultivated soil, a wooden structure of considerable antiquity partly overgrown with moss, probably a barn, then three or four wooden houses sporting television aerials and a line of telegraph poles... He assembled these observations in his mind, tried to make sense of them. Tried to see what it was two elderly women were pulling in a wooden trolley. 'Potatoes?' he asked, swaying. They went by without a word. A dog barked once rather drowsily. A tousle-haired little girl stared at him through the struts of a front gate. He leaned down and looked at her. She had beautiful blue eyes. They exchanged a long silent stare. Then she turned and ran away up the front path. He pulled off his cap, waved it in front of his face, replaced it and stumbled on.

The junction turned out to be shaded by more trees. It demonstrated its right to be a junction by having a dumpy-looking concrete milestone pointing to Moscow and a tarmac-ed roadway. Two trucks were stationary beside a brick building that advertised itself as a 'Restaurant' from which loud talk and a man's deep bass voice singing 'Moscow Evenings' could be heard. A stream of distinctly dirty water had crept down from this building along a crack in the tarmac-ed forecourt and formed a smelly puddle in the roadway. A dog approached it, sniffed it and turned away.

The road continued to the right. 'All right, Lydia Grigorievna,' he said, 'I can see it.' The air rasped in his lungs from the heat and dust and his lips were sawdust- dry. He took off his sunglasses and wiped the sweat out of his eyes.

What did he see?

Tree shade. Huge ink spills of shadow on smooth tarmac shone through the replaced sunglasses. They looked initially like water. He padded through them. Despite the seemingly watery shade the air was pervaded by the smell of the tarmac beginning to melt in the heat. No wonder few people were about. He had gone some hundred meters along the road when he heard voices. There was the doorway of the church whose gold cupola he had seen earlier, wide as a cave entrance and beyond it a vista of cool whitewashed interior. Old women in black were busy in the doorway preparing flowers.

He thought they waved at him and called. It was hard for him to understand their shouts. He shuffled across a broad apron of tarmac in front of the church. Although he wore sunglasses, his eyes stayed pinched up tight against the dazzle.

At first he did not believe what he saw. Oh, God, he thought, how typical! He tried to focus. The barrier suspended across the road swayed with each step he took towards it. The shouts had stopped. Now he could feel the eyes of the women on him.

It seemed domestic, what he saw. Someone sitting on a chair. It struck him as strange, someone sitting on a chair. Why was someone sitting on a chair?

He screwed up his eyes tighter. The image came into focus. A young soldier sat tilted back against a wall, his legs straddling the barrier counterweight. His peaked cap covered half his face and an automatic rifle rested on his knees. He jerked the cap back up to his forehead.

'*Dokumenti.*'

Bob stared at the red lips as they spoke the word with such authority. He took off his glasses and again wiped the dribbles of sweat. The face looking up at him was round, brown-eyed, russet-skinned. Stubborn, he thought, and insolent.

Muttering the word 'documents' to himself, he replaced the sunglasses. He summoned as much saliva as he could to mount his own challenge but he could not help his voice sounding exhausted and thin. '*Kakie documenti?* What documents?'

'*Dokumenti*' came the stubbornly reiterated demand and the rifle was shifted a little threateningly.

He had only the Merlin document. It would have to serve. He felt in his trouser pocket and brought it out. The red cover was dry but the interior leaves were stuck together with damp.

Out of the corner of his eye he noticed that one of the black-clad women from the church had approached. She was gesturing for him to come away. He saw the young soldier idly glance at the document and prepare to hand it back unread.

'Devil take you! Stand up!' Bob shouted, suddenly angry. He had not come as far as this to be treated so casually. He seized back his Merlin document. 'Stand up! Can't you see who I am?'

The red lips opened in dumb amazement.

'Eh?' came Bob's shout. 'Can't you see I am an officer of the Committee of State Security?'

The chair fell over as the young soldier scrambled to his feet.

'I am here on an official visit.' Bob's voice had risen to a yell. He knew boldness would serve him better than diplomacy. 'Stand up when I speak to you!'

13

He could not tell her about the panic that gnawed at the pit of his stomach as he waited for the phone call to be made from the guard post and was then given permission to walk down the gravel lane between the trees. There was this voice insistently telling him it was very likely all a trap and he'd best be careful not to look round or appear in the least hesitant. Because the rifle across the boy's knee was no doubt pointed in his direction.

Luckily the lane curved and he was hidden from view. True to instructions, a wooden dacha appeared to his right visible through trees. He presumed it was the first of the holiday homes and walked on, only to discover a much more formal entrance to the second such dacha with a wooden gate, now open, and recently tarmac-ed driveway leading to a large wooden building set back some fifty paces from the lane. Obscured though it was by the overhang of trees, a large 2 carved in the gatepost encouraged him to assume this was his goal. He found his footsteps on tarmac in the silence of the trees became quite loudly audible as he approached the wooden porch steps. Startled, a woman's voice suddenly exclaimed:

'*Tak chto vy, angliiskii diplomat, schitaete sebia ofitserom KGB! Molodets! Molodets!*'

It was followed by a loud laugh. She was in the shade of the porch between the outer front door and the inner. Strong-voiced, as if delivering a speech, she had said:

'So you, an English diplomat, consider yourself an officer of the KGB! Well done! Well done!'

The ensuing friendly laughter seemed apparently unconcerned with his hardly very diplomatic, bedraggled appearance. She beckoned him in with an elegant motioning of the fingers and then, in the shade of the cool hallway, stopped and looked at him closely. He supposed she had expected his arrival, otherwise she would not have referred to him as an English diplomat. The scrutiny was hazel-eyed and sharp.

'And you have reached us, that is the main thing! They telephoned from the barrier. Officer from the Committee of State Security – I was shaking in my shoes, I can tell you! What does he want? I ask myself. So I am watching out for you. Congratulations, you have arrived! Now come into our dacha.'

She was long-faced with very straight eyebrows and hair drawn back tightly from her forehead and held in place by a comb. She swept ahead of him in a green striped dress that swung bell-like from her narrow hips and showed off her slim figure. Forty? Fifty? He could not be sure.

'You know my Peter, do you?

He had to admit he didn't.

'What do I call you, Mr Diplomat? Robert?'

'Bob.'

'Bob.' She pondered the sound of the name as if unsure of it. Then she nodded. 'So, Bob, I am Peter's mother – Ariadna Ivanovna. People call me Radna.'

He had to make a quick re-adjustment on hearing this. Peter, the 'Great Peter', obviously could not be one of Lydia Grigorievna's elderly Russian worthies. If Radna were his mother, he could hardly be much older than Bob himself. Conjuring with this likelihood, he was led into a large cool room furnished with several ancient leather armchairs, a sideboard of sorts with dusty mirrors and one of its feet supported by books, a writing-desk, bookshelves, the corner of a large blue-tiled stove protruding next to a door and nineteenth-century portraits in oils filling the wall spaces between the tall windows. It smelled dusty and unaired. She apologised.

'Shut up all winter. Our first visit. You are our first visitor, Mr English diplomat. My Peter, by the way, has gone for a swim. Which way did you come here? Did you get a taxi?'

He had to explain that the route he had taken was unorthodox.

'Oh, you came by the old way! That used to be our short cut to the station!' In a low voice she deplored the way they had been hemmed in by fences and guard posts. 'So you got soaked?'

He agreed. She did not bother to enquire further. Instead she continued in a low voice:

'Oh, the way we treat people nowadays! Even my Peter, who is so important to us all, even he is restricted, you know.' She shot him a knowing, confidential rather wide-eyed look, as if she were not exactly sure she should trust him with confidences. 'He is essential to our rocket programme. I suppose you know that.' His effort to look trustworthy came to nothing as she almost immediately picked up a hand bell and rang it vigorously. 'Without him there would be nothing! Nothing! And they treat us all as if we cannot be trusted. There is no morality left. My Peter is very upset by it all. You must meet my mother and my niece.'

She had scarcely spoken before an elderly woman entered the room with a tray of rattling glasses. She put it down on a round wooden table and looked solemnly into the newcomer's eyes.

'I have never seen an Englishman before.' She seemed satisfied enough by what she saw. 'Liza will want to talk to you, she is learning English. Liza dear, here is an Englishman.'

Liza was an evidently shy brunette of eight or nine with

pigtails who hung back by the door. She was dressed in shorts and an embroidered shirt to show off her pretty legs and slender neck.

'My niece,' Radna said.

'Of course the Englishman is here to spy on us. You've come here to spy on us, haven't you?' the grandma said a little severely, her elderly lips puckering into a smile.

Bob tried to make a polite protest.

'Ah, well, you speak our language, that is a good start.' She made a whistling sound. 'You are all spies, I know that.'

He mentioned Lydia Grigorievna.

'Ah!'

'He has come to see Peter,' Radna said, making a rather grand gesture with her right hand. 'We told you about it, mother dear. You never listen to what we say. Are there enough glasses? Peter has his friend, you know.'

'I listen to everything,' the old woman protested. 'Everything.' She had an intelligent, lined, handsome face and a way of turning it to one side after speaking, like many people who are slightly deaf. 'And if I cannot hear, I ask Liza. She is my ears. And a very good pair of ears, too.' The old woman called her forward and patted her on the head. 'Say something in English to our visitor, dear.'

Liza stood very still. 'How are you, sir?' she said.

'Thank you, Liza. I am very well.'

'Today is hot, yes?'

'Yes, very hot.'

The exchanges foundered at this point. The girl blushed prettily and looked wildly from aunt to grandmother. Bob, awkwardly clutching his baseball cap, used his free hand to run his fingers through his sweat-damp hair.

A loud male voice boomed its way in from the porch.

The 'Great Peter' had arrived, judging by Radna's 'Ah, he's here!' and the sound of feet rushing up the porch steps. He came into the living room almost at once, confronting them in a floppy straw hat, garish red-striped Bermuda shorts and plimsolls. Large sunglasses were pushed up on his forehead. Of medium height, slim, with a muscular chest and a shirt tied round his neck by its sleeves, he looked at first glance like a teenager, but his real age showed more clearly when he swept off the floppy straw hat to reveal a head of dark curly hair and narrow, handsome, rather ascetic, thirty-year-old features that had a slightly delicate, feminine air to them. His eyes, of dark brown, immediately fastened on Bob in an intense, assertive way, though he continued with what he had been saying to another young man who came in behind him barefoot and dressed only in black swimming trunks.

'Nothing, Vania! Not another word! Hold your tongue!' He used his sunglasses to point. 'I showed you the room to go to. Now go to your room!'

The sharpness spoke as much of natural authority as of irritation. He gave a wave of the sunglasses and the young man slipped away.

'So we have our visitor, I see. You are the English diplomat, are you?'

His mother began a kind of introduction.

'Yes, yes, mother, I can see...'

He extended a hand and Bob shook it. The handshake was muscular, slow and calculating, designed, it seemed, to assess Bob's character, though he had no idea what it intimated except that, through the physical contact if nothing else, it suggested clearly enough that here two worlds were meeting and he, the Great Peter, was likely to be calling all the shots.

'And now, Peter dear, you want to be alone.' It was strange hearing Radna address her son with the English pronunciation of his name – Peter – accompanied by the Russian endearment.

She turned to her mother with an agitated wringing of her hands. 'There is the dining room... Lemonade and kvas, yes?'

Between mother and son there was clearly an awkward, rather uncertain, affection that seemed to embarrass both. Bob read the relationship and the signs of agitation as possibly due to his presence. To the old woman, on the other hand, they were interpreted as a kind of instruction and she immediately called upon little Liza to run and tell whoever it was in the kitchen that refreshments should be prepared at once and taken to the dining room.

'Come,' said the Great Peter in English.

The room to which he was led smelled of dust and was gloomy, shadowy and cool like the first room. Interior shutters had been drawn across the windows. Maybe they had been drawn all winter, but now, against the sun, they caused broken shafts of light to criss-cross the floorboards and make regular patches of light and shade across the green baize cover of a large table. The effect on Bob was to give the room a sense of secrecy and conspiratorial threat. It left him feeling he had been brought into the presence of some covert judicial proceeding in which the dozen or so tall-backed chairs set round the table played the role of a panel of judges. Hanging above the table and glistening eerily was a large cut-glass chandelier. It had attracted a swarm of slowly buzzing flies. Another corner of the large blue-tiled stove gleamed dully by the door.

'Sit.'

The instruction was again in English. Bob felt he should wag his tail.

The Great Peter sat down opposite him. He had his mother's habit of staring. He stared for a minute or more directly into his guest's eyes without saying a word. It quickly developed into a kind of competitive staring match. Bob did not blink, did not withdraw his gaze. He was grateful enough for the chance to sit down and let the other attempt to penetrate to his soul. He raised one eyebrow.

This made the Great Peter smile. 'Good,' he whispered. 'Good. I think I know you. We are related.'

Bob could only mention Lydia Grigorievna again, at which the other blinked several times, abandoned his staring and ran the palm of his hand along the surface of the green baize. 'Yes, she is related. She said you could be trusted. That is why you're here. I am going to trust you.' A fly landed on his forehead and he struck it with his hand. 'Devil take it!' He returned to his whispering. 'My grandmother's house, you see. She shuts it up all winter. It is of the old world. Before the revolution.'

Bob wondered at the relevance of this piece of news, but the Great Peter had no trouble with it at this stage, it seemed. What he had trouble with was the fact that Lydia Grigorievna's generation, like his grandmother's and his own, had lost their true ideals. What ideals?

Again came the Great Peter's intense look. 'The ideals,' he whispered very solemnly, 'of free personality.' He licked his lips. 'And of life regarded as sacrifice. Those sacred, Russian ideals. We have lost them. They were the fundamental ideals of our intelligentsia.'

'Were they?'

Bob knew any doubts or contradictions of his would be based on ignorance, but he excused this to himself by thinking it was natural for Russian conversations to begin by referring to serious issues. Still, he resented the assertive manner of such whisperings. The Great Peter reacted by breaking into a warm smile.

'Of course I know they are dormant! Because they are not visible, let alone conspicuous, in our Soviet life – or in your bourgeois life – does not mean they are not true. Freedom and sacrifice are the ideals at the heart of a good life. They must be aroused, you know. They must be lived. I want to make them come alive!'

At which point Bob had to assume he was being lectured. This Great Peter was either blessed by a kind of craziness or so deeply imbued with the conviction that he was right it sounded ridiculously grandiose, especially whispered so intently. Leaning much closer to Bob, he became suddenly more confidential:

'There is something I have learned by heart. Let me tell you it. It comes from Dostoevsky, the words of his monk Zosima. It is what the good life really means. Here it is: "*Each one of us is undoubtedly answerable for all people and things on earth, not only because of the universal sinfulness of the world, but each one singly for all people and everyone on earth. To be conscious of this is the crowning achievement not only of the monastic way of life, but of every human being on earth. For monks are just like other people, except that they are as all humanity on earth ought to be. Only when this comes about will our hearts become tender enough to have an insatiable, eternal, universal love. Then each of you will be strong enough to conquer the whole world with love and wash away the sins of the world with your tears.*"' He paused, blinking several times, and then asked rather timidly: 'Impossible, isn't it? But I think we must try to remember it. Ah!'

The door opened and a girl came in carrying a tray. She put it down on the table beside them. It contained jugs of kvas and lemonade accompanied by plates of *zakuski* – sardines, sliced sausage, cucumber, moist rye bread.

'Thank you, Sonia.'

The Great Peter now spoke loudly. The sound of his voice tended to emphasise the girl's presence, for she clearly attracted Bob's attention by remaining standing at the end of the table and looking at him very solemnly. The shadows that seemed to swarm about the room made her loom above him in outline rather than make her instantly real. Her eyes, though, were bright sparks in the apparently child-like features. Some flash of recognition came to him. She was the angel in the white fur hat! That's who she was! He half-rose from his chair and was about to claim he knew her when she spun round and sashayed elegantly out of the room, confirming her identity by giving a quiet but recognisable laugh as she closed the door.

'Who is she?' It was dawning on him what had happened.

'Sonia, my cousin. There was no need to stand up. I know you English like to be polite, but she's just part of the family. Please sit down. I want to explain something.'

'She's a ballet dancer, isn't she?' Bob resumed his seat.

'She was a dancer, yes. She's given that up.'

'She wants to go to America?'

The Great Peter frowned. He lifted a jug and poured out lemonade. 'Drink. Eat. How do you know she wants to go to America?'

'We met.' Then Bob added in a sudden decisive assertion: 'You knew that, didn't you? You arranged it! You've got the photograph!'

His momentary anger seemed to pierce the formality of the other's pretend ignorance. The jug was lowered back on to the tray along with a nod of the head.

'Yes, it was arranged. I am answerable, true. But...' He pressed his lips together before giving a wave of the hand and adding: 'I'm not free. None of us is free. The Committee for State Security fixes these things. I wanted to know for sure whether you were the relative Lydia Grigorievna said you were. The Committee, KGB people, wanted to have evidence that could be used – oh, you know, to be scandalous, embarrassing, humiliating. Your career as a diplomat would be...'

'So it's the scar! That's what matters!'

'The scar, yes.' He looked directly into Bob's eyes. 'It is my sin. It is all my sin.'

This extraordinary confession or claim, spoken with such intense sincerity, was hard to hear. Bob's initial impulse in response was to laugh, knowing now what role the Great Peter had been playing and preparing, naturally enough, to challenge it. Instead he found himself overwhelmed by the other's ferocity of manner through standing up abruptly and turning his back. He was facing the interior shutters when he began speaking again.

'I was wrong. I shouldn't have.' The fairly loud whispering was resumed, loud enough for Bob to hear, although all he could see was the silhouette of head, shoulders and towel-draped bare back surmounting the striped Bermuda shorts. 'I made Sonia do it for me. She and I, we often change places, you see. I wear her clothes. She teaches me what to do as a woman. She is a dreamer, of course. We Russians are all dreamers after our fashion. It is all sin, I know. I have infected you with that sin. That is why I wanted you to come here.'

'Well, I'm here!' Bob announced a little testily. He was finding the Great Peter's talk inappropriately private and confessional. After all he had come here on the instructions of his grandmother and the materials he had received. He deserved more than these intimacies, offered in such lecturing tones. He drank some of the lemonade that had been poured out for him.

'My ultimate aim in life,' said the Great Peter, swinging round and once again sitting down, 'is to become a monk, to be the man who achieves that perfect love that can wash away the sins of the world with his tears. And the one sin to be washed away is what you English suffered. You English, especially those in London, were the first people in the history of the world to suffer the sin of rocket attack near the end of the Great Fatherland War. That is why I wanted you to have the materials. You have received the materials, haven't you?'

Yes, Bob admitted he had. 'I've kept them. I've kept them secret. I didn't know what to do with them.' He drank most of the lemonade. It was oversweet but deliciously thirst-quenching. The glass was refilled. Distantly in another part of the house a telephone rang. The Great Peter took no notice.

'So you know what I do, do you?'

'No.'

'I co-ordinate all the phases of a rocket's trajectory, from start to finish.'

This sounded too grand even for his uninitiated listener. 'Isn't that, well, a little...'

'We use advanced computerisation and I design the programmes. I am the only expert who can do it from start to finish. Of course you do not believe me.'

Bob opened his mouth but said nothing.

'I do it all!' The Great Peter's bright white teeth crunched into cucumber. 'You may believe it or you may not, that is your choice. The material which has so far been passed to you will prove it, provided the experts who see it are clever enough to understand my calculations. Very few of our experts can, that I must admit. Sometimes I even wonder whether anyone else in the world can understand what I am doing. Weren't people puzzled by Einstein's theory of relativity? It demanded a revolution in thinking. I demand a revolution in thinking about rocketry, about rocket control systems, about gyrometrics – that is what I call it: *progressivnaia girometrika*, "Progressive Gyrometrics" – and it will not be easy even for experts. Another language. Another way of thinking.' He drew in a breath sharply. 'But I know it will be, it must be shared, my knowledge, I mean. I know it is no use to humanity just used in our Soviet rocketry for selfish, national purposes. But how? That is what I have been asking myself. How can I share it with the world?'

There was an ache of sincerity in these questions that forced Bob to believe them. Equally there was a degree of obsession bordering on madness that seemed to infect everything he said.

'I had a thought, you see,' the Great Peter went on. 'A simple, silly, idealist's thought. I thought why don't I shoot it at you? Why don't I arrange for one of our rockets to fall literally out of the sky, just fall into your hands? Your experts would then know what I have done. My invention, my progressive gyrometrics, would then be demonstrated to the world. Or would it? Perhaps it would need explaining, wouldn't it? What if I were the only person who could explain it? It would be no use unless I was there. It might not be correctly interpreted. I would have to be there as well. Do you see my problem? Do you understand what I am trying to tell you?'

'You're trying to tell me,' said Bob after a moment's silence and in a querying tone matching his uncertainty, 'you want to defect, is that it?'

It was the wrong thing to say. The other raised his eyes to heaven.

'A bourgeois nationalist thought! You are as narrow-minded as our bureaucrats!' The Great Peter thrust his mouth so close to the other it was as if he were about to kiss him. 'Look! If I let the world know my work, I expect the world to do something for me. Is that wrong?'

'No.'

'You must help me. I wish to become a monk. That will be part of my bargain. But that does not mean I am defecting. Did my great-aunt Lydia Grigorievna defect because she had lived in London? Yes?'

'No.'

'Good. So I will not defect. I will simply join those who were my family. Family ties are above all other loyalties. They are what love means. Love crosses all boundaries. Love, real love, is free. Love, real love, is a deep bond, a spiritual experience, a relationship of pure being. The freedom to love whoever we wish is the only real freedom. All the politics and ideologies and religions should be founded on that.'

The Great Peter looked intently into the English diplomat's eyes and the latter read in the look a sincerity so passionate and confident of itself that the softly uttered words seemed to be carved on the very air of the room. Then the Great Peter hastily turned his head.

'I have said too much,' he added. 'I know I have. Forgive me. Can I trust you?' The eyes were narrowed now. 'Can I?'

Bob flinched from their renewed intentness and the hot, kvas-tainted breath.

'I trust you.'

It was a whisper. Enough of a sound to satisfy, it seemed. The Great Peter drew back a little.

'So do you want to know why you?'

'Why me?'

'Why you in particular, my English relative. I can see you are a sincere, honest person. I can always tell what people are really like. So why you? I will tell you.'

'Lydia Grigorievna?' Bob suggested.

'Only partly, my friend. Only partly. True, you are part of our family. The reason why I wanted to see you in particular is that, if I arrange what I plan to arrange, then the rocket will be a rainbow linking our two worlds. You see, that is how I think of it. Like a rainbow. A rainbow linking your home and my home. Do you understand what I am saying? It will be the reverse of all the rockets that fell on your country, won't it? It will do no harm.'

For the first time since reaching the house Bob felt the onset of terror. How much power did this Great Peter really have? How the hell could he talk about such infinitely complex matters as rocketry with such confidence? How could he even believe that he could exercise such control? Or was he mad?

Beads of sweat broke out all over Bob's scalp. If he had been listening to someone who was insane, mad, that is, in terms of normality and sanity as he understood it, then his whole day had been misspent. This expedition into a forbidden zone had become nonsense. It was all an elaborate KGB fix. Like that girl in the white fur hat. But this very thought somehow had a calming effect. He faced the Great Peter and asked:

'You mean the rocket will fall on England?'

The other's face acquired an ironic smile, more of pity than affection. 'Not really, no.'

'Then where?'

'Oh, in the vicinity.' Noting his listener's anxious reaction, the speaker's tone became emollient. 'I can make it come down wherever I like. And it will be possible to retrieve it. Then experts will be able to study it. It will change the balance of power, you know. There will be a much greater chance of peace and friendship. It is something I can do for the good of the world. But we have to strike a bargain, you see.'

'What bargain?'

'Show them my data.'

'Yes, I can do that.'

'And then I will tell you my greatest secret, my greatest wish.'

Bob did not ask to know it. He knew he would be told. It would be confirmation of his suspicions about the Great Peter. So he was a genius but mad.

A short silence followed. Bob blinked nervously as he waited to be proved right. But when the words resumed they were not exactly what he expected. The Great Peter spoke up towards the drowsy flies still making their idiotic circuits round the chandelier.

'I wish to be the dagger of the God of love, that's what I wish. That's my secret. I will avenge the wrath of the Lamb with a heavenly dagger. It will have the shape of a cross. And then the world will be changed. It will be filled with love. It will be an eternal, insatiable love that humanity will never want to lose.' Suddenly he raised a hand to his lips and stared with horror at Bob. 'Oh, I shouldn't have said that! How could I have said that? No, no, I have to make myself pure, absolutely pure, before I can say that! Yes, I must make myself pure! Please forgive me for saying such things!'

14

Had he understood at that moment or any later time what the Great Peter meant by these words and his talk of a bargain, he, Bob Jermin, could perhaps have acted differently. As it was he politely listened, as if he were being ranted at by a salesman or a charity worker, in the hope that soon enough the spiel would be exhausted. It did end, because Radna put an end to it. She announced that food had been prepared. It was to be outside at a table under a specially prepared awning since the dining room had been occupied so long by the two of them. And what is more, there had been a phone call, she announced, and Peter should get dressed properly. He laughed at this and went off upstairs. For Bob, though, it meant he was released from the gloomy room with its chandelier and flies and directed into the hot sunlit garden at the back of the house.

It was the beginning of a long mid-afternoon meal in the shade of the awning. Bob found himself in the shade of apple trees. This time the talk was about family matters with one exception – the Great Peter was absent and where was Sonia? Sonia had gone swimming in the lake. She would be coming home later. So Bob never saw her again that day. No, the talk came from the womenfolk and was about Lydia Grigorievna – 'Always so flighty!' claimed Radna's mother. When she was oh no more than eight or nine in Petrograd she had known 'Aunt Lydia'. During the civil war. Hard times. Hard choices had had to be made about staying or leaving. Then the rumour was that Aunt Lydia had met this English officer. She had betrayed the family connection. They only heard much later she had gone to England.

Liza, her pigtails flying, rose up on an old swing and then came swooping down and each time the rusty hinges screamed like echoes of her cries. An elderly maidservant or nurse stood by attentively.

And Radna had talked too. In confidence. Under the rustle of the sun-twinkling leaves and the buzz of insects. Sipping lemon tea and continually fanning her face, she told how she had brought up the Great Peter by herself after his father had died, how her son was a genius, how she had known this from his boyhood, how she had sacrificed her own stage career to ensure his happiness and how she loved him deeply and devotedly. But she admitted that the greatest love she could now show him was to honour his wishes and let him go.

'He will want to leave me and all of us here, you see, and go out into the world somewhere because he thinks his genius will only be fully recognised there. He will lose everything here, me, his grandmother, his cousin, his friends, his respect as a great scientist, and what will he gain there?'

Bob mentioned how he wanted to become a monk. It was foolish of him to blurt this out and he received a soft, appreciative pat on his bare arm.

'Oh, perhaps, perhaps,' Radna said. 'If so, that will satisfy him. It will be his private emigration. That is why he wanted you to come here. Because he was sure you could help him. But we Russians have become so used to emigration if we have the chance. If we are not cast out of our homeland, we perversely choose to leave! And what becomes of us? We drift, we are flotsam on the surface of other societies. We hardly ever mix fully. There is something in us that makes us superfluous no matter how hard we try to assimilate and belong.'

To belong — that was it! It was the soul of all their lives.

He felt it was the truth at that moment with the sort of

conviction that can justify any sacrifice. Simultaneously he knew he could never belong with that degree of faith. It was not in his nature. Too binding, too exacting. He could respect the Great Peter's wishes but acknowledge his was a genius tinged with madness. To speak of him as mad, though, here and now, in the presence of his mother and grandmother, would be utterly wrong. It would violate that very belief in the ties of family and their faith in themselves that gave their lives spiritual meaning. Then Radna exclaimed:

'Ah, here they are!'

There came the sound of tires halting on the loose sandy surface of the tarmac driveway outside the front of the house. Some vehicle had arrived. Bob supposed this was what the noise meant while Radna, without a word, rose quickly and padded off up the verandah steps to disappear into the interior shade of the house. There were raised voices inside. A momentary, sharp sense of alarm overwhelmed Bob at the thought that KGB agents might be about to seize him. After all, he was in a forbidden zone. Instead, in total reverse of such a thought, the Great Peter, now fully dressed in white shirt and trousers, with a light jacket over his arm, sprang down the verandah steps, leant over and kissed his seated grandmother on the head. Then he came face to face with Bob. Bob stood up.

The face confronting him, seen now in the brightness of afternoon sunshine, had a thin, ascetic look, although youthful and made slightly anonymous by dark lenses that accented the nose and finely shaped mouth but could not conceal the pallor of the complexion. It was easy to sense the power of character at this closeness. There was something slightly unnerving in the stonily rigid expression and the authority of the whispering.

'It's a bargain, my English relative. I may need your help. If so, you will help me, won't you?'

Bob could only blink away the severity of the question. 'I will try.'

'Good. Now I have to go. I can't take you with me. Orders, you know what I mean? But my mother will show you a way out of our, er...' The Great Peter gave a brief grin '...out of our forbidden zone. That's a promise.' Suddenly he pressed forward, hugged Bob warmly and kissed him on the lips. 'A dagger of God, remember!' Releasing him just as suddenly, he opened his shirt for a moment and where, in the hugging, Bob had felt some hardness, he now saw that the Great Peter was wearing what looked like a white wooden cross. Instantly, without further explanation, closing his shirt front, he shouted: 'Now goodbye... goodbye everyone!'

Calls came from the grandmother and Liza and the maidservant. He waved to them all, turned on his heel, ran up the verandah steps and was gone. The sound of a vehicle leaving could be heard and a moment or so later Radna re-emerged from the house and returned to the table. Bob, who had remained standing, sat down beside her.

'He has to obey orders,' she explained. 'Such a shame on a public holiday.' She settled herself in her chair as the maidservant refilled their glasses with tea before taking away the samovar. This modest activity brought silence to the table until Radna turned towards Bob, saying in a low voice: 'You will help him, won't you?'

He nodded, though he had no idea what such help could mean. 'I will try.' The acknowledgement sounded scarcely more than a mantra and seemed rather pitiful in the heat of the afternoon. Liza meanwhile wandered away on her own among the apple trees and the grandmother fell asleep, her chin resting on her chest. Radna kept her voice low.

'When his father died, you see, I only had my Peter and I treated him as if he were as fragile and precious as the kind of egg-shell porcelain they make in China. But he is not fragile.

He is strong and passionate. He has demons, you see. He has to fight them and curb them and make them serve him. He can be very fierce when he senses injustice. And when he loves, like he loves that Vania of his, he can be fierce. Oh, he and Sonia are like wolf cubs, the two of them. So for him to be a monk, yes, I can see what he wants, I can see it. He believes very much in that monk Zosima in the *Karamazovs*. He wants to be as perfectly human as that *starets* Zosima. He will try of course, try hard, but he never will be as perfectly human as that, I think. The essential thing is to want to be, that's the essential thing. To try, to go on trying, to make something perfect out of one's life, to try to do that ...'

Her voice trailed away into the insect murmurings of the surrounding air. A very faint metallic stirring of leaves in a sudden light breeze emphasised the quiet. She had been saying a farewell, Bob thought. The ensuing silence was like an epigraph to the talk of the afternoon. Very distantly he heard the hum of an aircraft but there was no sign of it in what he could see of the immaculate blue of the sky. Above his head the yellow and green foliage bloomed like an emerald smoke and sunlight scattered stars of light through it. In the long episode of silence, due more than anything to the need to respect the grandmother's sleep, Bob felt the encroachment of a readiness to belong in the very peacefulness of the afternoon and a sense in that peace, however momentary and romantic, of the embrace of Russia itself, its history, its vast, unconquerable grandeur.

Then came Radna's whisper.

'It's time we went. Are you ready?'

***

She accompanied him on the short walk to the barrier where her authority was obviously known and she was allowed through without any questions being asked about Bob. Nor was there any problem about getting on the bus that stood waiting on the tarmac forecourt outside the 'restaurant.' Scarcely more than a half-a-dozen other passengers were seated in it. The driver and his conductress were apparently in the 'restaurant.' Radna whispered self-importantly that they would leave 'on the hour', no matter that it was a public holiday; and she turned out to be right, though it was more than ten minutes 'after the hour' that driver and conductress were finally fetched and brought to the bus, both in a holiday mood and unapologetic for the delay.

More confidential whispering in Bob's ear made it clear that Radna was going to make sure he reached the train station safely. It was her mission, she said with a wink. There was no mention of a forbidden zone but he knew what she meant and was grateful. He sensed, if uncertainly, that he had passed some test. He had been admitted into the family circle, a fact to some extent authorised by Radna's willingness to escort him on this final journey.

When it actually started, the journey was slow. The broken road surface caused a continuous rattling. They bumped and shook their way through rather arid rural scenery and occasional stretches of woodland, always accompanied by drooping telephone lines and the inevitable sun's heat that gently baked them despite the flow of air through open windows. His journey on foot earlier that day began to seem hardly more than a stroll. No wonder, he thought, it had been called a short cut. There were of course several stops at various places en route, but the traffic was light. He and Radna hardly spoke because they were seated near the front close to the ancient clattering folding doors. All she communicated was that they would shortly reach 'the lake stop' when the bus would be bound to get filled up. She was right to the extent that a party of children, a school group or something of the kind, brought their laughter and chatter in a rush into the old bus and quickly dominated it regardless of orders from shrill-voiced adults.

So, crowded and groaning a little with the weight, the bus trundled its way to a stopping point near the station. Here, in addition to those spilling off the bus, were other hordes of holidaymakers pressing forward to go through the guard post entrance. Radna literally pushed Bob to join the children exiting and so he joined them as if he were one of their teachers and stepped down into the supposed anonymity of the crowd. Maybe the fact of being among so many children made him conspicuous. In any case, he was tired and therefore not alert. He did not notice a car parked virtually next to the bus.

What happened next was unexpected and left him speechless. Had it all been planned? Was Radna to blame? Seized from behind, he was suddenly pulled into the car's open rear door. As he tried to shout a medical tape was pulled over his mouth by a man in dark glasses. He was then bundled into the back seat, his arms were pinioned and the rear door was slammed shut.

Immediately, with a blazing horn, the car pulled away. He only had time to glimpse the interior of what he recognised as a *Chaika*. Reacting to the forward jerk of the car, the side of his cheek hit something hard, maybe the back of the front seat. An instant later he had been blindfolded and tape had been wound round his ankles.

Struggle as he might, he could not release his arms and was held awkwardly sideways on the rear seat. The car smelled thickly of cigar smoke, body odour and sweaty clothes. No doubt it had stood some time in hot sun with closed windows. He supposed the windows were still closed. Then, adding injury to insult, he received a sharp blow. Delivered at short range, it crashed into his ribs like a bullet and winded him. He could scarcely groan through the tight bind of the medical tape.

'Mister Dzhermin, we know where you have been. You have been in forbidden zone.'

The voice came, it seemed, from a man in the front seat. His breath smelled of vodka-tainted Havana.

'Diplomats must obey rules, yes?'

Sickened both by the pain of the blow and the sheer indignity of it, Bob felt angry enough not to nod. He had diplomatic immunity. An official complaint could be lodged. The thought was obliterated by a repeat of the question.

'Diplomats must obey rules, yes?'

There was another sharp, bruising blow that nearly buckled him. It was delivered expertly to ensure maximum pain. He nodded.

'We know everything. You were wrong, Mister Dzhermin. It was wrong to go where you have gone today. It is not allowed, you understand? We know everything.'

So if you know everything, why this? A futile thought. The car was going at such speed he found himself flung first against one body, then another, though the grip on his arms did not relax. The voice continued.

'You do not learn your lesson, do you?'

Maybe a sign was given because he received another expertly delivered blow. He again nodded his head.

'You must learn your lesson, you see. You must not think you can do what you like in our country. We know you have important contact. But no one, you see, can break laws. Most certainly English diplomats cannot break laws. You are representative of bourgeois-capitalist encirclement. You know what that means?'

He nodded again. It was better to agree. The two men in the back seat had him completely at their mercy. When he tried to struggle, a husky voice close to his ear warned him not to. Each blow had brought stabbing, knife-sharp pain to his ribs, the increasing fear of fracture, a gulping struggle for breath, a watering of the eyes, a mute sense that his spirit could snap any moment and an overwhelmingly bitter awareness of his helplessness. Had the Great Peter done this? Had Radna? Yes, it was better to agree. He felt he would soon wet himself or worse.

'So you will be good boy, won't you? And if you are not, you will be *persona non grata*. And of course you will have no idea who *we* are, will you?'

His thoughts had raced over that one already. Whoever they were, they were doing this with impunity.

'And of course you are not very important, Mister Dzhermin. We may open car door now and you will fall out. At one hundred kilometres an hour who will care that you have some bruised ribs? Most bones in your body will be broken. You will have had accident in forbidden zone. Great pity. Very great pity.'

The car swayed violently.

'But it will be your fault. Great pity you died young. But you were in forbidden zone. It might perhaps cause international incident. More likely, your embassy will say nothing. Quickly it will be forgotten. People will not know about you. But we do not wish to hurt you, Mister Dzhermin. We just wish to warn you.'

He expected another blow. None came.

'And what about your girlfriend? Will she be sad?'

Who?

'You think we don't know about her?'

Who? Another blow. He groaned and came near to bursting into tears.

'Oh, yes, we know about your American girlfriend. She will be sad for one day, maybe two. But after that she will find another boyfriend. And it will be great pity for her to suffer some injury, yes? She might have to go home to United States. Or she might not be able to walk again. How can you dance with her then? How can you go to restaurants with her? How can you do that?'

A long stream of Havana cigar smoke was blown into his face. He tried to shake the smell out of his nostrils. He only succeeded in shaking teardrops into his blindfold.

'You will not be able to take her to dinner so often, will you, Mister Dzhermin?'

He thought about it. It was the make-or-break point. If they didn't dispose of him, he would warn Grace first thing. The car's noise at speed made the voice speaking from the front seat hard to hear, so the interrogation or whatever it was lapsed. It left a space for Bob to relax slightly. He felt sure the first thing was not just to warn Grace but also let her have the materials. He had to. It galvanised him to think that these thugs from the KGB, from the Committee of State Security, or whoever they were hadn't mentioned the materials. So maybe they didn't know. But that was *his* secret. So long as he had that secret he was untouchable.

The thought was ridiculous of course, yet it somehow bolstered him for the rest of the journey. Eventually he was quickly untaped, the blindfold torn off and he was literally thrown out onto a grass verge. He blinked and stared round him. It was evening. There were shadows everywhere. He scrambled to his feet and found a bench. Too dazed even to watch the car speed away, he sat and stared at the traffic bouncing past him on the undulant tarmac of the boulevard.

It was somewhere on the outskirts of Moscow. He guessed that much. From an open window in a nearby apartment block came the amplified voice of an opera singer. A pink neon sign on the other side of the boulevard, part hidden by trees, advertised *Univermag*, a small supermarket.

He felt sick. Sickened by pain, by humiliation, by the hideously brutalising effect of the blows on his ribs and his self-respect. Whatever finer feelings he might have had about meeting Radna and the Great Peter were now literally beaten out of him. He sat on the bench and stared down at his feet. Breathing was a succession of gasps accompanied by shooting pains. The evening air around him was still and hot and lightly perfumed with traffic smells and fried onions. God knows where the onions were being fried. Moscow always had so many smells.

Gradually he felt anger returning. Anger at himself for having let himself be caught, knowing he should have been more careful. But anger most of all at the threat of injury to Grace.

He despised them for that. Suddenly he felt sure they were acting freelance at best.

No, they weren't thorough enough!

After all, they hadn't searched him!

They hadn't taken his money!

They hadn't found his Merlin document!

He stood up, clutched his ribcage and laughed in short, shallow bursts despite the pain. He saw a taxi and hailed it.

15

It was easy for Grace Hampson to imagine that the network she and Bob had created might give her a secure place in TT's affections. It might even gain the esteem of the State Department for a while. Until, that is, Ed Kalthorst and his sidekick from the CIA, R.C. Smithson, started asking questions.

It was Ed first. He had a pleasant, ordinary face, round-cheeked, clean-shaven, unspotted, a sophomore's face, she thought, intelligent enough in a bright-eyed way. He could be amiable, diplomatically likeable after a fashion, with a smooth tone of voice, but suspect, because beneath the All-American look lurked, as she knew only too well, the equivalent of a King Kong who wouldn't be content with just holding his Fay Wray but would exact all the sexual pleasure he needed from her once she was his victim.

As for Raoul Cyrus Smithson, the black attaché, he was his own man, patronised by Ed, sure, no doubt for racial reasons, but astute, careful and strong. Grace liked him. She knew he was to be respected. He didn't give himself any of Ed's superior airs. He worked unostentatiously at whatever he had to do and filed useful reports, one of which TT had let her see as an example for her; and she'd been impressed that this tall, strong man with a smile as wide as the Hudson River had written such supremely elegant, succinct prose.

Okay, so the two of them asked to see her. Brutus had found a temporary seat for himself on a chair beside Grace's desk and was hastily moved. Ed took his place. R.C. plunged himself into a swivelling black leather armchair, smiled courteously and crossed his legs.

'Grace, this is just a friendly visit, you understand,' Ed began. He smiled with unctuous amiability. 'Your report to TT has been circulated as a courtesy to R.C. and myself. You don't mind if we ask questions, do you? For example, can you tell us who this Miss N.A. is? She claims to have known Brezhnev and several other top-ranking people so, er, intimately? And how does she actually pass you the material?'

His superficially innocent gaze had a distinctly sardonic gleam. She knew exactly how to deal with it.

'I'm not telling you. And that's flat. TT has told me not to. Go ask him if you want to.'

'You and, er, a certain member of the British embassy, Robert German, is that right? have jointly reported...'

'Bob's name is Jermin – J-E-R-M, not German.'

'Right. To me that sounds pretty much the same. So you and Bob whatever have jointly...'

R.C. intervened a little bluntly with a question. 'What's this Bob Jermin done?'

'He's been very helpful. He's been studying the Moscow scene. It's not just through newspapers or the media generally, you know, he's made contacts...'

'So as I understand it,' Ed said, 'you and he sort of go out to a meal somewhere, in some restaurant, and the material sort of comes to you, is that right?'

'We have ways, yes.'

'But you're not prepared to tell me what they are.'

'I'm not. No.'

'But if they're *that* secret, how can anyone validate them? Could you and your boyfriend be making it all up?'

'No, certainly not!'

'I mean we would like an itsy-bitsy teeny-weeny, you know, bit of proof, Grace.'

'There will be proof. In due course we will have proof for you, Ed. In due course.'

She doubted that he or R.C. would go to TT. They were CIA rookies tasked with keeping an eye on Soviet rocketry. What TT authorised on the ambassador's say-so was none of their business. Ed Kalthorst could be suspicious if he wished, but it had only been through TT's courtesy that the report had been shown to the CIA on a share-all arrangement ordered by the ambassador. She was darned if she would tell Ed anything. She had TT's unequivocal support and so long as she had that she knew Ed could do nothing.

Bob had brought her his material. TT had arranged for it to go to Washington. But she knew she had to come up with some 'validation', some 'proof', pretty damn quick, otherwise their report and their supposed network would be blown to pieces soon enough.

It had been risky, far too risky, and once her visitors had gone, she felt a chill of fear. Not so much because of Ed's accusations but because of what had happened to Bob on the recent public holiday and the bruising he had shown her. She knew it would deter. If their imaginary network had been sussed by the Soviet authorities and threats had been made personally against her, that much was lost. There would be no more planning. At least for the time being there wouldn't. Her only hope for the immediate future was that Bob's materials would somehow prove utterly reliable. It would justify everything if they did. But the chill of fear overwhelmed her.

Here she was seated at her desk that she always kept very neat. She had flowers on the windowsill that she always kept watered. She was surrounded by the whole smart unreality of cream-walled office and imitation teak furnishings and bluey-green metal filing cabinet.

So why did it feel alien, uncompromising, hostile? Why did she suddenly feel she did not really belong here at all?

No, she told herself, that's not it. This self-questioning was silly. It was Ed pushing his luck. No, she wasn't going to be frightened. It was the situation, she told herself. The Moscow situation, that's what it was. She put Brutus back on his chair as if to regain her self-confidence.

When her eyes moved accidentally towards the wall mirror, her face looked back at her with such youthful brightness, the hair coppery and smart, the eyes blue as the ocean off Pacific Palisades behind the spectacle lenses, the dusting of freckles like specks of gold leaf and the firm-edged, shapely red lips carved more beautifully than any classical statue's, and she felt at ease with herself, in her body, in her womanhood. She had a secure sense of herself that she wanted to flaunt.

Like the very first time she had gone to the restaurant in the National Hotel to have dinner with Bob. Then she had flaunted herself. Yet that wasn't what she most remembered. What she most remembered was catching sight of his hand against the white tablecloth as he played with some crumbs of rye bread. His fingers were what had first caught her attention. Their unselfconscious movements and their slender shape had been sensual invitations. She did not know exactly why. In all other ways, his looks, for instance, his smile, the things he said, the very conspiratorial way they were engaged in doing something utterly false, Bob was fun and she would willingly join him in that fun so long as the fun played well for her reputation with TT.

But of course that was only part of it. The movements of those fingers on that tablecloth were like the first sexual stirrings. She felt the tips of her own fingers burn when she was reminded of it. Oh, he hadn't been showy, not full of intense sweet talk like some she had known. Maybe it was because he didn't take himself too seriously. Or maybe because she'd grown more relaxed. There was no need now to explain the scars, the legacy. None of that mattered.

What mattered was that he treated her so well. He held her so softly. His touch to her skin had a thrill to it as keen as the sharp, engulfing feel of the first morning plunge into the pool at Pacific Palisades. Then there was the sheer sweetness of the loving, no longer urgent and anxious as at first but easy now, sensually enriched by the force of the ecstasy that made them lose control.

She loved that. It challenged everything. To be out of control. To be completely out of control and still perfectly free.

The intercom buzzed on her desk. It took a moment to recover her poise.

'Grace Hampson. Administrative Executive.'

Julie's voice, TT's secretary, asked her to see Mr Thoreau.

'I'll be there.'

She had not yet prepared the guest list for the Fourth of July. Maybe that was what TT wanted to see her about. She prinked her hair quickly in the mirror, debated about lipstick, thought better about renewing it, adjusted her skirt and put on her full-scale efficient look. A not-too-conspicuous notepad and pencil were essential accessories. Armed with them she sallied out of her office and down the long corridor between the glass partitions.

TT was at his desk and scarcely acknowledged her. He was poring over recent despatches. She assumed they very likely concerned her and the network. The air conditioning in his office maintained a temperature several degrees lower than in the rest of the building and she felt its chill as a kind of affront to her. He looked up at her and smiled.

There was about his manner now a faint paternalism that

reminded her of her father. It oppressed and unnerved her for a moment. He was wearing his sleeves down, the blinding whiteness of his shirt and cuffs contrasting more than ever with the deep suntan on the backs of his hands. She watched his fingers as they held up a sheet of paper as if for her scrutiny. They were unmoving, undemonstrative, fixed, like the aquamarine gaze of TT's eyes when they were finally lifted to study her out of the suntanned mask of his face. His lips opened with a very faint suggestion of wonderment or maybe disappointment. He nodded for her to sit down.

'Grace, my dear, Washington is reappraising. Do you know what that means?'

'Reappraising?'

'Your network.'

She was transfixed by the working of TT's Adam's apple. It moved slowly up and down just above the neat knot of his necktie depicting stylised sailboats on squiggles of rippling water. He spoke in his slow way with a crackling of saliva and appeared to lick the words as if approving them for utterance.

'I reckon, Grace, you could say they're... they're mistrustful.'

Grace gave a little shiver. 'Mistrustful, TT?' Her voice was small.

'Yes, my dear. They want to know why it is there is so much material flowing towards them right now. They want to know why people out here haven't made your kinds of contact in the past.'

'Well, maybe they haven't done what we've done.' It was pert and obvious and she tried to sound confident. TT took it at face value.

'That's my own thought, Grace, my very own thought. Till I arrived here and you and your English friend started asking the right sort of people the right sort of questions, there couldn't be any such materials available, could there? That's how I think about this.' He shook the wad of papers comprising the Washington despatch and reinforced his meaning by giving a thoughtful shake of the head. 'How could they know about Mr Average Moscow until some pertinent research was done on the ground? I am a great believer in starting at ground level, Grace, as you know. And you and your English friend have gone right down to rock bottom in setting up your network. I like that! I like that very much!' Then there was a sigh followed by a sniff. 'You see, these analysts they have back there in Washington, Grace, they're paid to be mistrustful. It's likely your network's part of Soviet propaganda, that's what they think. But I don't believe that. I like what you've done.'

'Thank you, TT.'

He dropped the papers on the desk in front of him and clasped his fingers together. 'Now this is strictly off the record, Grace. Perhaps I was unwise in letting the CIA people see your material. I did it at Chuck's suggestion and he's our ambassador and a suggestion from him has all the force of an order. You know what I mean? So Ed Kalthorst and, er, Mr Smithson have spoken to you, haven't they? Right. So what they want is some kind of proof. Isn't there some way you could give them that proof?'

'I don't see how. I told Ed Kalthorst...' Grace glanced down at her fingers and noticed that one of her nails was broken '...I told him we'd be endangering the contacts. And it's all a matter of trust, TT, as you know.'

'Sure. I appreciate that. But what if you could bring in Ed Kalthorst on one of your network meetings and show him how it works? You know the sort of thing. Or even let him meet with one of your networkers, then there'd be no doubt.'

Grace knew she was in a fix. She tried to maintain her poise as long as she could. She bit her lips and stalled.

'Can I ask Robert – Mr Jermin – before I give an answer?

He and I are both in this together, TT. I'll have to consult with him.'

'Why, of course! Of course!'

'There is something else.'

'What?'

She knew she ought to mention she might be in some kind of physical danger. Bob's warning about violence had kept her awake at night. 'There is a likelihood...'

TT waited for her to finish. He unclasped his hands in a slight indication of impatience.

'There is a likelihood that he and I are in some physical danger from the Soviet authorities, TT. As a matter of fact, he has been attacked.'

She let it slip and TT picked up on the remark at once. 'How?'

She gave a brief description without mentioning the forbidden zone.

'I'm sure the British embassy will lodge a protest,' TT said. 'As for you, my dear, don't worry, we'll look after you.'

He gave her a fatherly smile. It did not comfort her, but it was something.

Faces were turned towards her through the glass partitions as she returned down the corridor from TT's office. She was still a relatively new girl, of course, and the designation of Administrative Executive naturally presupposed a special relationship. Therefore she deserved the knowing, even smirking, covertly lascivious and possibly envious looks on the watching faces.

Fear like a pain had lodged itself at the pit of her stomach. When she reached her own office she at once locked the door from the inside. She stood facing the half-closed blinds over the window and hugged herself, feeling her ribs, reminded of Bob's ribs and thinking it was a punishment of sorts that she should share his pain. She also knew there would be no protest by the British embassy. After all, he had been in a forbidden zone, hadn't he? He should never have been there, of course. Probably it had never been authorised, so he couldn't admit his injuries, could he? If it hadn't been authorised...

She recognised how all this might affect her. The one, not very convincing defence for the supposed network was that any contact with Mr, Mrs or Miss Average Moscow had to be kept secret at all costs, let alone have anyone like Ed Kalthorst involved in it. How long could such a defence survive if Washington acted on its suspicions of fraud? Not long. It would mean, among a great many other things, the endangering of her self-image as independent, a career person, someone who could buck the whole system. And on top of it was the complicating issue of Bob himself, whom she could not just tear out of her heart. Whom, in fact, suddenly, she needed, felt more deeply about, was more alerted to, had more in common with, than anyone else in the world. To whom she would have liked to turn at that moment and say, as she would have said if she had been in California:

'Let's go!'

Let's go out into the desert, let's go to Arizona, let's fly to Mexico, let's find a motel somewhere and spend day after day by the pool! Let's be free, Bob, you and I, forever and ever!

Not in Moscow! Through the slits of the blinds were the rusted metal roofs of Moscow houses, the rectangular concrete apartment blocks, a pimpling of trees, streets like little canyons, most of all a knowledge that there was no escaping into that alien environment.

Snap out of it! she suddenly told herself. You're not in prison! You can go-go-go if you want!

Turning round abruptly, she saw on her neat desk the list of things to be done and heading it was 'Fourth of July guests.' TT had asked her for suggestions. Okay, so there would be

Bob and all the usual guests from Western embassies and extra helpers would be needed, meaning help to serve canapés and drinks and Bob had said his maid Sophie might help. She smiled at the thought.

***

'America' was the problem. The citadel of capitalism represented by the embassy of the United States of America was all things infernal – more infernal, indeed, than militiamen, the *upravlenie*, meat lines, poor-quality footwear, a surly husband, damp accommodation, leaky plumbing and mice. Sophie had her own ideas on things and would not enter the American embassy for dear life. *Niet*! was her answer to Bob when he mentioned it. Moreover, she was in her fashion protective towards her 'Mister Bob' and her 'Mister Charles' and had long suspected that her 'Mister Bob' was not being faithful to his true love, Marsha, because of his association with the American embassy.

The weather was hot and thundery with heavy rain when Bob returned to the Sadovaia apartment one late afternoon. It made the stairwell surrounding the elevator shaft unusually dark. When he let himself into the apartment, Charles Evesham being away on one of his trips, he was surprised to find no light on in the hallway and Sophie standing immediately inside the door. He asked what had happened.

She muttered something about the bulb having failed, but that seemed an excuse or perhaps an overture for her change of heart and a renewed readiness to help over the American offer, or so he supposed, until she quite suddenly started making flame-like motions with her hands.

'A guest,' she whispered.

'Where?'

'In the sitting room.'

More flame-like motions of agitation and alarm. In the

gloom of the unlit hallway, silhouetted as she was by dull light from the internal corridor, her eyes flashed with indignation and hurt. Her obsessive nature often brought on these tantrum-like states during which she would take a violent dislike to something said or some slight inferred from a casual remark. This time she evidently wanted Bob on her side.

'Sophie,' she went on whispering, 'does not know, Mister Bob, how he got past. They should not have let him in.' To emphasise this, she pointed vigorously downwards, indicating she meant the militiamen on duty at the entrance four floors below. The diplomatic apartment block was not exactly Fort Knox, but it was certainly closed to unauthorised persons, meaning ordinary citizens. Bob knew what she meant. He asked how long the 'guest' had been there.

'A few minutes.'

'What's his name?'

'Oh, I don't know.'

'Is he English?'

She could not say, but shook her head, which puzzled him. Apparently the 'guest' had arrived shortly before his return. She had rushed to the door at Bob's return thinking it might be the *upravlenie*, meaning the manager of the whole diplomatic apartment block, a man known as Ivan the Terrible, who would doubtless have been told about an intruder and would therefore be entitled to use his passkey.

There was a pecking order in all this. Sophie spied on Charles and himself, true, and informed on them, but she was more in awe of the *upravlenie,* who spied on her and had the power to hire or fire. She would of course be held responsible if an intruder or unauthorised person were found on the premises.

Bob hung up his raincoat. Once in the sitting room, he saw a man standing by the sideboard where the photographs were displayed. His back was turned and a little bent forward, so that his slim shoulder blades lifted the cloth of the blue raincoat like wings about to unfurl. A rain-cowl hid his face and all Bob could see was the glisten of raindrops down the blue cloth tautened over the bent spine. Even when he finally turned round recognition was difficult because Bob found himself instantly in a tight Russian embrace with the wet raincoat pressed hard against his shirt and jacket. It felt more like an over-enthusiastic baptism than a welcome. Then came recognition.

'Great Peter, what the...'

'No, no, not!'

'What?'

They drew apart, the visitor trying to brush away some of the wetness, saying in English 'Not great, no, no. I am Peter,' while grinning brightly though evidently uneasy at being there.

There was something about him that did not invite 'greatness'. It was as if the repudiation of his title or nickname, and his wet clothing, diminished him. He looked slimmer and sallower, with an air of uncertain triumph.

'You not expect me?'

'Well, no. How did you get in here?'

'Official card. I show it.'

Bob gave a chuckle. 'So you walked in?'

'I walked in.' Then he frowned. 'But they check, you know.'

'I see.'

'Yes, they check. I know here is forbidden. For me here is *zapretnaia zona*, yes?' This time he smirked. 'So I need help, because I must warn you. I must warn you.'

'Please, Mister Bob,' interrupted Sophie, standing by the door and again busy with her flame-like hand waves. 'Tell him to go, Mister Bob.'

The pleading, almost hissing sound of her Russian brought a sharp authoritative glance from Peter. He flung out his arms. 'It's what I want to get away from!' he cried in Russian but in an almost childish, girlish tone of voice that startled both his listeners.

Silence instantly ensued, as if in the aftermath of an explosion. The sitting room was simultaneously filled with an ultra-loud sound of rainfall and a distant swish of traffic audible through an open window.

Peter deliberately ended the interval of silence by using the same girlish tone of voice to hold up Marsha's portrait and ask who she was.

It was too much for Sophie. She rushed forward, retrieved it and clutched it to her. 'Only Sophie touches Miss Marsha!' She looked round at Bob for approval with tear-bright eyes and hurriedly replaced the portrait on the sideboard, even blowing on it to remove any taint. Peter treated this dubious act of hygiene with smiling contempt.

'Congratulations!' He broke into Russian at Bob's admission of her identity, seeming not to care whether Sophie heard or not, and seized Bob by both arms. He demanded his full attention.

'Look! I did not want to have to say this straight out! I wanted to be able to discuss it, not announce it.' He paused and swallowed. 'I am taking a great risk. As I said, I wanted to warn you.' His voice had grown softer and the noise from street almost drowned his words, but the effect lent a degree of such confidentiality to what he was saying that his audience listened all the more intently. 'You must inform your ambassador, your government, your people! The entire world must know! A rocket will be fired! I can tell you where it will come down! I can tell you exactly! And what it may do is ignite all the combustible material from a gas rig...' His voice had now fallen to a whisper '...but I know how to stop that, at least I think I do. Hopefully it will not happen.' He paused and looked with a serious, anxious face from Bob's face to Sophie's and back again. 'And do you know why? Because they want to make it seem I am just crazy. They think I am only fit to go to the West. If the rocket does damage, then it's because I did it. So I can go. "Go, comrade genius!" is what the fools say. "Go to the bourgeois, capitalist world! See how they will admire you! We don't want you here in our beautiful Soviet world! You cannot be trusted!" He tightened his hold on Bob's arms. 'But you know, don't you, that I have a different aim in life. I wish to purify myself.' He gulped and drew in breath sharply. 'You are family, remember? Remember?' The moist amber eyes did not beg. They studied Bob in an intent, forceful way, much as they had studied him in the darkened dining room. 'Remember what I said – I want to be a dagger of God? But I am dead if I am found here. Literally.'

Sophie made a distinct sighing sound.

'Help me!' he whispered.

There was a loud, prolonged, authoritative ringing of the doorbell.

Sophie's cheeks changed from red to white in one instant.

'*Upravlenie*! Mister Bob, what do we do?'

***

Ivan the Terrible, the apartment block manager, was a squat, pale-cheeked, corpulent man who carried about with him a mixture of odours easily detectable at just about arms length. Although he claimed to be a veteran of the Great Patriotic War and wore a badge to that effect along with a ribbon-held disc round his neck denoting his managerial authority, his personal appearance was in general quite un-military. Dressed now in a not very clean white shirt, a canvas jacket and trousers tied at the thick waist by a leather belt with a large metal buckle, he gave himself a managerial air by raising the v-shaped tuft of beard on his chin, pouting his lips and gazing straight ahead of him with fixed, unblinking eyes. A line of ash from a cigarette just removed from his mouth had fallen on the lapel of his jacket.

'You have admitted an unauthorised person!'

The words were barked through the rectangle of the open front door. He stared at both Sophie and Bob as if they were so much vermin and proved the point by dropping the cigarette on the tilework of the landing and squashing it underfoot.

'An unauthorised person!'

His suspiciousness entered the confined space of the hallway along with his tobacco-laden halitosis. He pushed his way past Bob and entered the corridor. Glancing in the sitting room, he inspected the bathroom, the kitchen and Bob's bedroom. He insisted on opening Bob's wardrobe.

'You are the only people here, yes?'

'Yes.'

'And in this room?' He indicated Charles Evesham's bedroom.

'Mr Evesham is away. He always keeps his room locked.'

'Keeps his room locked.' Ivan the Terrible scorned the idea.

He stood in front of the locked door, tried to force the handle, rattled it up and down and failed to open it. He was clearly conscious of losing face as he did this and instead of prolonging an unsatisfactory state of affairs gave up with the announcement he would be back shortly to make a forcible entry.

'That is not allowed,' Bob protested.

'I am the manager,' said Ivan the Terrible crossly.

'How do you know,' Bob asked, 'that there is an unauthorised person in this apartment?'

Ivan the Terrible pointed down below just as Sophie had done, indicating the guard post. He then did his best to pretend he knew nothing.

'You mean to say,' said Bob, 'you have no listening devices installed?'

There was some muttering at this.

'You know you are overstepping your authority,' Bob said.

Ivan the Terrible made as if to spit on the floor but thought better of it. He muttered something about abuse of diplomatic privilege and left.

As soon as he had gone Sophie, in a fit of near hysterics, demanded that the 'guest' be thrown out at once. She ended by bursting into tears and fleeing towards her habitual refuge in the kitchen.

Bob knew she was right. Peter could not be allowed to stay in the apartment a moment longer. There was only one way in and one way out, that is to say through the apartment's front door and the block's front entrance. As for the locked door to Charles Evesham's bedroom, Bob had the spare key, given him by Sophie in the few moments before the 'guest' was secreted there and Ivan the Terrible had entered. He pressed the key to his lips. It inspired him.

'Sophie!'

He ran after her down the corridor.

'What?'

'You must do something for us!'

'What?'

'Do it for my sake and for your sake! He is family and I am part of his family. We need your help.'

The kitchen door was partly closed and he spoke through the slit at her peering face.

'What?'

'Take off your clothes,' he said in a very soft, coaxing voice.

'Sophie must…'

He saw her eyes widen.

'Sophie must take off her clothes?'

'Yes.'

'Why?'

He explained what he had in mind. She listened with the knuckles of her left hand clenched against her mouth. He knew it could cause further hysterics, but he pointed out that if the *upravlenie* were to find their 'guest', their unauthorised person, still in the apartment it would be bad for all of them. On the other hand, if Sophie were to go to the American embassy for training for the forthcoming Fourth of July celebration, the 'guest' could escape. Sophie herself could slip upstairs to where her friend Tania worked, like her, as a housemaid, and he'd bring her clothes back.

She contemplated him through the slit with glistening eyes. It took very little time for her to unclench her left hand, blink several times and finally nod. She saw the benefits of his plan more clearly when he explained that she need only take off her skirt, stockings and shoes and hand over her raincoat.

The spare key was then inserted into Charles Evesham's bedroom door and Peter sprang up from where he had been seated on the bed. Told about the need for disguise, he instantly saw the point and began to undo his shoes.

'It'll be risky,' Bob said.

'Sure, but I'll take the risk.' Peter smirked. 'So where?'

'The American embassy. Training for the Fourth of July.'

'Training. Ah.'

'Yes. And be as female as you can.'

'Female?' Another smirk.

Bob meanwhile went back to the kitchen. Sophie had been quick. Her arm came round the door offering her skirt, her stockings, her lace-up shoes and her pink plastic raincoat along with a plea for urgency that he echoed. In fact, Peter and Sophie were approximately the same height. In the pink plastic raincoat, belted at the waist and with the hood raised, Peter conveyed enough unisex conviction to make the narrow, shaven features look less than obviously masculine. His eyes, for instance, were no less brown than Sophie's. He was of course less broad at the hips and the skirt could not be made to hang properly. The shoes were a poor fit but passable. He was not a class act in such cross-dressing, especially since the stockings were wrinkled and needed a good deal of pulling upwards and smoothing round his thighs, but he was inventive and theatrical enough to embrace the role.

'What are you going to call me?'

'Sophie of course.'

A grin. 'What about lipstick and powder?'

'No way.'

The facetiousness of this was annoying while Bob made a cursory scrutiny of the result. It could convince, he felt, provided no one looked too closely or asked for documents, which Sophie in any case refused to surrender. She was prepared to do no more than exchange her 'on the off chance' plastic bag for Peter's raincoat.

There was no time to fuss or finesse. Bob opened the front door and listened. Nobody was about. The lift was not working. Sophie, in slippers and blue raincoat, took the opportunity to run upstairs to the next landing. They heard her say a few words to her friend Tania. At that moment, three or more floors above, someone started to descend the echoing stairs quite slowly. The noise blanketed any more sound of voices and led to the closure of a door.

The fact that someone was descending on foot probably

meant that the lift was occupied or not working. Bob was just reaching out to press the button when Ivan the Terrible's voice could be heard. It boomed away at the foot of the dark stairwell. The actual words were inaudible but no sooner had they ceased than the lift gates clashed together and a second later the cage began its noisy ascent.

The combination of footfalls from above and the lift ascending meant their own descent would be less noisily obvious. Bob clutched the handle of his umbrella, exchanged a look with Peter and pointed downwards. Without a word they ran down two flights, clinging as closely to the outer walls of the staircase as they could. The rectangular top of the cage rose slowly towards them. Its interior light came up the wall, passed them, rose higher to the next landing and then higher still. Here the gates were pushed back. They even heard the distant ringing of the electric doorbell as Ivan the Terrible pushed the button to Bob's apartment.

They ran quickly down the remaining flights of stairs and entered the entrance hallway where the only light came from glazed double doors at the far end. It happened that two men came in from outside talking loudly and shaking raindrops off umbrellas. Bob and his companion were wished '*bonne chance*' in '*l'orage effroyant*' as the noise of exterior rainfall came in like thunder and drummed down on the paving outside. The awning of the guard post shed little waterfalls that contributed to a quagmire of huge puddles fed by downdrains off the roof of the apartment block.

Precipitately Bob opened his umbrella. He did it too quickly and the tip of one of the ribs struck a militiaman in the back as he sheltered under the awning. The man turned towards him a frowning face encased in a kind of yellow sou'wester.

'*Kakoi chort/*'

It could have been worse. He recognised Peter dressed as

Sophie and smiled. Familiarity was the last thing they needed. Bob pointed towards the taxis.

'*Akh, pri takoi pogode…* I weather like this…' The man gave a shrug.

In weather like this taxis would be in such demand they would hardly need to wait in ranks. All Bob could rely on was the reputation of foreign diplomats as good tippers. To his relief he saw a solitary taxi was waiting at the head of the rank showing a green light.

There were no other pedestrians about. Vehicles poured along the wide *Sadovaia* sending up clouds of spray. So long as the signals remained green at the junction the taxi would remain where it was. Even so, Bob moved as quickly as possible to the pick-up spot and stood there under his umbrella with Peter beside him. He waved frantically.

There was a clap of thunder. In the meantime he knew the passkey would have been used and Charles Evesham's bedroom would have been forcibly entered. Simultaneously the taxi's windscreen wipers began to arc to and fro. He felt the first wave of real panic. The wind along the *Sadovaia* began to play havoc with the pink plastic raincoat. It tossed the umbrella about as if doing it for fun.

Slowly once the signals turned red the taxi edged forward. It made its way across the wide wet tarmac. Slowly it passed under the swaying overhead trolleybus lines. Slowly it swung round and splashed through a choppy sea of puddles and runnels. Finally it came to a stop.

Bob thrust his companion into the rear seat. Panic almost affected his voice. He was scarcely able to say the words 'American embassy' before the driver nodded, repeated '*Amerikanskoe*' and added '*Lardno.*' The taxi lurched forward and carried them out into the renewed traffic flow.

They moved in fits and starts in a dense mass of vehicles from one set of traffic signals to the next. Save for the driver remarking on the rain and the intercom crackling about other custom, no one spoke. Bob had to clench his teeth tightly. Curtains of rain could be seen sweeping across the face of tall buildings. The window beside him started leaking.

He closed his eyes. He had a sense of things ending. There was no knowing at all what would happen once they reached the American embassy. Equally he hoped that Ivan the Terrible would have no idea they were going to the American embassy, save that the photo of Grace Hampson in his bedroom made him resigned to the likelihood of two and two making four.

On the other hand, it could be positive. After all his companion would be their only *real* contact, his and Grace's only truly living, breathing 'proof' or 'validation' of their imaginary network. If their network were ever to be laid to rest with any dignity, it depended on this *real* contact proving how real he really was.

And what was his 'proof' likely to be? A rocket on England? A 'friendly' rocket on England? And what on earth could he mean by talking about purity and becoming a dagger of God? Or was it all nonsense? Was it simply one consequence of the obviously contrived meeting with the girl in the white fur hat, that wicked little angel called Sonia, supposedly Peter's cousin?

He opened his eyes. The transvestite Peter still sat beside him, knees together, clutching the plastic bag tightly. Their eyes did not meet. He was reminded of Radna's words and recognised both the risk and the promise. The risk was this journey and the disguise, the promise little more than proof of the devotion supposedly owed to the family. And why? Was his companion doing this out of devotion to Zosima's ideal of love, whatever form that might take, or because he was arrogant enough to believe his genius needed recognition worldwide, or for the divine but selfish reason that he strove for the purity of sainthood? Or because he was mad?

Bob broke out in a cold sweat at that instant because the raincoat's pink plastic hood had ridden up Peter's face to reveal an un-Sophie-like eyebrow. He snatched it down, but not quickly enough. The driver's eyes in the rear-view mirror gave him a strange look that quickly morphed into a crude smile.

Almost at once the tall frontage of the American embassy came into view. Due to the forthcoming celebrations for the Fourth of July, large concrete blocks were being installed outside the embassy entrance. Grace had mentioned they were presumably intended to deter suicide attacks, but the work had entailed the drawing-up of a cordon of militia to ensure that all traffic was diverted away from the entrance. It was enough to scare their taxi driver even more than it scared Bob. The taxi turned into the nearest free curb space and both passengers were promptly ordered out.

The driver seized the high denomination note thrust at him and instantly drove off, leaving his passengers facing an open area of paving swept by squally rain. They were left with no choice. To reach the embassy they had to get through the cordon of militia and a gap in the concrete blocks where an entrance way for pedestrians was being erected. It would mean showing documents. No work was actually taking place in the rain but Bob knew Peter's lack of suitable documentation would stop them.

Suddenly the wind seized his umbrella and almost snatched it from his hand. It shook with such frenzy it was turned inside out. Two-handed he tried to fight it back into shape but could not get sufficient leverage on the handle. With a useless umbrella and water splashing into his face, he felt wretchedly wet and hopeless.

It was at that moment that his companion decided to make a run for it. He pelted ahead of him in a streak of pink wetness in the hope of getting through the gap in the concrete blocks. Naturally this alerted the militia. Their shouts and the blowing of whistles were enough of a warning. Still fighting the umbrella, Bob glimpsed their faces clearly. Rain dripped from their noses and the peaks of their caps under yellow sou'westers. Then the umbrella's ribbing collapsed and a jumble of bent struts became as lethal as a flail.

He waved it to and fro. It was as if he were swatting raindrops. He reached the gap a few paces behind Peter, still waving the broken umbrella, but the militia had formed into an untidy line beyond the blocks and were clearly determined to stop them. When two of the men tried to grab him, he struck one hard in the face and the other received a backlash from the flailing metal struts that caught him in the mouth. His scream caused the others to draw back a moment. It was enough for Peter to dash through the opening in their line and make for the embassy steps.

Through a crescendo of whistle-blowing and shouts Bob swung his flail wildly. He did not know whether he struck a pursuer. He knew he had to save Peter. Facing into the rain, which plastered his face with tiny wet kisses, he ran and ran towards the embassy steps. The men were at his heels. He could hear their footfalls. One seemed to be calling out his name. He flung away the umbrella and the tiny wet kisses of the rain kept on beating against his cheeks.

By which time he was within half-a-dozen paces of the embassy entrance.

He heard a sharp explosion that he thought at first must be thunder. It echoed and was followed by another. A stabbing pain shot up his left leg. He stumbled.

A black sergeant of Marines recognised him, held him up as he fell forward and shouted out to the militia:

'Hey, stop that! This is United States sovereign territory, know what I mean!'

Bob could not even gasp. He could say nothing. He thought his lungs had burst. The sight of his own blood dripping on the embassy steps and turning into crimson curlicues and little red inkblots as the rain diluted it was so astonishing he could not believe it, until the pain returned more acutely and he lost consciousness.

PART III

16

Ed Kalthorst of the CIA was faced by the thin, sallow features and intelligent brown eyes of someone of, say, thirty years of age who looked like a woman and spoke like a woman when her real gender seemed difficult to identity under the raincoat hood. If she were a man, as Ed Kalthorst insisted she was, then he/she was remarkably unfazed by wearing a woman's pink plastic raincoat and rayon stockings on what were shapely if rather thin legs.

Could this really be a Soviet transvestite? Okay, so there was no denying he or she had all the right accreditation. You are not prevented from entering the territory of the United States embassy in Moscow by a cordon of militia unless you are genuinely a fugitive. Nor does the English diplomat accompanying you get a bullet in his leg from an officer of militia. Unless, that is, you are who you say you are.

But, hey, this was too obvious. Ed Kalthorst was no fool. What if this fugitive were genuinely a member of Grace Hampson's network? Okay, so it would be all the proof, all the validation she needed? And if he/she were a member of her network, then this was a coup beyond compare! A Soviet rocket scientist, their sole expert on the latest control systems as was his claim, right here in the embassy of the United States and apparently ready to undergo a preliminary debriefing on the eve of the Fourth of July! It was off the wall!

On the other hand, was he crazy? Was this fugitive a Soviet

plant? Things just didn't happen this way normally. And the story he told was scarcely believable.

R.C. didn't believe it. Mostly they agreed on things, but R.C. was even doubtful about the sex of their interviewee. 'He's a female,' he insisted, though in the course of the interview the transvestite displayed a stubborn streak. He refused, for instance, to take off the hood of the pink plastic raincoat. This was allowed in view of a small piece of documentary evidence he supplied to justify himself. It was a sheet of paper folded up into a small pellet so it could be quickly swallowed if necessary. It gave the calculations and co-ordinates for what was claimed to be the trajectory and landing site of a Soviet ballistic missile known as *Raduga*. The launch, which would be experimental, was scheduled to occur within forty-eight hours.

'Why in the North Sea?'

'Because it will be retrievable.'

'I see.'

'But there is another reason.'

'Which is?'

'England was the first country to endure indiscriminate rocket attack in time of war. I want to show that my system makes targeting exact. But I do not want anyone to be hurt. I am against all war. I want people to love one another. I want *Raduga* to be a rocket of love. If you trust me, I will trust you.'

'So what do you want us to do?'

'When my *Raduga* is retrieved, I want you to help me to go to the West so I can explain my *progressivnaia girometrika*.'

'I see.'

In fact, neither Ed Kalthorst nor R.C. Smithson saw very much, let alone Grace Hampson until she had had a chance of speaking to Bob. Once he confirmed that the interviewee was genuine, or as genuinely a very distant relative as he claimed to be and genuinely a rocket scientist, it was TT who insisted that the Great Peter should be permitted to stay in the embassy. Meanwhile R.C. could hardly deny that the interviewee was a man. A couple of nights under fairly secure guard in accommodation on the topmost floor of the embassy building offered proof enough. Any surviving doubt centred on his membership of Grace's network.

Matters were quickly decided by the Washington reaction. Initial scepticism after scrutiny of the material concealed in the fake *Krokodil* led to a quick, positive reassessment. The fact that its author was already in the Moscow embassy and his 'experiment', the rocket known as *Raduga*, had been retrieved from the predicted site in the North Sea meant he was seriously important. It also meant that TT's authority was enormously enhanced. All queries about the network virtually ceased.

R.C. remembered the egg on his face. He remembered that ambassadorial authority imposed the strictest silence. The 'cargo,' as it was called, was not to be mentioned. If rumours were to fly about, which was inevitable, they were to refer to a depressed Soviet maidservant who had sought refuge in the embassy of the United States. This kind of desperate defection was rare but not unknown and coming so close to the celebrations for the Fourth of July hardly figured very prominently even in embassy gossip. It did not figure at all in the Soviet media and only one foreign correspondent referred to a somewhat garbled version that attracted temporary attention internationally. More surprising still was the fact that the retrieval of a Soviet rocket from the North Sea attracted no attention at all. R.C. himself remained in the dark about what came to be known as 'the *Raduga* affair' for a good many years after the collapse of the Soviet Union. He had many other concerns to deal with. When in the course of his work he raised the connection with *Raduga*, the prevailing secrecy surrounding it meant it could not be discussed. He had been officially barred from re-opening the matter.

As for Robert Jermin, the injury to his leg necessitated overnight medical treatment in the small hospital bay of the United States embassy, but as soon as possible he was transferred to the British embassy. Within a couple of days he was flown to Berlin. The treatment received initially at the United States embassy prevented any spread of infection and allowed R.C. time to interview him and write a report. Naturally this corroborated the fairly sparse account learned in the initial interview about the identity of the so-called Great Peter. When confirmation came of the successful location of the *Raduga* rocket and its retrieval, the puzzlement over the reasons for allowing it to be fired, let alone the strange official silence surrounding it on the Soviet side, left those few people in the know highly suspicious. There were theories, of course, but very little in the way of fact.

***

Arnie Wainwright, impressed by R.C.'s account of the visit to the Silber residence, backed up by Officer Boswell's report, decided that the threat to the life of the U.S. president on the eve of the presidential arrival in London needed to be taken seriously. The man with a passport in the name of Kingman was detained a couple of hours after R.C.'s and Officer Boswell's visit. It was authorised both on the grounds of the threats he had issued and the possibility that his passport was invalid. What he later claimed under interrogation proved to be essential for the security of the president's arrival in England.

***

By the morning of the president's scheduled arrival, Bob had begun to change his mind. Where exactly the photograph had come from, for instance, had to be attributed to a Russian source, there could be no doubt of that now. Of course the Foreign Office knew of it and had used it as a principal reason for his dismissal. It was naturally enough a principal reason why he quickly enough lost close touch with the Foreign Office, though not with Charles Evesham, who had long since retired. They contacted each other in a regular sense only by Christmas card and the very occasional lunch at a club in Pall Mall. In any case, it was very unlikely that he had any connection with the Great Peter, even though his locked room had been the haven for the latter's brief concealment. The only reason Bob thought of Charles Evesham or the FO at all was out of desperation, due to the photograph. Where the hell had that thing come from?

After he had been shown the pictures, however indistinct, of a man's face, of someone who might have been the Great Peter, he may have initially doubted. He could well imagine that the KGB set up the meeting with the girl in the white fur hat in the Metropole Hotel and that whoever was in charge – perhaps R.C.'s Koursaros –had kept a copy. The one who shot him in the leg, perhaps. Very likely the one in the car who smoked Havana cigars and must have known about his visit to the Great Peter in the forbidden zone on that extremely hot day. But he'd put all that behind him.

Bob, Mr Robert Jermin, successful businessman, had put all that behind him. He had never seen the Great Peter again. All he had known was that he had become someone called James Pinckney, had died apparently almost the same day as his grandmother, Lydia Grigorievna (Wilbur Oldfield had told him as much) and had been buried as an American citizen somewhere in the United States. Yes, Wilbur Oldfield, the Anglophile American who had been his sole contact about *Raduga*, told him all he knew about the retrieval of the rocket while swearing him to eternal secrecy. As for the Great Peter, the same secrecy had accompanied Bob's account of his brief acquaintance with him. All that was long ago, by at least thirty years, and Mr Robert Jermin, the successful businessman, had put it behind him.

The more he thought about it, the more he convinced

233

himself that it had been the successful businessman who expressed doubt, not the young English diplomat. He had been the businessman trying to cover himself, trying to deny his younger self's truth. But after thirty years it was not wholly surprising that the Great Peter's appearance should have changed. To the contrary, judging from what he'd seen, it was surprising how little that change seemed to be. The more he thought about it, the more he came to that conclusion. Then, towards the late afternoon, he got a text from Wilbur Oldfield: Kingman had been singing. He claimed the assailant would strike later that day. It became essential therefore that the site of arrival be moved from Heathrow. The new site was a secret known only to a very select few and thought to be as secure as possible to ensure the safe arrival of the president of the United States.

Security reigned to the extent that limitations were hastily placed on everything. No pictures of the airfield were shown on television, nor anything of the actual arrival. Apart from glimpses of what looked like the interior of an aircraft hangar with people lined up for a welcome, the initial reception of the president by royalty seemed to happen at some distance and have very little of value for the accompanying voice-over commentary to note. The familiar face and figure seen almost daily on television screens finally came into view, smiling and waving among a sea of bobbing heads. It was not until the iconic features appeared in close-up on the raised platform from which a speech would be delivered that the president could be said to be truly part of the scene. Here were the shrewd eyes, the familiar voice speaking, the deftly made-up features, the immaculate clothing so devoid of creases encasing the middle-aged form, the little gestures lifting up extravagant words as if conjuring stars out of the air, the movement of the face following the lips as if visually trumpeting the statements, the pauses that acknowledged the enriching privilege of the audience in listening, the smile that comforted in its purposefully gilded smartness, It was as if the world had been remade for that instant. It had been blessed for that presence, the immediate perfection of those words, of those gestures, those smiles. The watching world could but admire and submit to its authority in acquiescent conviction that here was greatness.

Polite applause greeted the presidential compliments in expressing happiness at arriving in England, 'the United Kingdom,' as it was described, at the opportunity during this stopover on the way to Geneva to renew 'the special relationship' the president so cherished, as did the American people, and generally to demonstrate the close ties that united the two nations. The words were satisfactorily conveyed to the immediate company but created an echo for those a greater distance away. This caused a disturbance which meant that when the president finished speaking and was being ushered out of the hangar, presumably towards the waiting helicopter for the journey into central London, a crowd broke forward, partly protesting at not hearing everything, partly, it seemed, at quite naturally seizing the opportunity to greet the president in person. Suddenly surrounded by a crowd, in the midst of it, rushing forward, came a figure holding aloft a small wooden cross. Television pictures showed this object being held aloft, showed it approaching the president, showed the whiteness of the wood as it was thrust downwards. Practically simultaneously, as startling for one moment as the sight of the white cross above the multitude of heads was a loud cry and then several shouts of horror. Some kind of disturbance had occurred. A further, louder, thunderous roar followed. It became obvious that someone had fallen to the ground.

The assumption that there had been an attempted assassination or wounding momentarily paralysed everyone. In fact, the thunderous roar almost immediately faltered. It transformed itself quickly enough into a wave of applause when the president was seen waving as the official entourage reformed and left the hangar. It made it appear that the event was a normal part of the presidential visit. Everyone should have expected something like that to happen. It was a relief discernible fairly clearly even in the reaction of commentators at such a breach of security. Questions naturally centred on who had been carrying the wooden cross and who had fallen. But to everyone's surprise a very efficient blanket secrecy temporarily governed all answers. It was apparently what the president wanted and what the British authorities wanted, because the president, after all, was unhurt and a certain degree of official embarrassment was involved both by Washington and London. For the time being secrecy was the watchword despite an explosion of speculation in the media.

Bob and Marsha had watched the television coverage that evening. What should he do, Bob wondered, if the glimpse offered by the sole shot of the fallen figure did resemble the Great Peter? If he claimed to know who it was, who would he be talking about? Someone known to the Americans as Pinckney? Someone who had officially died? And if the American president were unhurt, did it matter all that much?

The trouble was people did want to know. Bob Jermin surmised he would have no peace until they did. Especially as pictures in the media of the white cross above the multitude of heads went round the world almost instantly as the most memorable image of the presidential visit.

17

Opening her eyes, Marsha saw uncertain summer sunlight flickering beyond the curtains. It had stopped raining but the fresh leaves of the chestnut rustled sufficiently to suggest there was a slight breeze although what roused her was the sound of tyres on gravel in the driveway. A car had stopped outside the house. Then footsteps crossed the gravel.

Suddenly she was upright. She jumped out of bed and ran to the window. Between the curtains she had a clear enough view of the driveway to see the car. Was it Georgina home from university for some reason? Simon, their son, would surely have let them know if he were coming. Then another car stopped beside the first.

Flinging on her dressing-gown and stepping into slippers, she tiptoed quickly across the bedroom so as not to disturb Bob. Once out on the landing, she paused to listen.

She detected what she thought was a slight movement in the porch, beyond the front door, and ran downstairs. Halfway down she saw a shadow through the stained glass of the front-door panel. Someone was standing there.

Loud as hammer strokes came tapping on the stained glass. A face seemed to be peering in at her.

'Mrs Jermin? Marsha?' A man's voice.

The tapping came again. He was looking in at her through a lighter, yellow area of the stained-glass rose pattern.

'Yes?' she asked in a much quicker and firmer whisper than she thought her voice capable of at such a moment.

'Mrs Jermin, Marsha, I think, I do apologise.' The voice was faint but distinct and clearly American. 'I am Wilbur, remember me?'

'Don't move!' she shouted.

Already the buzzing had started. In a few seconds the alarm would burst into life. She rushed round the hallway to the cupboard under the stairs, switched off the alarm and then dashed to the front door. It opened to reveal an elderly Wilbur Oldfield whom she hadn't seen for donkey's years and scarcely recognised but had at least done her the courtesy of remembering her name. He had on a light fawn raincoat. Otherwise, save for a head of nearly white hair, he was, she recalled, a friend from Bob's past whom she had welcomed to the house more than once.

'Marsha, I really must apologise…'

'Come in, come in,' she was saying as she held the door for him. 'Oh, there's someone else, too!'

'Yes, this is a Mr Kalthorst who came over with the president. I'm sorry we're so early.'

He introduced a slim, similarly raincoated man of about fifty who offered a firm handshake and a courteous smile before declaring himself as 'Ed, Ed Kalthorst, Mrs Jermin, very glad to meet you, but with my apologies as well as Wilbur's for disturbing you this early.'

'Ed is part of the president's entourage,' said Wilbur quickly, 'and we're here to see your husband. Have there been any newsmen in touch with you, Marsha?'

'Newsmen?'

'Yes, from the press or television?'

She was so astonished by the question she couldn't take it seriously. It was unnerving enough anyhow to hear the word president. 'No, I don't think so. I mean Bob may have had some contact. I haven't. I mean why should I? Let's go into our sitting room rather than have this conversation out here in the hall.'

'If you haven't and your husband hasn't,' Wilbur insisted, 'then we've got here in time. Which must explain why we're so early and behaving in this rude American way.'

She opened the door into the sitting room. 'I remember you, of course. You came to dinner here, didn't you?'

'I did. And it was very enjoyable.'

They trooped after her into the sitting room and she flung back the curtains. Daytime showed a reasonably tidy room even if, in the suddenly admitted sunlight, the furniture looked startled and dust motes hung like fine suspended rain in the searchlight beams of early sun's rays directed at the fireplace and several pictures on the walls. Marsha used a handset to ignite the gas fire.

'Please do sit down. You'll be wanting to speak to Bob,' she was saying, 'so I'll have to... Oh, here he is.'

There were rapid footsteps on the stairs and in a moment Robert Jermin appeared in the doorway in dressing-gown and slippers, his hair briefly combed into some sort of order.

'Yes, I heard your voices down here, so I felt it only polite to join you.'

The visitors, who had already begun to seat themselves, both rose. There were handshakes along with greetings. Unshaven as Bob was, he at least enjoyed the authority of being host for this moment and welcomed Wilbur Oldfield particularly vigorously. 'What on earth brings you here at such an early hour, Wilbur? Have you had breakfast?'

A little sheepishly the admission came he had had an early breakfast, but he went on to say: 'I'm not the one in charge here. Ed's the one in charge. I said I knew where you lived, so I drove down here and Ed followed. There are security reasons why we didn't phone you and we're here because of what happened to the president.'

'What happened to the president.' Bob took up the refrain. 'Well, what happened to the president? And how can I…'

'That's exactly why we're here to see you,' said Wilbur. 'Ed, explain.'

Ed Kalthorst, seating himself with his raincoat open, so that it spread in a kind of arc either side of him on the room's principal sofa, Wilbur Oldfield beside him, wore the slightly embarrassed look of a man overdressed for the occasion who nevertheless had urgent news to impart. He spoke with a degree of forcefulness to which he felt entitled by his position, as he went on to explain:

'Mr Jermin, I have been privileged to act the role of supervisor of presidential security in the White House since the inauguration of the new presidency. To secure the president's safety at all times has been my chief concern. What happened to the president yesterday was of course shocking and quite unexpected, but luckily no serious injury was inflicted. A scratch is how it has been described. If that's the extent of the physical injury, then there's not likely to be much of a problem. But the assailant is the problem. Who is he? He apparently had a heart attack and has been hospitalised. He was prevented from injuring the president seriously by the quick, timely reaction of a colleague of mine. I had personally appointed him to keep an eye on a Russian oligarch who had been issuing threats. The colleague is known to you, I think. We know him as R.C. – Raoul Cyrus Smithson.' He opened a newspaper. 'There he is! Celebrated as the chief protector of our president! A national saviour!'

Bob admitted at once he met him yesterday, while Marsha exclaimed that their daily paper hadn't arrived and wouldn't be arriving for another hour or so. She asked if everyone would like coffee. It turned out that everyone would like coffee and she went off to the kitchen.

'You apparently said yesterday,' Ed Kalthorst continued, addressing Bob, 'you didn't think the man pictured at Mr Silber's residence was our late Mr Pinckney but we're now pretty certain he is. The evidence of that Mr Koursaros has been very helpful. A monk from Mount Athos, that's the most likely identity! A monk, wielding a white cross with a sharp point!' Ed Kalthorst's raised voice had a squeaky edge of amazement to it. 'He tries to wound the president during what I have to say was frankly, Mr Jermin, a very poorly organised occasion. Still, as we all know, the president wasn't hurt. But we're left with an assailant, close, I believe, or so I am told, close to cardiac arrest. Now who is he? We believe he may be a Soviet rocket scientist who defected to us and worked with our people for a couple of years before allegedly dying. So we have a dead assailant attacking the president with a wooden cross used as a lethal weapon that only causes a scratch. Has a ghost ever been known to do that?' Both the speaker's hands were held out in a flourish of bewilderment. He continued in a more serious tone: 'Probably not. So what we want to know is, does he have collaborators apart from that Mr Koursaros, is he part of a bigger plot, who is he, dammit, what's his message, etcetera, etcetera. So what with the media screaming to know who this assailant is and our ignorance of his role and intentions, we've come to you, Mr Robert Jermin, because he, the assailant, insists that he will only speak to someone he trusts and the only person he trusts is you, Mr Jermin. Yes, *you*! Will you please help us! We're desperate. And we haven't got much time.'

The look on Ed Kalthorst's face was more than earnest, it had an intensity and passion that made Bob feel he was being handed responsibility for the safekeeping of a holy grail. Luckily at that moment Marsha entered the room carrying a tray with a coffee jug and cups. They tinkled enough before being set down to reduce the tense atmosphere caused by the pleading in the speaker's last words. 'Anyone take sugar?' Marsha asked. No one took sugar. The coffee was quickly distributed. She then announced she was going to get dressed. Ed Kalthorst laughed apologetically.

'I'll be through in a moment,' he said. 'There's just one more thing.'

'Of course I'll help,' Bob said, as anxious as Marsha to get dressed, but grateful for the sharp, hot taste of the coffee. At which Ed asked:

'You've not spoken to anyone from the media, I hope, Mr Jermin? Since the president's arrival, since his speech yesterday, I mean.'

'No.'

'And you obviously haven't seen the weapon used by the assailant?'

'No.'

'Well, here it is!'

Triumphantly Ed held up a phone screen showing a small wooden cross. At a first glance it might not have looked made of wood because its whiteness had a resemblance more to ivory. A greater degree of magnification quickly dispelled that impression. He handed the phone to Bob.

'As you can see, the central shaft has been carved to a point at its base. What kind of a wound it might cause I'm not sure. And at one time words or some kind of message had been inscribed down the length of the shaft, but there's nothing there now. Anyhow, the assailant used it to strike at the president. I suppose he wanted to cause some kind of wound. In fact, thanks to my colleague, Mr Smithson, all he caused was a scratch. This cross, the weapon, was seized from him. Does it help you in any way? Does it to remind you of something the assailant may have said? Does it identify him in some way?'

'He said something about being a dagger of God,' Bob admitted, his right arm raised making clutching movements with his fingers as if the air would release its meaning to him. 'I remember that crazy expression.'

'Okay, so he thought of the cross as a weapon,' Ed said. 'That makes sense.'

'No, I don't think he did.' Bob said. 'Or he never said anything like that. He wore it, that's all. Look, I must get dressed. Please excuse me.' He half rose from where he was sitting.

'I think that's enough,' intervened Wilbur, pressing a hand to Ed's arm.

'Does it identify him?' came the sharp question. 'That's what I want to know.'

'I certainly saw him wearing it. Yes, I suppose it identifies him.'

Bob handed back the phone and stood up. He knew he had to keep his promise to the Great Peter. But Wilbur asked quietly: 'If Mr Jermin saw him wearing it, that's sufficient evidence in my view, isn't it?'

Ed Kalthorst didn't reply. He merely stared down at the image of the cross and nodded. Wilbur added: 'I think that's evidence.' He was looking up at Bob. 'I mean if I saw someone wearing a cross like that, I'd be fairly sure it identified him.'

'Thank you,' Bob said. 'May I get dressed now?'

'Sure, sure, sure.' Ed apologised for having spoken sharply. 'It's just that I'm not used to dealing with ghosties or the undead or whatever.' He knew this sounded silly, smirked and pocketed the phone. Wilbur took him at his word. 'So far as we know, the assailant is still alive and will hopefully talk to Mr Robert Jermin.'

'I said I'm willing to help,' Bob agreed. 'I'll be as quick as I can.' He left the room.

Ed Kalthorst at once took the opportunity to agree with Wilbur Oldfield's whispered comment:

'I told you, you've got the right person.'

'I think you're probably right. By the way, who's the painter?'

'Marsha is.'

'They're good.'

He stood up and strode over to where a wall space was devoted to several water-colour paintings that he studied closely for several moments.

'Very good. Why didn't you tell me?'

Wilbur Oldfield tried to be as reasonable as possible. 'You only wanted to know about what the assailant called "the member of my family", about Robert Jermin, not his wife. You wanted to make sure he was the right one.'

'True, true,' Ed conceded. 'Oh, my God, here's a Hockney! It's a signed drawing! And this is – Oh, I can't believe it! Do you know who this is?'

Wilbur Oldfield could not deny his ignorance.

'It's a Chagall!'

Ed Kalthorst exclaimed the name as if he had a mouth full of chocolate. Suddenly there came a ringing sound. He had the phone to one ear. 'Right,' he was saying, 'right, I'll be there.'

He had apparently had a summons from the president. He had to leave at once.

***

'Let me say thank you,' Wilbur Oldfield said. He entered the motorway. Early morning traffic swept by at speed before he joined the steady race of vehicles going towards London. Full sunlight now excited sparks from windscreens and brightwork, flashed on paintwork, glowed along the light coloration of the road surface like the faintness of the car's tyres making the speed sound grey and stiff the faster they went. 'You see, there's the embarrassment of it. I mean, first of all, how did this mad monk or whoever he is get so close to the president? You wouldn't know the answer to that, no more than I do. And if all we could say was that, well, we think he's dead, because that's officially what he is, how the hell does a ghost attack the president with a wooden cross? No, no, we've had to keep it all officially secret until we're sure who he is, the one you call the Great Peter. And was he working alone?'

Bob, seated beside Wilbur Oldfield, had to listen. He had no answers for the time being. He could not be sure of his own readiness to identify the supposed assailant even after being shown pictures of him in a hospital bed. He had looked at a clean-shaven face, thin and earnest, the lips finely shaped, the eyebrows straight and the eyes just as intent and masterful, but the lines on the forehead, the white hair, the stretched skin over the facial bone suggesting asceticism, sadness and old age. It had come as a shock. Was this really the Great Peter he had known? How could he be sure? And now he was being taken to see him, how could he, Robert Jermin, be at all certain the Great Peter would recognise him as the young English diplomat, his alleged 'brother', after almost thirty years?

'I know we've not been in touch recently,' Wilbur was saying, 'so you've no reason to know what *Raduga* was intended to do. Since the archives have been opened, we've had a clearer idea. What the Soviets intended to do was to drop this rocket onto sensitive oil installations in the North Sea. They knew they could do it. They knew they could sever an important pipeline if they wished. The shock effect seems to have been the main thing. The effect on NATO thinking, for instance, the implications of it for NATO defence strategy. Or just the sheer mischief, not to mention the havoc it might cause.'

He paused in his speaking due to a series of red rear braking lights from the traffic ahead. It was one of those unexplained slowings in motorway traffic that prove quite temporary and quickly resolve themselves.

'But they had a real problem of their own,' he resumed. 'The guidance system. They knew it worked. They had it in their possession. But what about its inventor? Could they really be as certain of him? Could they trust him? What if they discredited him? What if they arranged to let him defect to the West but his invention could be shown to be defective? He would be treated as a typical crackpot scientist, wouldn't he? And he wasn't easy to deal with in any case, insisting as he did on this and that. But he was clever. He had made certain the explosion that was supposed to damage the sea-bed pipelines and destroy the rocket itself never happened.

'Mind you, we couldn't exactly crow over the retrieval of this lump of metal, however intact, we couldn't proclaim it a great victory for the CIA, the West, for the future of mankind and all that jazz because, first off, the rocket turned out to be an old design and, secondly, the "cargo" came out of Moscow all too easily. We couldn't believe he was who he claimed to be. The Soviets seemed to want to let us have him.

'Naturally everybody was suspicious of everybody. It took a lot of debriefing and two years of experimentation before our people were able to convince themselves finally that he was the genuine article. By which time the technology had become more sophisticated and the "cargo" a lot more uncooperative. So Pinckney was officially allowed to die. Unofficially he was allowed to go to Mount Athos. That's the story so far. Or rather that's all we know so far. And I suspect it might be all we ever know if we don't get to London pretty damn quick.'

Perhaps, Bob thought, Wilbur is right: *that's all we will know.* 'You mean he'll be dead?'

'Correct.'

18

Probably there were, Bob reflected, the two kinds if life, '*la vie triviale*' and '*la vie tragique*', and the latter was the necessary antidote, the necessary reminder that most activities could quickly seem trivial enough once tragedy took command. He could easily have said it was none of his business. It would have been quite within his rights to do so. After all, the president hadn't been injured. There was no imperative need to renew the supposed family connection that made him so essential to the Great Peter, even though he knew he would be breaking a promise if he did so. No, the passing parade of sunlit facades of offices and shops, the parked vehicles, the surrounding traffic, the people going about their daily business on either side of the car's windows – no, it all added up to a kind of proof that the normal and trivial still dominated life. He could close his mind to everything he saw and simply pretend to himself that tragedy was always individual, the trivial always general.

Like the car's radio announcing that the president was in good health and spirits and ready to continue with the scheduled arrangements, while the assassin was not yet identified but remained in intensive care under close medical attention, tragedy nurtured itself on headlines. It grew larger in its emphasis on the assassin's state than on the universal praise expressed for the CIA agent, R.C. Smithson, who had prevented him from striking the president again. Its tentacles might reach out as far as him, Robert Jermin, and even be present along with Wilbur Oldfield in the closed world of the

247

car, but the life of the trivial and normal, the viable, endurable life of the everyday, moved past them outside with a kind of constancy that demonstrated the promise of immortality more obviously than any tragedy could. It did not seem stoppable. The trivial life would always reassert itself in the end. This was what made it such a blessing, such an absorptive, endurable state of being, which the tragic always threatened to make meaningful and terrible.

His life, what was it? What would it be now if he wasn't seated in this car next to Wilbur Oldfield? There were clients to be seen, phone calls to be made and taken, emails to be received and answered, meetings to be attended, as on most mornings of his working life. His involvement in an official investigation into the attempt on the life of the president of the United States might not carry much weight in the world of international insurance brokerage. It might not be a good thing for his reputation. But trivia? No, it was not a trivial thing, except that tragedy pre-empted it and made it seem important. Tragedy was in charge here.

Tragedy was in the very dutifulness of following the instructions that brought him here. It was scarcely nine o'clock in the morning and, as Wilbur had said more than once, they weren't known, they were as ordinary and inconspicuous and much like concerned hospital visitors as possible, hence the bouquet of flowers on his lap and the insistence on Wilbur's part that he was too old and too long retired to be recognisable to the media, the press or to anyone. He was not important. He would make his way to the hospital as if visiting a sick friend.

The international news media besieging the hospital would pick up on anything, Wilbur had insisted, which was why he had not phoned ahead this morning. They were reminded of the fact when the hospital entrance came within sight. Apart from TV news vans ranged immediately opposite the hospital gates, the courtyard beyond and the main entrance were choked with camera crews, newsmen and police. It seemed that a statement was about to be made. As if in anticipation a flock of pigeons suddenly rose and circled excitedly, white wings against grey concrete, in front of the hospital building.

The birds wheeling and the forward surge of the crowd were all Bob saw as they drove straight past and turned down a side street. A thought importuned him: what if the Great Peter was already dead and this was what the statement was about? He felt a flood of relief succeeded immediately by contrition and a sense of emptiness.

This sense of emptiness sustained him. He felt he was without a will of his own. He was ready to be greeted, shown the way, led, accompanied to wherever he should go so long as it meant merely stepping through a rear entrance to the hospital, past paramedical staff and trolleys, seeing ahead of him the rectangular shape of Wilbur Oldfield's back in the fawn raincoat, noticing names of wards and white arrows and signs for exits and lifts and smelling the chemically unreal air that always lingered in hospital corridors. So long as it meant being conscious of a tight security presence in the form of those he assumed were plain-clothed officers gathered in pairs beside swing doors and, most conspicuously of all, down one long internal corridor lit by concealed strip lighting that seemed to accentuate with a charcoal blurring the hollows of the watching eyes and the stippling of stubble round chins, not to mention a uniform chalky pallor given to the faces of nurses and women officers regardless of their natural complexion. So long as it meant not having to think or make decisions.

At the end of this corridor and subjected to constant inspection he was led to a waiting-room. He did not remember exactly who he met. There was someone from the Foreign Office, someone else introduced as being from the State Department, someone from Downing Street, but Bob found himself quickly closeted with a Chief Superintendent who explained what they wanted, at the same time adding that his own title was usually shortened to Chief Super.

'Mr Jermin, thank you for coming. I'm afraid this may not be easy. You have met with representatives of the United States security services who have told you a bit of the background. We have had to trace you and ask you to come here as the most likely person to fit the description given by the man we have in custody. He refuses to talk to anyone else. You speak Russian, don't you?'

'I do.'

'Be warned, sir, this is a long shot. We're not entirely sure of his identity. As you probably know, he has been named as Pinckney by the Americans, but they have also declared him as officially deceased.' The Chief Super was consulting a notebook. 'He has resided incognito for at least the last dozen years in a monastery on Mount Athos. So he's been a monk. Yesterday evening he attempted to stab the president of the United States while the president was attending the welcoming ceremony. He had a heart attack and was hospitalised. That's the story so far.' The Chief Super cleared his throat and tucked his notebook away. 'What we want to know is: Did he have any associates? Did he act on behalf of a larger organisation? What are his connections?'

He paused. Having spoken to this point in the neutral, clipped way of a senior police officer who aimed to express himself as succinctly and clearly as possible, he now rubbed the palms of his hands together with a rapid, dry, washing motion as if he were literally washing them of an obligation. He drew in a breath sharply through clenched teeth.

'If he doesn't say anything, that's all right by us. We will be grateful to you for having tried. I'll accompany you.'

He led the way through two sets of swing doors. A middle-aged woman in nurse's uniform and a plain-clothed man introduced as a doctor, a stethoscope round his neck, were seated beside the only bed in a small, dimly lit room filled with electronic monitoring equipment. Intravenous drips hung from the arms of a metal trolley on one side of the bed along with a mobile ventilator and fixed to the rear wall were the customary monitoring units for blood pressure and heart beat accompanied by an array of tubes. At least two CCTV cameras were visible.

The room was surprisingly quiet. Save for an air-conditioning hum, there were no indications of life apart from the regular dancing movements registered on the monitor screens behind the bed. The one window seemed to have grey shutters fixed across it. The air was hot and static and pervaded by a prophylactic smell that Bob found at first sticky and offensive but grew used to after a while.

The patient, or 'the man in custody' as the Chief Super had described him, was evidently asleep. A single sheet was drawn right up to his chest, leaving his arms, shoulders and neck bare. Thin as they were, enough was visible to show the slight but regular rise and fall of his breathing. As for the face, it was turned upwards with the help of several pillows but they naturally enclosed it and Bob had to lean down close to see it clearly. What he saw were the same features as those in the photograph Ed Kalthorst had shown him except for the tubes inserted in the nostrils, although the overall effect in the room's dim lighting was to make the patient look less than adult, smaller and wizened, as if it were a strangely old child lying there. The skin on the temples and upper cheekbones was wrinkled and mottled in a light shade of ochre. The lips were delicate and well-formed as they always had been, but a fine dark stubble, scarcely more visible than charcoal dust, shaded the whiteness of the jawline. The hair curling above the forehead was thin, wiry and white-tipped. One thing only was missing – the appearance of the eyes, now closed. Bob knew he would never be certain of identifying him as the Great Peter until they were open.

The hot still air, the self-important, mouse like dartings of instruments, the slightly resentful manner of the nurse and doctor, all contributed to a sharp increase in Bob's anxiety. He struggled to reach a handkerchief in his trouser pocket. He had begun to sweat. The doctor put out his hand to stop him reaching the pocket. Instead the nurse offered him a tissue. Simultaneously the Chief Super asked:

'So?'

It was coming back to him. A high-speed drill was burning its way into his leg.

'I think it's...'

He re-experienced the gunshot wound. It was more of an identification than any movement or word from the patient. The sweat poured down his face.

'What?' asked the policeman.

He could feel the sweat like rain on his face. The tissue had become a damp ball from his dabbing. The lighted windows of the embassy building were yellow blobs in the distance. He saw the pink plastic raincoat and hood darting ahead of him over wet paving stones. Then the pain in his leg was re-enacted. He saw blood-red curlicues dissolving in the rain at his feet. He felt profoundly sick.

'*Piotr Nikolaevich!*' he blurted out suddenly, leaning far forward to see into the patient's face.

Nothing happened. It was unreal. The sound of his own voice speaking the Russian name in the thick, cotton-wool atmosphere of the room seemed quite divorced from him personally. He glanced at the nurse, the doctor and the policeman and read the same look of impatience and disbelief in each pair of eyes. The suspicion of false pretences shone in each of them. He repeated the name.

This time he spoke more slowly and gave equal weight to each syllable. The sound was more authoritative and less aggressive. It produced a noticeable disturbance in the rhythmic flashing on one of the screens. The lips moved a fraction and the rise and fall of the chest seemed to pause.

Even though the thin throat may have seemed to move, more conspicuous was a clenching motion of one hand that was explained by the doctor as the patient pumping a heart stimulant. Bob decided it was time to identify himself. Leaning down very close into a private place by the topmost pillow, he whispered what might have been endearments except that they contained as many of the names as he could remember from his visit to the house in the forbidden zone as well as his grandmother's name. He ended by mentioning the word *Raduga*.

'I think I was your sole hope,' he whispered. 'I sent the materials and I took you to the American embassy, remember? After that I never knew what happened.'

Both eyes opened. They were as intensely dark and brilliant as he remembered them, though bloodshot round the rims and glittering feverishly in the untrustworthy strength of the lighting. Whether or not they recognised Bob's face looking down at them was hard to say, but he was sure it was the Great Peter lying there. He said so.

'You're sure?' the Chief Super asked.

The lips parted in a very faint smile. The patient's hand reached out slowly and pointed at his own face. '*My name - Piotr Nikolaevich.*' It was in Russian as was everything he said. The hand then seemed for a moment about to stretch towards Bob's but changed direction and instead made the Orthodox sign of the cross in a slow fluid motion. 'God be praised. Thank you, thank you. You are my brother and my friend. I am close to death, as you can see.'

Bob felt inadequate to this. Was he here to torture a dying man by asking him questions? Tears spontaneously pricked his eyes. At the same time he could not help noticing that the patient's left arm had a series of puncture marks running from the wrist up to the elbow. They were small indentations in the skin, like insect bites, the most recent still red and sore. He pointed to them.

'No idea,' said the doctor. 'Self-harm, I guess.'

'Ask him where he's been staying,' the Chief Super muttered.

Bob put the question. Instantly came the whispered reply, 'I am not saying.' The patient looked from Bob's face to those of the others, flickered and darted away. He mentioned a name.

'Who?'

Bob had misheard, but impatience and disdain stared from the elderly features, as if the question deserved no more than a curt, dismissive rejection. At the same time there was another tired, fluid motion of the hand making the sign of the cross and a groan of pain. The pumping occurred again. 'God be praised. I did what I wanted.'

The Chief Super interposed: 'Ask him if he has accomplices.' Bob ignored the demand and asked instead:

'What did you want?'

'To be a dagger of God.'

The answer so startled him that he failed to translate it and was even more surprised when Great Peter made the strange gesture of holding up his arm to deliberately show the line of puncture marks. No explanation came. In fact the eyes were closed again. It looked as if the patient might have fallen asleep to avoid further questions, only for him to surprise Bob by saying quite clearly:

'You thought I was dead, didn't you?'

The Chief Super asked what he'd said and the doctor leaned down closer to the patient as if anticipating the worst.

Bob said: 'You mean Pinckney?'

'Yes. But I wasn't. I died, you see, in my earthly body and like a rocket I ascended into heaven to be among my spiritual brothers, God be praised. To be the servant of the God of love.'

There was more of the pumping action. It seemed pointless to ask what he was talking about. He was talking, which the seemed the most important thing. It had to be assumed that someone near death could be excused for talking nonsense.

'Robert,' came the soft voice from the bed, 'I will talk to you because I trust you.'

The brown eyes blinked slowly up at him. Their brightness seemed to grow with an apparent renewal of confidence and strength. Bob returned their gaze as openly as he could, distracted only by noticing in the corner of his eye something hanging over the metal bed-head. He could not be sure what it was until it dawned on him it was a small microphone ready, he assumed, to catch and record every word spoken.

'I had genius,' the voice was saying. It made a soft, rustling sound as if it were no louder than a light breeze stirring leaves on a hot afternoon in a forbidden zone. 'But I had a little genie within my genius... a little imp of mischief...' A pause. 'I did not want to lose him... ever... *Ozornik*! You know what I mean? There is nothing within me without him. He is the reason why...'

'What's he saying?' the policeman asked. Bob waved him away.

The rustling of many leaves followed, a stream of whispered words, some lost, some seeming incomprehensible, all building into a torrent of meaning, that could only be snatched at like leaves blown about in a high wind.

'Remember what Herzen said... our first revolutionaries... warrior champions, they went out knowingly to face certain death... to purify the hearts of children born into an atmosphere... into an atmosphere of executions and servility... they were legendary warriors... clad in pure steel from head to foot...'

'What's he saying?' the policeman repeated.

'It is our legacy... our intelligentsia legacy,' the voice continued as faintly as fluttered leaves, 'to fight tyranny, the tyranny of rulers, the tyranny of ignorance... our dream was a new man able to liberate himself, a dream of Godmanhood, of women liberated, of all people free... the Will of the People, the People's Freedom, *Narodnaia volia*... God be praised!'

Again he crossed himself slowly, his right hand moving in the same fluid gesture. He closed his eyes.

'Ask him!' the Chief Super urged impatiently. 'Ask him who his accomplices were!'

Bob knew he could not hurry whatever the process was. He was drawn into it through an obligation of trust to the patient. He was more and more convinced that his role had become that of a guardian or confessor rather than the policeman's collaborator or informant. He turned his head away, annoyed by the pressure on his tear-ducts and the nagging sense of personal inadequacy in trying to understand, let alone translate, the scattered meanings of these whisperings.

'You want to know why, don't you?' the quiet voice suddenly asked.

'Yes.'

'God spoke to me. When you are in heaven, God's word is all. He spoke to me in my very soul. He said I was to be an apostle of love. I was to make a sacrifice for the remission of all sins. So I decided to go to the girl of my dreams.'

'Who?'

'You took me to the American embassy, remember? The girl at the embassy.'

It dawned on Bob that he must be talking about Grace Hampson, but he could not believe it. He stared down at the apparently sleeping face. Then, to his astonishment, the eyes opened and shone brightly. He could not suppress a treacherous impulse to dismiss the mention of 'a girl of my dreams' as nonsense. He was reminded of all his doubts in the darkened dining room at the dacha when he had listened to the Great Peter's words, but the eyes fixed their gaze on him and were mesmerising in their sudden brilliance.

'My life... my identity... my soul,' the voice whispered, 'all gone! I was officially dead. God said No, you are not dead! You must be resurrected. You must rise up and use your cross. You will use it to spread love. You will use it as Zosima said you should. When all is permitted and you are free... you struggle with the nihilism in your own soul... and you enter the portals of hell... I would pass through those portals... I would open up the world to God's word... God's word that is full of love. People would listen...'

The strength which had been visible in the eyes now seemed exhausted. Speech became increasingly hard.

'They would, people would...' The whisperings now came in short bursts and less than coherently. 'They would understand... the twentieth century... a century of purgation... the next... liberating... an age of a Great Idea...'

He gathered strength for a final effort.

'My own *Raduga*, my own rainbow, would bring people together... It would be the portent for the future... and people would listen. How did the Son of God have His words heard ... if he hadn't died on His cross?'

He asked for water. The English words came as a surprise. They interrupted Bob's attempt to translate what he had just been saying. The nurse quickly brought a plastic cup to his lips. He sipped and again crossed himself. The Chief Super muttered something about the whole thing being a waste of time. Maybe this irritation communicated itself to the man lying on the bed even if he did not hear it.

'No!'

He shouted the word in English and began struggling to

raise himself to a sitting position. The action was so sudden and unexpected that the nurse gave a yell. She tried to refix some of the unfastened tubes while the doctor ordered the patient to lie down but he rose up so defiantly it was hard to stop him.

'Listen, I want to tell you why!' The words were uttered in English in an American accent, more as if he were gulping for air than expelling it, so that what he said came in little blocks of sound. 'I wished to be... dagger of God... of God of love.' He raised his hand slowly and solemnly as if he were about to cross himself, his eyes ablaze with a feverish conviction. Instead the gesture seemed more one of threat than benediction. The hand rose above his head and remained there. A pinging sound started. 'If the president knows... (Ping) how full of love ... (Ping) the world will be... (Ping-ping) then humanity... (Ping-ping) all human beings... (Ping-ping-ping) all humanity... (Ping-ping-ping) will never want... (Ping-ping-ping) never want... (Ping-ping-ping-ping) to lose it... (Ping-ping-ping-ping) never... (Ping-ping-ping-ping) ever lose that love... ever... Where is my cross? Where is it?' He pawed at the tubes fixed to his chest or those already loosened. 'Where is it? What has happened... to my cross?'

The words ended in a shrill cry, just as the pinging built into a loud ringing like a fire alarm. He seemed seized by a racking pain, tried to expand his chest, struggled, literally fought for breath and was suddenly still. The nurse shrieked, covered her face, recovered instantly and clasped her hands. The doctor rushed forward in an attempt to make the patient lie back but drew back himself at the patient's momentary stillness.

To the surprise and annoyance of all four people in the room, the swing doors flew apart practically at that instant. A group of people in raincoats proclaiming that they were from the media, some holding up cards or notices in justification, some with cameras in their phones already flashing, burst into the room. Presumably the patient's cry had attracted them.

The Chief Super tried to force them back, a phone already to his lips, and the doctor angrily protested at their violation of a dying man's final moments.

There was no stopping them, it seemed. The world needed to know what was happening to the likely assassin of the president of the United States. Who was he? What did he want? Why did he do it? Who were his accomplices?

Bob realised then why this small room had been chosen as suitable for this patient. It was obviously inconspicuous. No police had been stationed outside. Nothing unusual would draw attention to it. Except of course for the shrillness of the patient's cry. Meanwhile the doctor had carefully drawn a sheet over the collapsed shape of the patient's half-raised shoulders and head as he had fallen back on the pile of pillows.

Bob, on the other hand, could not take his eyes off the third of the four monitors behind the bed-head. The soft pinging sound accompanying the final whisperings had produced a dancing line that suddenly became boringly horizontal and still like the patient. The fire alarm stopped. Simultaneously uniformed officers entered and began clearing the room.

In the ensuing noise of shouts, protests and general mayhem Bob found himself being virtually frogmarched into the adjoining corridor. He could not say a prayer for the soul of the Great Peter, nor could he explain why he was there. He was clearly no part of the hospital's medical staff and therefore fell into the category of intruder, to be manhandled out of the room. Someone he recognised then seized him by the arm.

19

He caught his breath a moment, held his head back, filled his lungs. The air in the small room had been extraordinarily dry. Now, in what looked like a consulting room, with a desk and easy chairs, he found himself coughing and was shown to one of the chairs. He wanted to talk about what the Great Peter had said, explain it, justify the words before they lost all meaning to him personally or became no more than data in some tribunal evidence. He heard the Chief Super say:

'I'm glad you got him to talk, sir. Thank you. We were instructed not to attempt to revive him. Of course, we'll be studying the recordings.'

Oh, of course! And what good would it be to know the dying words? He resented the idea as intrusive, yet he knew they had a perfect right. The patient had been a prisoner in custody, a self-confessed, would-be assassin of the president of the United States. They had a perfect right.

'Mr Jermin, I believe you know Mr Smithson.'

The coughing fit passed with the help of a small bottle of water. The chill liquid cleared his throat as he lowered the bottle to face R.C. A pretty woman in police uniform had been speaking.

'Yes. We met, er, the day before yesterday, in my office. You've become famous.'

The statement had a tinge of query about it. Raoul Cyrus Smithson smiled at him the kind of smile he had been depicted giving in the newspaper photograph Ed Kalthorst had shown him, except that there was now more of a self-effacing grin in the curve of the lips. A brief nod reinforced his acknowledgement of a compliment.

'Yes, I was on the spot. But your man, the assailant, I held him, that's all. He'd been running toward the president and he had this white cross in his hand. He posed a threat. My judgement is he was in no fit condition. A cardiac arrest, they said. And now?'

'The same,' Bob admitted. He coughed again and took another mouthful of the water.

'You mean he's dead?'

'Yes.'

'And he was who we thought he was?'

'Yes, he was.'

'I won't ask what you got from him because that's not why I'm here. No, I'm here... Oh, how rude of me!' R.C. suddenly said. 'I should have introduced Miss Boswell, Officer Joan Boswell, who's been looking after me here in London.' He then made the introduction and Officer Boswell rather demurely nodded. 'You see we're going our separate ways very soon. I'm going back to New York this afternoon. I've relied on her more that I could have imagined.'

Bob was aware at that instant of a relationship between them that had grown beyond official loyalties. He was reminded himself how much he missed Marsha. The pang of the reminder chimed with R.C. adding:

'I'll miss her. I'll miss her very much. Oh, but that's not what I should be saying! No, sir, I shouldn't be saying it. What I should be saying is that Mrs Van Straubenzee wants to see you.'

'Who?'

He had no idea what the name meant. All he knew was that

R.C. suddenly had a cellphone to his ear. He smiled at what he heard.

'She's free right now and will see you. You knew her back in Moscow,' he somewhat idiotically insisted. 'She's keen to see you, Mr Jermin. It may be a long time ago.'

A long time ago? What was he on about?

'This way.'

Bob could only think about Marsha while Officer Boswell was busy beckoning him to follow R.C. out of the room. The latter was saying:

'She is a senior presidential aide, one of those responsible for the arrangements. She told me she wanted to see you earlier but there wasn't any time. It's just two doors along.'

Uniformed and plain-clothed police in the corridor stood aside for them to pass and R.C., evidently known to them and treated with respect as a result of his overnight fame, gave a polite preliminary tap on a door before opening it and inviting Bob to enter.

It was a small, cramped office that had presumably been vacated by its staff due to the emergency. Two desks or work stations faced each other, both equipped with computers and keyboards and a desktop clutter of files and tissues along, in one case, with artificial red tulips in a plastic vase. The walls were covered with charts and much of the floor space was devoted to filing cabinets. Despite this, there was enough room for upholstered typist's chairs and a metal table on which sat an electric coffee percolator with a jug on a hotplate. As a result, the air naturally smelled of coffee. If it was used to that, it seemed unused to another perfume that Bob recognised instantly and seemed to have a drenching effect on the whole room.

She was, he felt, too exotic. Her perfume itself was a silent hurrah. It merely underlined by its very presence the wave of shock and excitement that swept over him. R.C. did no more than usher him in and left him to face her as she surveyed him with those sunlit-sea eyes, their blue heightened in its brightness by the lenses of the smart silver spectacles and leaking out in a strange way into the calm crow's-feet of surrounding lines and the smooth patina of the freckled complexion. Her lips had the same carved classical shapeliness but accentuated a little by the ageing effect of the small smile lines chased so subtly into the corners of the mouth.

'Grace!'

'Didn't you know I was here?'

'No, I didn't. Hampson, yes, but Van... Van...'

'Van Straubenzee. Yes. Well, I was married. But I'm not now. I've simply kept the name.'

She still knew how to dress, that was obvious. The long navy blue jacket and skirt were not power-dressing for power-dressing's sake, they were smart like her personality and her still coppery hair. Her steady way of looking at him was matched by a kind of trustfulness and challenge in the mature pose of her figure. It was as if she asked to be looked at for what she was in herself, not for what she might be in terms of authority as a presidential aide. There was in this naturalness a slightly defensive appeal.

'No, Grace, I didn't know you were married.'

She noticed in the remark a modest tone of reproach and countered it with: 'We've both moved on, haven't we? Will you have some coffee?'

'Thank you.'

'I wanted to explain about Mr Pinckney,' she was saying as she poured the coffee. 'He was given that pseudonym once he was in the States. You probably knew that.'

'I did, yes.'

She handed him a cup of coffee and replaced the jug on the hotplate. 'And you've just been with him, haven't you?'

The words 'been with him,' spoken so casually, affected him so deeply he felt a momentary shock at the power of grief. To hide the shock he blew on his coffee several times before sipping it, felt another cough beginning and swallowed. He knew his eyes must be full of tears but he looked at her calmly and took another sip. Then he told her the Great Peter had died.

'Really?'

'Yes.'

She returned his look quite steadily for several moments and then lowered her eyes. 'I mean I want to be sure. I mean I was told Pinckney had passed on. But of course I knew that wasn't right.' She took in a deep breath. 'Oh, Bob, I'm so sorry! I'm so sorry! I suppose it's...' She pulled a paper tissue from the box by the computer and turned a little from him as she raised it to her face. 'Forgive me, I've caught one of your hay fevers, one of your English summer colds.'

'He was only hanging on by a thread,' he said.

She nodded. 'Yes. I see. So it was painless?'

'Yes, I suppose it was painless.' He saw she was relieved by this. It was almost as if he could sense she wanted to put the fact behind her as something as disposable as the tissue that she now crumpled and let fall. 'It's you and me, isn't it?'

'What?'

She looked sideways at him. 'Grace, for his sake,' he said, 'for the sake of old times and love and forgiveness...'

'What?'

He drank another mouthful of the hot coffee and felt the coughing come to a halt. Then he put down the cup. 'So that his soul may rest in peace... Is that a silly thing to say?'

'No.'

He was glad she said that. 'And for our sakes...'

Was that really what he meant? But he said it in the

conviction he was right. And to his own astonishment as well as hers, he stepped forward and took her in his arms with an urgent, clutching motion and held her body against his. She stiffened in the very unexpectedness of his action and then yielded. He felt a slow, gradual release of stress between them, a slow, gradual easing of tension. She put her arms round him and held him tight as well. They stood there holding each other and noises of voices and feet tramping along the corridor and an ambulance or police siren from outside entered their silent embrace.

He was consumed by the odd thought that the soul of the Great Peter was finding its way to heaven. He felt it needed the comfort of Grace's closeness to speed it on its way. If there were no choirs of angels, there was at least the perfume, not drenching any more but soft and endearing, and he knew it was not as strong as he had supposed. He felt her body and her vulnerability in his arms. A kind of renewal of love, as subtle as a pain entering his body, made him gasp out suddenly:

'The silly thing is he wasn't even a friend. He claimed me as a brother because I belonged to the family. That was all.'

'He was a friend to me,' she said.

'What do you mean?'

'I mean he gave me my career.' She withdrew her arms and pulled another tissue.

'How?'

'I don't mean anything more than that. Bob, sit down.' She blew her nose. This time the tissue was thrown into a metal wastepaper basket. 'Sit down. It's about that I want to...'

'What?'

He sat down in one of the typist's chairs and she in another.

'About the fact that I saw him when he reached our Moscow embassy. Remember? The maid coming for the Fourth of July celebration? The first real evidence of the network? It was a helluva big thing for me, that whole *Raduga* thing. It gave me a big start career-wise.'

He saw the milled-steel look again. 'I'm sure it did. And I got shot in the leg. It put an end to my career.'

'Bob, I...' She gave him a puzzled look. Maybe she had forgotten they had both been in it together. She pursed her lips. 'Oh, my God, yes! Of course! Of course! I hadn't forgotten, it was just that I'd been concentrating on *him*, because you'd confirmed him as a rocket scientist and I got to know him as that.'

'No, go on telling me,' he said. 'He talked about you as the girl of his dreams.'

'He talked about me as the girl of his dreams?' she repeated, half-smiling at the surprising flattery.

'Yes.'

'He never told me that. He was always rather cold, rather distant. You mustn't get any ideas that aren't absolutely politically correct about this, Bob. There was no emotional link between us. Nothing like that.' A brisk sideways movement of the upright palm of her right hand seemed to wipe the air clean of any such idea. 'When he had been interrogated at the embassy and it was recognised that he was really important as evidence of our network, all he said to me was that he wanted to become a monk. Purifying himself or something like that. I mean he wasn't very cooperative. Of course he became much more uncooperative once he was in the States, but for me he was important and I owed him. That's why I was so astonished when I learned he was being brought to London. It was a couple, maybe three days ago.'

'Did you know he'd issued a threat?'

'Yes.' She raised her eyes to the window and the sight of pigeons wheeling against an office building opposite and sighed. 'Yes, I knew that. That's why I got back to Ed, Ed Kalthorst, in

Washington, remember him?' He nodded. 'He sent out R.C., Raoul Smithson. They'd both been the first to interview him. You must've known about that.'

'I did,' Bob said.

She looked challengingly at him. 'They were the only two CIA people who'd had close experience of the Cold War at that time. Like you and me. And when it came to Mr Pinckney deceased, well, who better than those two? As for the Mr Pinckney himself who suddenly turned up in London, not deceased at all but as alive as you and I are, dressed in his old-fashioned suiting and looking so pious, I thought if I owed him, shouldn't I help him, especially as all he wanted was to meet the president? I said he probably couldn't actually meet the president but if he was with me he could get close. There was something so sincere about him, you know, in the way he looked at you. It was mesmerising. He said, yes, he'd issued a threat to assassinate the president, but it was a pretence, the only way he could persuade that oligarch to help him. He wouldn't have helped if he'd simply said he just wanted to *meet* the president. I understood that. Anyhow, he wasn't armed with any weapon. He showed me his cross, but I never thought he could be a danger. All I knew was he had lived on Mount Athos in fasting and prayer. That's not likely to make you into a trained assassin, is it?'

'The Russian intelligentsia had a tradition, you know.'

'Yes, I know that!'

'And he was obeying God's word.'

'Okay, rub salt in, Bob!'

'Sorry. But he didn't do more than issue a threat, did he?'

'Small mercies, sure. But I am the senior presidential aide in charge of arrangements for the visit and I invite a potential assassin to be my guest when he first arrives! How does that read, eh?'

'It reads like this, to my mind,' Bob said. 'It tells us, for instance, how he managed to get so close to the president. It also,' he waved aside her attempt to interrupt, 'it also shows there was no conspiracy, no evidence of collusion. You trusted him for good reason because you felt you owed him. Grace, that doesn't read too badly as a justification for what you did. To me it reads like the spontaneous, warm-hearted behaviour of someone who is basically a very decent and a very nice person.'

'You reckon?' She laughed and then blushed.

'I reckon very much.'

'Bob, you always did have a way with words!' She inhaled deeply. 'More coffee?'

'No, thank you.'

She pulled out another tissue. Her gaze avoided his for several moments. There was a short hiatus.

'Bob,' she said, 'you're the one who's really owing. It's why I wanted to see you.'

'We don't owe each other anything,' he said.

'Don't we?'

He knew he was wrong. He also knew he was trying to suppress feelings that were building up beneath the crust of his respectability and self-control. He picked up a paper clip and ran it to and fro between forefinger and thumb.

'I married Marsha. I've got a son and daughter and a business and I'm okay.'

'And you're happy?'

'Yes, I'm happy.'

'I'm glad about that, Bob.' She took his hand. 'It was watching your hand at that restaurant we went to. You were playing with some crumbs, like that paperclip. That's what started it. It's what made me...' She blinked. Her manner changed. 'Oh, did we really invent that network?'

'Yes, we did.'

'You remember Penthouse Suite A?'

'Of course.'

'I moved somewhere else after you left. To another apartment in the embassy.'

'Did you stay on long?'

'No, only about six months. TT left, but the State Department gave me a tenured post. I went back to Washington and started on my career. I did marry but it wasn't a success. No, my life story's not as complete as yours. And that's the truth.'

'And my truth is I loved you,' he said. 'Yes, Grace, I loved you. You and I, you and I were what mattered.'

She started shaking her head. 'I loved you too, but it was the Cold War, remember?' She withdrew her hand and stood up. Loud voices giving orders for people to make way could be heard in the corridor. 'I often thought about you. Then, when I really thought about it, I knew we couldn't.' She paused to blow her nose and dispose of the tissue. 'We knew each other for what? Three, four months, that was all. If you make a commitment to someone, it should be for life. I knew that about my marriage. But I'd made a commitment already – to be good at my job.' She sniffed and pulled another tissue. 'There've been relationships, people I've liked, sure, but I've never met anyone else I felt the same way about. And you weren't there. So my career has been the real commitment of my life. And now look what's happening to it! It's ironic, Bob, isn't it, that you should have been there at the beginning of it and now here you are at the end as well!'

'Oh, Grace, this isn't the end of your career!'

'Maybe not the complete end but when scapegoats are needed, scapegoats are found.'

'People will forget.'

'In the end maybe. Not right now.'

'Grace, if I...'

'No, Bob. I don't want you involved in this.'

He stood up as well. He wanted to kiss and comfort her, because what came from her was not her perfume so much as the scent of loneliness. He stretched out his arms.

She had turned away, the tissue raised to her face. He knew it was futile to try to offer comfort, especially as, idiotically, the moment she blew her nose there was a tap on the door and it opened.

'Grace,' said R.C., 'you're wanted down in the lobby. A press release is being prepared.'

'Thank you, R.C.'

The Chief Superintendent was standing out in the corridor, with Wilbur Oldfield beside him and a woman in a smart raincoat whose eyes seemed to be fixed on Bob's face as he and Grace stepped out of the little office room.

'Yes, Bob, you're right. I've still got a career.' She kissed him on the cheek.

This was Grace's farewell. She patted him on the arm in a sisterly way, her face as composed and handsome as it should be when she had to meet the media. He knew this was her milled steel persona and couldn't help admiring the confidence of her smile as it roved over the Chief Superintendent's face and those beside him with a practised charm. She was indeed committed to this, he felt. With R.C. at her side she strode away down the corridor, her neat navy blue skirt trimly echoing her strides like the beating of a drum.

'Mr Jermin,' the Chief Super was saying, his hat held under his arm, 'there's no need to detain you any longer. We are very grateful to you for your help. Shortly we'll be in touch with you for a statement, but for the time being I'll leave you in the hands of Mr Oldfield here.' The woman beside him nudged his arm. 'Oh, dear, how forgetful of me. I've got one more duty to perform. It is to introduce Mrs, er, Emerson – it is Emerson, isn't it? – yes, Mrs Emerson, whom I think you knew when you were in Moscow.'

'Yes,' the woman said, 'thank you, it was in Moscow. It is *Robert* Jermin, isn't it?' She spoke with an American accent.

The name, her voice, her appearance meant nothing to Bob at that moment. He was still thinking about Grace. He had never expected to see her again and had even consciously tried to force it all to the back of his mind. All the carefully constructed defences against the memory had proved no more impermeable than a sandcastle against a suddenly incoming tide. He saw her now as standing there against the tide on whatever beach of memory he was imagining and having to be courageous against the world. On the other hand, here was this woman whom he was sure he'd never seen before in his life, with a name quite unknown to him. Emerson? Emerson?

The policeman raised his hand in a kind of salute. 'Thank you, Mr Jermin.' He put his hat on and marched down the corridor in the company of two other uniformed men.

'*Pomnite*,' the woman said, '*u menia byla shapka... nu, belaia, belaia shapka, pomnite?*'

EPILOGUE

This time what stirred the pool of memory was anger and shame, matched by intense curiosity. *Wikipedia* came to his aid. It was at Marsha's suggestion once he'd got home that he looked up the name, because the actual meeting at the hospital had ended rather abruptly with Wilbur Oldfield insisting his car could not be kept in one of the ambulance bays any longer and the woman called Mrs Emerson saying she would be in touch. That she could possibly be the girl in the white fur hat simply made little sense. But of course as soon as he'd mentioned the possibility Marsha had the photograph ready for inspection and he'd been drawn to it as well in all its inexact, over-exposed, black-and-white candour. There he was naked, the scarring on his stomach quite clearly visible, his face momentarily turned towards the curiously fixed expression on the girl's face as she seemed to peer out of the small window frame of the hair falling either side of her cheeks.

Then it struck him. Of course she had been named Sonia, a cousin. Their eyes had met when she'd brought food and drink to that dining room at the dacha. Overwhelming that crevice of memory in the aftermath of seeing her standing beside the Chief Superintendent had been Wilbur's sudden determination to keep Bob out of the way of journalists in general. Her Russian words as well as her suddenly shouted: 'Okay, I'll be in touch!' were all that remained of her as he was quickly rushed into a lift and carried down he couldn't remember how many floors to somewhere at the back of the hospital and into Wilbur's car. Then Wilbur said as he drove: 'That Chief of police, he told me everything. Not a serious assassin was his verdict. Was he right?'

'He was right,' Bob said.

'But he had genius, right?'

'Yes, and he had a vision,' Bob said.

'A vision of what?'

'Oh, heaven, I suppose. No, I'm wrong. It was a vision of love.'

'Hey, that is something!' Wilbur shook his head.

It almost ended their conversation, except that before Bob was overcome by the urge to sleep he asked for no apparent reason the following rather odd question:

'Have you ever met an angel?'

'An angel?'

'Yes.'

'No,' said Wilbur after a pause, 'I haven't met an angel.'

But Bob had fallen asleep in the knowledge that he'd met an angel. Later, with Marsha half-smiling, eyebrows raised and pointing at the naked girl, he tried to recall as much as he could of this unknown Mrs Emerson, how she had looked standing next to the Chief Superintendent. Had there been any resemblance to the angel he had encountered in that shabby hotel room? None he could recall. She had been wearing a neat little rain hat along with the smart raincoat. Curled white hair was the icing as it were to a stately middle-aged face that had a sheen of smartness to it but no lipstick so far as he could remember. The eyes had no colour, shaded in any case by the rim of the rain hat. The only distinctive thing about her had been the voice, so sharply American when speaking English but so un-English in speaking Russian.

But it had the reek of money. A Silvester J Emerson was named as a Wall Street 'celebrity' with 'holdings' in IT, in the entertainment field and a range of businesses under the overall cover of Emerson International Corporation or EIC. Bob had seen it quoted regularly in the Financial Times. Maybe, he surmised, the unknown Mrs Emerson had had enough authority of her own without brandishing any of her husband's credentials to impress the Chief Superintendent or perhaps he had simply recalled the importance of Ralph Waldo Emerson, the transcendentalist (which was more than Bob himself could have done) and been helpful. On the other hand, if she were the bad angel of his encounter, then the name didn't really matter. It merely seemed too much of an irony that she should be there at the final meeting with Grace when she had been a kind of prelude to the first meeting so many years earlier.

Marsha had said that it was for him to make up his mind. She would not influence him. He trusted Marsha because he loved her with a true constancy not due simply to their years of marriage and parenthood, but also because he enjoyed her moods, admired her many gifts, loved her cooking and her seriousness and her sudden laughter, found the shape of her face enchanting and the sparkle in her eye a source of infinite grace. He liked the way she walked and sat and smiled and made fun of him. He genuinely admired her talent as a painter. Most of all he admired the way she enriched life.

The United States president had meanwhile passed a satisfactory night at the US embassy without any report of injury or infirmity due to the assault. The death of the assailant due to heart failure had meanwhile been announced. As for his intentions or associations, no information had been made available and would await a full inquiry into the circumstances. This of course did not prevent an outpouring of speculation in the media. The president, though, followed the planned routine of a visit to Downing Street and an official lunch before his stop-over concluded with the resumption of his flight to Geneva.

***

'This way, sir, if you please.' He followed the boy down the quiet hotel corridor. It was one of those places in which the door fittings as well as the architraves had a gilded brightness that matched the gold buttons on the boy's uniform. He knew it all swanked of upmarket propriety and respectful solicitude, only at certain points brought to heel by the presence of cleaners' equipment or an open door giving a glimpsed vista of unmade beds and drawn curtains. Unmistakeable wealth of course would have secured whole floors of a hotel this grand. To be satisfied with a mere bedroom or suite, however fashionable and smart, in such a quiet and lustrous corridor would mean perhaps an overnight stay or a few nights at best. All speculations ended when the boy stopped at the last door in the corridor and tapped on its oak panelling. When the door opened he announced rather stridently, reading from a smartphone screen, that a Mr Jermin had an appointment with a Mrs Sonia Emerson and Bob had to quickly search his trouser pocket for the necessary tip. The boy gave a smirk, seized the coins and nodded his thanks. He was off down the corridor at speed while Bob himself received a courteous invitation from a black woman to follow her into the apartment. 'Mrs Emerson,' she explained, 'is enjoying the sunshine.'

This meant that she was sitting in a stylish bamboo armchair in what turned out to be a quite extensive balcony area overlooking a view of the Thames. It was glassed-in and warm. She smiled up at him as he was introduced. The look on her face bore a faint, elderly resemblance to what he remembered of the girl's look. A sharply defined array of lines in the cheeks and surrounding the eyes hardened the resemblance, although it did not obscure it. In fact he could not deny to himself how much of the youthful show of fun remained in the smiling eyes raised to him as he was greeted and offered a similar chair beside hers. He sat down.

'Thank you for coming,' she began saying, leaning back in her armchair. 'I am Mrs Emerson now. My husband Silvester is in New York. His business interests have kept him there. My reason for wanting to see you is quite private, you see. I simply want to know what his last words were, Peter's last words. That was why I was there, at the hospital.' She ended on a note of query with eyebrows slightly raised.

He understood from her authoritative manner that she had acquired as part of her own New York manner a business-like approach to conversation. The niceties were to be put aside. She wanted direct answers. He countered by not replying. Instead he extracted from the inner breast pocket of his jacket the neatly folded old photograph of their two naked images.

'You said you wore a white hat, didn't you?'

She was taken aback but covered the affront by opening a handbag and looking for spectacles. She found a pink framed pair that she slowly put on to look at what he was showing her. 'I see I had a good figure,' she remarked.

'You had a very good figure,' he agreed. 'You had had ballet training, you said.'

'Sure, I did have ballet training.'

'But you were more interested in Marlon Brando.'

She frowned and handed the photograph back. 'Marlon Brando?'

'You claimed I knew Marlon Brando.'

This left her still frowning. She looked away towards the Thames. 'I do not recall.'

'But the real reason for the photograph was the scar on my stomach, wasn't it?'

This elicited the beginning of a smile. It was exactly the same look he had seen her give when she sashayed out of the dining room in the dacha. 'Oh, for mercy's sake, you were a sucker, weren't you!' she suddenly declared. 'Isn't that right!

Sucker! The KGB, they got what they wanted! And Peter got what he wanted! And I got what I wanted! Well, almost. We could've had some fun, right?'

He blinked several times. The implication was too obvious. 'I suppose so.' He forced himself to smile.

'No, you were too stiff, too English. True, I got what I wanted and that was enough. Now tell me what did Peter say. Did he say anything about me? What were his last words?'

He shook his head. 'I'm afraid he didn't say anything about you or Radna or anyone. His very last words were about his cross, he wondered what had happened to it.'

She had leaned forward. Her mouth was open in respectful acknowledgement of what he had just said. 'His cross?'

'Yes.'

'You mean the white cross, the one made of Ash?'

'The one made of wood, yes.'

'How do you know that?'

'Know what?

'Know it was made of wood.'

He explained what he had been shown by Ed Kalthorst. She leaned back on hearing this with her chin jutted forward as if in momentary indignation, but she contrived to lessen the effect by nodding slowly several times. 'I see.' The spectacles were removed and returned to the handbag. 'Yes, he made two.'

'Two?'

'Yes, he made two. I've kept the other one with me all these years.' She spoke with the kind of female authority that he recognised was hard to challenge, especially since she had kept the handbag open. 'Here,' she added. 'This is the one he made for me.'

A white cross, hardly larger than a man's hand, the central

shaft carved to a sharp point, was passed to him. It looked exactly the same as the image Ed Kalthorst had shown him, except that in this case the inscribed message running down the central shaft was clearly visible and therefore readable. She had evidently not worn her cross as the Great Peter had worn his.

'What's it say?'

'It's in old printing,' she said. 'In Soviet times Dostoevsky was not printed often. We read his novels in old print.'

He knew what she meant. The message was in the old, pre-revolutionary alphabet, but each letter stood out clearly. It took very little effort to decipher it. *YOU,* he read, *WILL HAVE THE POWER TO CONQUER THE WHOLE WORLD WITH LOVE.* He read the message out loud and saw she was smiling.

'Oh, he believed it, he really believed it.' She gave the impression of speaking to herself, smiling at her own words and shaking her head in appreciation. She went on speaking in the same self-absorbed way with her gaze turned towards the view of the Thames. 'You see he hoped by becoming a monk he could, by trying, by trying and trying and trying, become full of love himself. He said he made his cross out of hard white wood, so its sharpness might pierce skin, not too much, but enough, and make himself pierced by love, by prayer full of God's love. I knew this cross changed me. I felt it. Love grew inside me. But he wanted power to change more than himself, he wanted power to conquer everyone with love. How could he do that? By perhaps putting love into one person of power, someone like the United States president. It was what God told him to do. He was not trying to wound or assassinate, he was trying to let love grow, let it conquer. It was his vision, his life's purpose. He told me all this when we met two days ago here in London.' She turned on saying this to look directly at Bob. 'But, oh, how old he looked! He was said to have a weak heart and I could believe it. I was not surprised when there was talk of cardiac arrest.' She held out her hand for the return of the white cross, received it and snapped the handbag shut. 'I loved him more than I've ever loved anyone. Now I love my husband. I love, I love, I love, I love, that is what it's all about. Always.' She patted the handbag.

He blinked several times. She had spoken with the sincerity of a child and now leant back, her head back and her chin raised, looking as innocent as the girl in the white fur hat had looked the moment he first saw her outside the Metropole Hotel. The wrinkled, elderly face had relaxed. He could tell from the way her eyes shone that she believed her words. They were confessional, gilded with the purity of her belief and as honest as the most intimate truth.

You will have the power to conquer the whole world with love.

There they were, he thought. The words were now beneath the skin of the president of the United States. They were the Great Peter's legacy. They were the teaching of the girl in the white fur hat.